Digital Book ISBN: 978-1-64873-235-5
Paperback ISBN: 978-1-64873-234-8
Hardcover ISBN: 978-1-64873-233-1

Printed in the United States of America

Published by:
Writer's Publishing House
Prescott, Az 86301

Cover and Interior Design by Creative Artistic Excellence Marketing Project Management and Book Launch by Creative Artistic Excellence Marketing creativeartisticexcellence.com

Stories From the Hidden World

Brian Jay Nelson

Table of Contents

Tale One:

The Spirits On The Lawn

...Darkness can never prevail

Where light is prevalent...

Santa Barbara, California Spring 2018

The pendulum clock in the almost empty waiting room ticked like a time bomb, as Jack Mendenhall watched, and patiently waited. He stayed glued, refusing to make eye contact with any of the few people in the room. He worried that someone may see past his dilapidated appearance, and realize his true identity. His illness had left him very gaunt, with pale skin, and bald head. His oversized clothes were a stark reminder of how his body had deteriorated.

He flinched from his self-imposed hypnosis when the door suddenly opened. A nurse holding a file peeked into the room and called out his name. As others in the room watched, Jack raised his hand and stood a bit unsteady. A concerned woman dropped her magazine long enough to steady his arm as he tried to get his bearings. Jack gave her an emotional nod and followed the nurse's lead through the door.

The nurse ushered him into an exam room and steadied him as he took a seat at the end of the table. Jack slowly watched as the nurse checked his vitals, and left the room without even casual conversation passing between them.

After a few long moments, his oncologist, Dr. Emiko Hayakawa entered with her file already open. Jack looked toward the floor in deep thought, as she glanced over the file. He could feel the clock ticking inside his chest, waiting for some reply, when she finally looked up with a stressful sigh.

Jack spoke up before she could find the right words, "I can already tell by your expression the news isn't all that great."

Dr. Hayakawa scooted a nearby seat closer and sat down. "The chemo and alternative therapies didn't work as well as we had hoped. The tumors have spread to your other organs." She hesitated, "I'm sorry."

"I know you did your best." He paused to let the impact sink in. "I'm working on a novel that I'd like to finish. How much time do I have?"

"It's very aggressive." She reasoned. "A few months, maybe less."

Jack forced a smile and nodded rapidly. "I guess I'll just have to put in some long hours to finish it then."

She placed a comforting hand on his shoulder.
"I continued with your prescription for medical marijuana, and I'm also giving you some Chinese herbs that will help to give you more strength." Jack lowered his eyes, and nodded, while she stood up, and concluded. "I've assigned a home hospice worker to help you through this." Then she handed him the information sheet. "Is there anyone else who can look in on you?"

"I have my housekeeper, Rosa," Jack answered. "She's been with me for a long time."

"I wish there was something more I could do, Mr. Mendenhall." She sadly smiled. "Call me if you have any questions."

"Thank you, Dr. Hayakawa."

Later that afternoon, Jack sat on a park bench overlooking the Pacific Ocean. He wore a fedora-style hat to protect his bald head from the sun, and he stared straight ahead, out over the ocean, lost in his thoughts. A young couple wandered by, walking hand in hand, and they paused near him to kiss. The pretty blonde girl fondly reminded him of someone he knew so very long ago. He leaned back to let the sun warm his face and calmly smiled at the pleasant memory.

Late that night, Jack sat in his dimly lit office, working diligently on his final literary work. His large, orange Tabby, Mr. Snagglepuss rested on the top of his desk, as he worked away on his Apple desktop. Jack suddenly paused, stared at his screen, and sighed with frustration.

"This damn cancer!" He exclaimed. "I can't even organize my thoughts tonight."

He glanced over at the cat. "So, what's your spin on all of this?" He asked with a smile. "You're supposed to be my writing partner."

The cat slightly raised its' head, and looked back at him, causing Jack to chuckle.

"You and I have been through a lot together. Haven't we, Mr. Snagglepuss?" He smiled.

The cat appeared to be listening to every word, and Jack reached over to give an affectionate finger scratch to the crown of its' head.

"I'm going to miss you, you old tomcat."

The exchange is interrupted by the loud chime of the grandfather clock in the corner announcing that it was midnight. Jack listened until the very last chime, then looked upward.

"Goodnight, Bella." He muttered.

His eyes filled with tears, and he gently closed them for a moment, before looking back at the cat with renewed energy.

"Yes, Mr. Snagglepuss! This will be an amazing story when it's finished." He smiled. "And, only you and I will know that it's not fiction." He leaned back in his plush desk chair and drifted away with his thoughts.

Greenwich, Connecticut. Late spring 1971

A white Lincoln Continental pulled to the front gate of a large estate. The engraving on the large stone pillar at the entrance read "BRICE MANOR". The car waited as the gate slowly opened, then continued to the main house. It parked out in front of the grand residence, where two large moving vans were also parked, and several men were taxiing boxes, and items into the house.

A young Jack was the first occupant to emerge from the backseat of the Lincoln. He was a tall, handsome, well-built, 17-year-old with thick, dark brown hair. He got out of the car holding a portable cassette player with earbuds in his ears and stared with wonder at the façade of the large residence. Brad and Maureen Mendenhall emerged from the car next. They were both well-dressed, with a very affluent appearance.

"So, what do you think of our new home, Jack?" His father asked.

Without saying a word, he gave an unenthused shrug and headed for the front door. Brad hurried ahead and pulled the earbuds from Jack's ears. "Look! I know you're upset about leaving your friends, and Sarah. But give this place a chance. It's where I want your mother and me to spend the rest of our lives."

Jack only gave an agreeing nod and went to put his earbuds back in. "What type of music are you listening to?" Brad asked.

"Yes!"

"No! You must've not heard me. I asked what the music was."

"Yes!" Jack exclaimed with an eye-roll. "That's the name of the band, dad."

"Yes, is the name of the band?" His father asked with disbelief, and Jack gave a sober nod. "Where in the world do these groups come up with these crazy names?"

Maureen approached, carrying a small overnight bag. "I need to get inside, and make sure they're putting everything in the right place." She hurried to the door, before turning back. "Are you guys coming too?"

"Go ahead, Maureen. We'll be there in a minute." Brad replied.

Brad turned to Jack after Maureen entered the house.
"Can we just talk about this for a minute?"

"Dad! It's no big deal." He replied. "All my friends are going to different colleges, and Sarah is going to Bryn Mawr. It's time for all of us to move on anyway." Brad gave an understanding nod and thought for a moment. "I'll tell you what." He chuckled. "Your mother is going to be driving these poor movers crazy, and I don't want to be around for that." He looked to the expansive property beyond the house. "How would you like to go explore the grounds with me?" Jack smiled and gave an agreeing nod.

A short time later, he and his father were strolling along the stone path in the unmown backyard. Off to their right was a dilapidated pool area, and tennis courts. On their left was a tall brick clock tower with the hands-on its' time-worn face stopped at noon sharp.

"Do you think we could fix that clock?' Jack asked.

"I'll have to have someone look at it," Brad answered. "I don't think it's worked for quite some time."

Jack looked ahead to the massive batch of overgrown weeds, and brush in front of them. "Where do you think this path leads to, dad? It doesn't look like anyone's cut the grass back here in years."

"The realtor said the previous owner only came here for a few weeks each summer. I guess he didn't want to bother maintaining that part of the property."

"I guess he didn't put much care into the rest of this place as well," Jack grunted as he continued into the deeper grass. "This whole place is a dump."

"Be careful!" Brad warned. "We probably shouldn't be rooting around in there until I can get someone to clear it with a bush hog."

Jack continued anyway to where the stone path ended, and he stumbled over something. "I told you to be careful, Jack."

"I'm alright!" he answered with an annoyed tone." I think I found an old foundation over here."

Brad moved closer to check it out as well. "The realtor didn't mention anything about that either." He said with a clueless shrug. "Maybe there was some sort of structure here at one time."

Jack stood and surveyed the area around them. He saw the remains of statues, and ornate pillars peeking above the high grass, and then his eyes followed to the far end of the property where the woods began.

"Let's go check out the woods. It looks like there may be a cleared path over there."

His father strolled over to join him. "They did mention that there was a path that leads to an overlook. It's supposed to be a great view of the ocean from there."

Jack and his father wandered down the cracked concrete path, where weeds had encroached to narrow it. The sea breeze created an eerie sound as it filtered through the thick grove of trees around them, and they both paused to take notice.

"Listen to that, Jack. It almost sounds like someone's whispering."

"Come on dad! You're creeping me out."

Brad chuckled as they continued, "Look ahead of us. There's some sort of structure." Jack stated.

"Maybe it's an old picnic shelter or band stand," Brad added.

As they approached and looked it over, they noticed four old-fashioned park benches around the outer perimeter that were now broken, with rotted wood. They also noticed the pillared lamp posts that lined the pathway, which were now all broken, and rusted.

"Somebody put a lot of thought into building this place," Brad commented. "Look at all that ornate lattice work, and that windowed cupola on the top."

Jack looked it over curiously. "See those steel tracks, dad?" He pointed. "I think they must've had sliding doors on the sides of this at one time."

"Probably to protect it from the harsh winters." His father shrugged.

They both stepped onto the elevated wood plank floor, and a portion of it collapsed under the weight of Brads' foot.

"Are you okay, dad?"

"Yeah!" He groaned as he pulled his foot out. "Just be careful on this wood. It's pretty rotten."

Jack looked up and noticed the faded artwork on the ceiling. "Look at that!" He exclaimed with enthusiasm. "Those are tigers, walking tail to tail around the perimeter."

"It sure is." Brad chuckled. "Just like in that Little Black Sambo kids' book." He pointed to the other figures. "There's a roaring lion over there, and a smiling face with a joker's hat."

"Those other two look like prancing horses," Jack added, looking toward his father in thought. "You're a good artist dad. Maybe we can restore the artwork."

"It's too far gone, Jack. This place is about ready to collapse."

Jack glanced further around the interior. "Whatever it was, it must've been a grand place back in its' day."

Brad took a final glance and nodded in agreement.

They exited the structure and noticed a small stone building several feet away, with overgrowth all around it, and a caved-in wooden door. They strolled over and peeked in to see a dilapidated, and rusted generator.

"That must've been the power plant for whatever this place once was." Brad theorized.

They continued along the path, and the whispering sound from the woods got even louder.

"That sound is giving me the heebie-jeebies." Jack stated. "I feel like there's eyes watching our every move."

Brad glanced around laughing, "They did tell me the woods were haunted."

There was a loud groaning sound, and the underbrush rustled off to their right. "What was that?" Jack asked with wide eyes.

They both paused listening carefully for a moment, "Probably just an animal," Brad replied with a shrug. "That overlook should be just a short distance ahead."

"I think you're right, dad. I can hear the waves hitting the shore." They strolled into a small clearing area, where a weathered park bench sat with a serene view of the

Atlantic Ocean. Just above the bench, stood a stately old oak that provided a nice shaded canopy.

"What a great spot to just sit, and destress," Brad commented.

Jack walked over to the edge and looked down to where the waves crashed against the rocks below.

"I wouldn't want to fall down there." He said.

"Just don't get too close to the edge, Jack."

There was another loud groaning sound, and a strong gust of wind blew from behind Jack, causing him to barely keep his balance. A branch from the oak pushed against Jack's shoulder, preventing him from falling over the edge.

"Hey!" He yelled back to his father. "That tree's branch pushed me back from the edge."

"It was just a gust of wind." Brad laughed. "Come on! Let's get back to the house before your mother sends out a search party."

An old Jack awoke abruptly in his California home to the sound of a television preacher speaking of the end times. He looked around the room with confusion, and then glanced down to see Mr. Snagglepuss snuggled close to his side on the living room couch. He lightly tapped the old cat to wake him up, then he sat up, and tried to clear his head.

He struggled to his feet, grabbed the TV remote, and turned off the annoying, ranting preacher. He set his eyes on a wall full of old framed pictures on the other side of the room. He strolled over, and his eyes wandered to each one. He saw the pictures of his family when they were all young and still alive. Then he looked to a black and white picture from the early twentieth century of a father, mother, and teen-aged daughter, posing in front of a clock tower. He smiled endearingly and straightened the frame.

He then took notice of a photo of an older woman sitting behind a desk in a public library. "Mrs. Wozniak." He whispered profoundly, as he wiped a tear from his eye.

He looked higher and saw the shadow box frame that contained a preserved panel of wood. On that wood was one of the tigers from the old structure at his parents' estate. He reached up, removed it from the wall, and looked at it with great admiration for a long moment, before looking away in emotional thought.

A short time later, he leaned over the kitchen sink, smoking his medical marijuana, and sipping on a cup of coffee. He heard the front door open, and he promptly extinguished the joint in the sink. "Rosa?" He called out.

A woman answered with a sharp Hispanic accent, "Yes, Mr. Mendenhall. It is me."

He nervously ran his hand over his bald head, as she energetically entered the room, waving her hands, with a repulsed expression on her face. "You've been smoking that weed in the house again."

"I'm sorry Rosa. I just didn't feel like walking outside this morning."

She set her shoulder bag on the counter, "Did you sleep well last night?"

"Barely," Jack replied. "I had a hard time concentrating on my writing. I sat down to watch a movie, and fell asleep on the couch." He raised his cup toward her. "Would you like a cup of coffee?"

"I'll get it." She ordered. "You just go sit in the dining room, and I'll fix you some breakfast."

"Yes ma'am!" He smiled.

Jack settled at the large table glancing at each empty seat as Rosa brought him a fresh cup of coffee. "Isn't it ironic that before I got sick, I barely had a private moment to myself?" He asked. "People stay away now like my cancer is contagious."

"It's human nature I guess, Mr. M," Rosa stated with a sigh. "People fear death, even if it's happening to someone else."

"Does it scare you, Rosa?"

She paused, "I've worked for you for twenty-five years." The tears welled, "You're like family to me, and I'd never turn my back on family."

"Thank you." He smiled, as she moved to the kitchen. "I feel the same way toward you as well."

Rosa only glanced up from the kitchen counter with a grin, before she brought Jack a plate of scrambled eggs, and sausage. She settled into a chair next to him and poured a cup of coffee for herself.

"Aren't you eating?" Jack asked.

"I had a bagel before I left the house. I'm not that hungry."

Jack took the first bite and pondered as he chewed it. "I put the house on the market yesterday, and finalized my plans with the attorney." Rosa looked down, "I'm leaving in a few days, and won't be coming back." She raised an eyebrow, "I want you to know that I've valued your years of loyalty, and friendship. I set up a trust so that you'll be compensated for the rest of your life."

She gasped, "Please! Don't speak of that now." Rosa held her mouth, "I've been so happy here, for so long. I can't imagine how empty I'll feel when you're gone."

Jack forced a smile, "I'll need you to continue taking care of the house until it sells." He stated. "And, please make sure that Mr. Snagglepuss is taken care of for whatever time he has left."

"I will stay for as long as you need me." She choked back the tears, "And, I promise I will take good care of Snagglepuss."

Rosa paused to regain her composure…. "God bless you, Mr. Mendenhall." She wrapped her arms around is neck, kissing him on the cheek. She turned to make an emotional retreat to the kitchen but paused, "I'm very concerned about you…. May I ask where you are going?"

Jack looked up with a warm smile, "It's almost summer in Connecticut. I'm going home, Rosa!" He nodded emotionally, "I'm going home!"

A few days later, Jack was on a jet bound for the place he left several years before, but where he always remained in his heart. While in flight, Jack leaned back in his seat, closed his eyes, and drifted away with his thoughts.

A young Jack sat at the Dining Room table with his parents for their first supper at Brice Manor. The large painting of Captain Brice Stevens, the original Master of the household, looked down on them from a nearby wall. Jack glanced up at it and studied it for a moment.

"I feel like the guy in that painting is watching our every move. It's creeping me out."

His mother giggled and raised her water glass, "To our first meal in our new home."

Brad followed suit with his wine glass. "Here! Here!"

Jack didn't bother to participate in the cheer. Why isn't Amy here?" He asked. "Didn't her classes end last week?"

His parents quickly glanced at each other and sighed. "She isn't coming home this summer," Brad stated with disappointment.

"Why?" Jack pressed. "Isn't she working at the agency during her summer break?"

His father began with a slow nod, and his mother finished for him. "She's staying with her boyfriend Philip, over in Staten Island." She answered as Brad shot a stern look toward her.

Jack set his fork down on his plate and went ballistic. "You have to be kidding me! He exclaimed. "She's still with that Communist loser?"

"She's nineteen years old," Maureen stated, taking a deep breath. "We can't tell her what to do anymore."

Brad put a hand up, and cut her short. "She'll get wise, and come around." He assured. She's a Harvard girl and a Mendenhall."

"That's true." Jack concurred. "But you have to admit that Amy can be a bit flakey when it comes to common sense."

Brad stared sternly at him from across the table. "At least she realizes what a great opportunity she has with the firm." He paused with emphasis. "Why can't you decide to come work with me this summer too? I'm sure we can find a position for you.

Jack defiantly shook his head. "I want to spend my summer working on my novel."

Brad shook his head as well, with great disappointment.

"You and that damn pipe dream about being a writer." He fumed. "If you want to write, why not do advertising copy?"

"Not this again!" Jack rolled his eyes. "I told you before, dad. I'm not interested in advertising."

Maureen shot a stern glance at Brad, but he continued his rant, "What's wrong with advertising?" Brad shrugged. "Mendenhall and Allen is one of the most successful advertising firms in the country."

"Oh, Brad!" Maureen exclaimed with a groan. "Let's not talk about this now."

Brad sternly cut her short once again, "No! We will talk about this, Maureen."

He stared at her with intimidation. "Our son broke a family tradition, and passed on a golden opportunity to go to Harvard." He stressed. "Instead, he's going off with all those hippy-dippy Liberals at Princeton."

Jack expressed his frustration, as Maureen persisted in speaking on her sons' behalf. "At least it's an Ivy League School."

"More like a Pony League School." Brad laughed.

"Well! It could be worse." Maureen angrily countered. "He could be going to Viet Nam."

"Heaven forbid!" Brad exclaimed. "Did I tell you that Charlie Sawyer's son came home from there in a body bag?"

Jack slammed the palm of his hand down on the table top in anger. "Do I have to listen to all this at the dinner table?" He asked with frustration. "That damn war is all over the news, and the country is going to hell."

Brad angrily pointed his finger at Jack. "It's all reality… Jack." He countered. "Not like the fiction you like to write." He took a deep breath, "Don't you realize that you could graduate into a job with a decent salary?" He reasoned. "Most of those poor guys in Viet Nam didn't have that sort of option."

"So, what you're saying is that I should take the silver spoon from my mouth, and use it to dig for gold?" He sarcastically asked his father. "No thank you! I can find my own success."

"Really?" Brad countered. "Let me give you another dose of reality, Jack." He leaned into the table and stared his son down. "You have about a one in fifty thousand chance of making it as a writer, and about a one in a million chance of being successful at it. Those aren't good odds, son."

Jack pointed back at his father. "I'll prove you wrong." He gave an assuring nod. "I'll beat those odds, and I will be successful." Jack stood up defiantly. "I'm finished here."

Brad threw his hands up in frustration, as his son left the table. Maureen moved quickly to calm her husband down. "Let him go, Brad. He'll find his way." Brad responded with a hopeless shrug.

The airline attendant gently nudged Jack's arm, and he opened his eyes, slightly startled. "Please fasten your seat belt, sir." She smiled. "We'll be landing soon."

Greenwich Connecticut. Spring 2018

A white SUV pulled up to the open front gate of a grand old estate. The window rolled down, and Jack peered out at the same Brice Manor pillar that had lived in his memory for so very long.

"I'm finally back home." He whispered to himself.

After a few long moments, he looked ahead toward the house with determination and continued up the driveway.

Inside the den of his residence, Cecil Duncan, a distinguished, middle-aged Black man, sat comfortably in a large chair. His leg was propped up on an ottoman, and it had a cumbersome brace on it. He listened with great attention to the financial report on the TV. The doorbell rang, and he groaned while struggling to sit up in the chair.

"I knew I should've closed the front gate this morning." He muttered to himself.

He braced on the arms of the chair and pulled himself to his feet.

"Sasha!" He called out and waited for her to answer, while the doorbell rang again.

"Oh! Where is that woman?" He fumed, as he hobbled as fast as he could from the room.

"Better not be some Jehovah's Witness."

He stiff-legged his way to the front door, and opened it, just as Jack was slowly making his way back to his car.

"Can I help you?" Cecil called out.

Jack turned and began to stroll back. "I'm sorry if I caught you at a bad time."

Cecil looked toward him with great annoyance. "If you're selling something, then you must not be able to read." He pointed to the NO SOLICITATION sign posted by the door.

"Nothing like that." Jack laughed and offered his hand, "I'm Jack Mendenhall. My family and I lived here many years ago."

Cecil's face lit up with surprise, and he shook Jacks' hand vigorously. "I'm sorry I didn't recognize you, Mr. Mendenhall. I'm a big fan of your work."

"That's okay." Jack forced a smile. "A lot of people don't recognize me anymore."

"I'm Cecil Duncan." He gestured for Jack to come into the house. "Welcome back to Brice Manor."

Cecil ushered him in, and Jack glanced around with childlike enthusiasm. "I really missed this place." He emotionally choked. "You've preserved it quite well."

"We tried to respect the history of the house while making it a comfortable home space." He replied with a pleasing smile, as Jack marveled in remembrance.

"I need to get off this leg," Cecil grunted. "Please come in, and sit down."

Cecil and Jack settled into chairs in the greeting room, and Jack gestured toward his braced leg. "What happened there?"

"I just had an operation on my knee." He shrugged. "Old baseball injury from my days at Princeton."

"I went to Princeton as well," Jack replied.

"I know all about that." Cecil chuckled. "You're a legend among the alma matter."

"Cecil!" A voice calls from the other room. "Who was that at the door, baby?"

Cecil's wife Sasha, an attractive, and very fashionable woman in her mid 40s breezed into the room.

"Oh! I'm sorry!" She exclaimed with surprise. "I didn't know we had company."

"Sasha!" Cecil replied with a quick gesture to Jack. "This is Jack Mendenhall."

Sasha's eyes grew wide with excitement. "Thee Jack Mendenhall!"

Jack gave a humorous bow toward her, and she answered with a bow of her own, with both her arms outstretched. "We love your movies, and your books too."

She enthusiastically stated. "Oh! Especially that one about the haunted lighthouse."

Jack chuckled, as Sasha continued to chatter on. She turned to her husband with exuberance. "Baby! I am so glad you got to the door before Mr. Mendenhall left. I was busy on the phone with a client."

Sasha noticed as Jack took a deep breath, and had a short coughing attack. "Are you okay, Mr. Mendenhall?" She asked as she approached him with great concern.

"I'm fine!" He assured. "Just a little fatigued."

"Can I get you a cold drink?" She asked.

"I'll take a glass of water. Thank you!"

Sasha left the room, and Cecil looked to Jack with equal concern. "I saw in the tabloids that you had been sick."

Jack gave a matter-of-fact nod. "Pancreatic cancer."

Cecil blinked his eyes and glanced downward, "I'm sorry."

Sasha brought Jack a cold glass of water, then settled next to Cecil on the couch, "I know you're both wondering why I'm here."

He paused to take a drink, while the couple listened attentively. "I wanted to make an offer to buy the woods from you. I noticed there's a fence around it, with a for sale sign."

They were baffled by his offer. "That property isn't ours to sell, Mr. Mendenhall," Cecil stated. Jack was equally baffled, and Cecil continued, "When we bought this property from your sister, she sold that plot separately."

Jack put his hand to his head, "What about the contract my father had with the city?"

"She never renewed it," Cecil answered.

"She sold it to a developer who had planned on building high-end condos," Sasha added and continued with visible anger. "We never knew about her plans until we already purchased Brice Manor."

"That sounds like something my sister, and her free-loading husband would do," Jack commented sarcastically.

"So naturally, we fought against their plans with the rest of our neighbors," Cecil stated. "Luckily, we had the city, as well as the Historical Society on our side."

"How long has all of this been going on?"

"Since 2001," Sasha answered indignantly.

Cecil nodded rapidly, "They fought us in court for over ten years until we finally won. Then they fenced it up, and put it back on the market."

"It's been that way for four years," Sasha added. "Nobody wants to buy a piece of property that they can't do anything with."

Jack leaned back, absorbing the aspects of the situation, "Except for me."

"With all due respect, what would you intend to do with it?" Sasha asked, and Cecil quickly chimed in. "I mean…., In your condition…."

Jack answered quickly with a sure nod, "I want to restore it to all its' original glory."

Cecil chuckled, and he and Sasha exchanged a baffled expression, "You mean, merry-go-round and all?

"You know all about that?" Jack countered with surprise."

"Hell yeah!" Cecil exclaimed, "I'm what you'd call a major history buff."

Jack reacted with excitement. "I have copies of the original photos of the property out in my car."

"For real?" Cecil asked with the excitement of a child. "I definitely need to see those." He exchanged another glance with Sasha. "We want to help you get this thing done, Mr. Mendenhall."

"Very well!" Jack got up and took a deep breath. "We can talk some more about it tomorrow. I've already taken up too much of your time."

"Where are you staying?" Sasha asked.

"I planned on getting a hotel in town." He answered.

Cecil quickly cut in. "Why don't you just stay here as our guest?" He offered. "I have the next two weeks off, and can help you get things arranged."

"I have a lot of things to do, Mr. Duncan. I have to finish the last chapter of a novel before the inevitable event of my death takes place."

"You can stay in the guest room in the North Wing," Cecil added. "You'll have a lot of privacy there."

Jack couldn't help but smile. "That used to be my bedroom when I lived here."

"That settles it." Cecil laughed. "That's where you need to be."

Cecil offered to shake on it, and Jack thought for a moment, before sealing it with a firm handshake. "Now, go get those pictures." Cecil joked. "I'm dying to see those things."

Jack chuckled as he exited the room. Sasha then stood up and listened for the front door to shut.

"Cecil!" She exclaimed. "Are you out of your mind? That man is dying. He needs to be in a hospital."

Cecil shook his head defiantly. "If he was as happy living here as we are now, then this is where he needs to be in his final days."

"What if he dies?" She countered.

"I think that's the whole point." He paused with emphasis. "I think the man came back here to die, and I intend to help him exit this world with dignity."

Sasha only sighed.

"Besides." He added. "How many people can say that they had thee famous Jack Mendenhall for a house guest?"

Sasha shrugged, "You are a wonderful man, Cecil Duncan."

Later that evening, Cecil ushered Jack into the guest room.

"I'm sure you remember this place." He smiled.

Jack stepped in and glanced around the room with awe. "Man! This sure does take me back."

"We kept almost everything as it originally was," Cecil stated. "I even bought the old antique rolltop desk from your sister."

Jack walked over and ran his hand across the walnut finish. "I wrote my first novel on this desk." He smiled, turning back toward Cecil. "Now, I'll finish my last one on it as well."

Cecil motioned toward the hall. "I built a small kitchenette in what used to be the other bedroom down the hall." He paused awkwardly. "There's not much in there other than beer and water. We don't entertain guests too often."

"That's fine! I'll go to the supermarket tomorrow."

Cecil nodded. "Whenever you feel like getting up, just come downstairs, and we'll fix you a good breakfast. He sighed. "Until then, if you need anything, just ring that bell on the nightstand over there."

"Thank you!" Jack said with a grateful nod.

"We'll see you in the morning, Jack."

"Goodnight, Cecil." Cecil awkwardly exited and pulled the door shut behind him.

Jack slowly sauntered over, and opened the window a bit, to let the night air into the room. Then he propped pillows against the headboard, and got comfortable on top of the bed. As he leaned back, he glanced over at the old rolltop desk, and fondly remembered that first day of summer, so very long ago.

A young Jack sat at his rolltop desk plucking away at the keys of his Corona typewriter. Suddenly he heard the distant sound of old-time music carrying through the night air. It flowed through the open window, and into his room from an undisclosed place outside.

He quit typing, and listened for a moment, before going to the window to check it out. Something odd caught his attention as he looked out into the darkness of the large backyard of the property. Astonished at what he saw, he ran from the room, and downstairs to get a better look.

He entered the outdoor patio through the ornate French doors of the house, and saw a glow of lights in the far portion of the yard. The music seemed much louder, and closer now. He stood, trying to make sense of what he heard, and saw.

The horizon was still faintly red from the sun going down twenty minutes before, but it was dark enough that he noticed the lighted face of the clock tower that read 8:45.

"That's impossible!" He muttered to himself.

He continued along the stone path in the back yard, and now saw a well-manicured lawn that was lit up with stringed retro party lights. It resembled an old-time carnival grounds. As he got closer, he saw several people wearing turn of the century clothing. There was a small orchestra of well-dressed men, playing music from that same time period.

He noticed the now restored statues of half-naked women, angels, and ornate pillars that lined the perimeter of the yard. There was a beautiful guest house that sat in the very spot where he saw the ruins earlier in the day.

Its two-story façade was supported by large wood carved pillars, and an ivy-covered pergola stretched across the front of it. "Outta sight!" He enthusiastically voiced to himself.

His eyes then wandered toward the woods, where he spotted two children joyfully running onto the wide path, that was lit by pillared, acorn-shaped park lamps. The warm glow of the lamps created a serene light against the darkness. Although he felt invisible, and quite out of place, he strolled through the ever-growing assembly, and toward the lighted path.

As he wandered onto the path, the orchestra music was drowned out by the sound of upbeat, happy carnival music. It almost sounded like someone playing a Hammond organ, or what possibly would've been some sort of calliope back then. He anxiously picked up his pace as more laughing children hurried by, and adults casually strolled by, giving him a curious once over.

When he rounded the bend toward the clearing, he was astonished to see a full-sized merry-go-round where he and his father had seen the dilapidated structure earlier in the day. He hurried over to it and anxiously looked up at the high wood-paneled ceiling inside. There he noticed the painted tigers around the entire perimeter and the other striking artwork in its' original condition.

He shook his head with disbelief. "This is amazing!" He whispered out loud.

A beautiful young girl, about the same age as him, strolled up, and happily watched the children, as they went round and round on the colorful, ornate, wood-carved horses. She had long blonde hair, sparkling blue eyes, and she wore a 1920's style white sequined party dress. Similar to the outfits he saw in old pictures of high society.

At first, she just stared straight ahead, lost in her amusement. Then she slyly cast a keen glance toward Jack. He felt his heart skip a beat, and he was instantly infatuated with her. He took a deep breath and approached. "Hi! I'm Jack Mendenhall." He nervously announced.

She reacted with surprise and said nothing at first. Jack felt frustration overcome him. He just had to get this girl to talk to him. "Can you tell me what's going on here, and how all this changed since earlier today?" He asked her.

She looked at him rather warily. "You're not one of us, are you?"

"One of who?" Jack asked with a shrug.

She curiously moved closer and touched him with the tip of her finger. A startled Jack jumped back away from her. "Wow! That was like an electric shock going through me."

She looked at him with amazement. "You're one of them!" In a brief pause, "You must be a seer."

Jack looked at her with a puzzled expression. "What do you mean? What's a seer?"

She became more relaxed, and eager to converse, which also helped ease Jack's anxiety. "Seers are very rare; mortals that can see and hear spirits like us." She giggled. "Didn't you know you had such a gift?"

Jack slowly shook his head, still confused by what she was saying. "This is all new to me."

He stood nervously, trying to search his mind for what he should say next. She sensed his uneasiness and giggled again. It was becoming obvious that she was somewhat smitten with him as well. "Let me get this straight." Jack began. "If you're a spirit, then when did you die?"

"In the summer of 1927." She replied nonchalantly.

Jack was thunderstruck by her statement and seriously addressed her. "Do you know what year it is now?"

"For everyone here, time ceased to exist when we died." She shrugged. "So, I really have no clue."

Jack looked at her with complete disbelief. "We're in the year 1971."

She giggled as though it was no issue at all, and glared at him with confidence. "That's forty-four years in the future." She looked up with great thought. "If I were still alive, I'd be sixty-one years old."

He shook his head in amazement and laughed. "I have to say that you're the prettiest sixty-one-year-old woman that I've ever seen."

She blushed and responded with a grateful smile, "You're the first seer that has been here for quite some time." She nervously bit at her lower lip. "Perhaps you're the one that Lady Joy said would come."

Jack is even more surprised and confused. "What do you mean?" He asked. "Are you saying there were others before me?"

"A few have wandered onto our gatherings over the years." She replied nonchalantly. "But I'd like to believe that you're the one we've been waiting for." She concluded with a sly grin.

Jack is even further perplexed by the conversation, but Bella quickly moved on to another subject. She pointed toward the carousel with excitement.

"Do you like my merry-go-round?" She asked.

"That's yours?" Jack replied with disbelief.

"My father bought it for me on my tenth birthday."

"That's quite an impressive gift," Jack stated with a chuckle.

She eyed Jack admirably, "I suppose now that I know who you are, the polite thing to do would be to introduce myself." She smiled. "I'm Isabelle Stevens, but everyone calls me Bella."

"I'm guessing that your father would be none other than Captain Brice Stevens."

"And, you'd be right." She proudly replied.

Jack is visibly smitten with Bella, and she found his obvious attraction to be rather amusing. She giggled, and once again, nervously bit her lower lip.

"Do you have a girlfriend, Jack?"

"I did." He shrugged. "But we broke up when I moved here." Jack looked down and shyly shifted his feet. "What about you? Are you with someone here in the spirit world?"

"I never had the chance to be with a man." Bella rolled her eyes and shrugged. "I was waiting for the right one to come along when I died."

"Really?" Jack replied with great surprise.

"Why does that surprise you so much?" Bella asked with a perplexed expression.

Jack stammered, hoping he hadn't been misunderstood. "Well! It's just that you're a really hot-looking chick, and I'm surprised some guy hadn't scooped you up."

Bella is quite baffled by his modern terminology and reacted with embarrassment. "I don't quite understand what you're saying." She wiped her hand across her forehead. "Am I sweating profusely?"

Jack took a deep breath and tried to rephrase his comment, "What I really meant to say, is that I think you're quite beautiful, and I'm sure other guys see that too."

Bella blushed and looked away in a moment of exhilaration.

"Are you and your family the new inhabitants of Brice Manor?"

"Yes, we are." He answered. "We just moved in today."

Bella breathed a sigh of exuberance, "As you've probably guessed, I used to live there as well." She smiled rather melancholy. "I used to love that house."

"It is quite nice." He politely commented. "But it is in serious disrepair. It'll probably take us a long time to fix it up."

Bella beamed with excitement, "I know that you're just the person who can restore it to its' original glory."

Jack glanced around with great doubt, "That might be a pretty large order to fill."

Bella took hold of his hand, and he was visibly stunned by the magical energy in her touch.

"Come with me, Jack." She urged. "You must meet my parents and the others. They'll be so pleased to meet you."

She ran ahead with the energy of a child, with Jack tagging along behind, while she held his hand tightly. They hurried down the path toward the party on the lawn, where several more people had gathered since Jack first passed through. Everyone was cordially conversing and dancing to the now lively music of the orchestra.

Bella led Jack toward a well-dressed couple, and Jack immediately recognized the man as Captain Stevens. He had the same graying black hair and a thick handlebar mustache that he remembered from his portrait. His wife Amanda was much younger than him. She also had blonde hair and had strikingly similar features to her daughter.

"Father! Mother!" She called out with excitement. "This is Jack Mendenhall. His family just moved into the main house." She looked back toward Jack with an exuberant grin. "They're the ones who are finally going to restore the property."

Brice looked at his daughter with an apprehensive expression, then turned his attention back toward Jack.

"I'm Captain Brice Stevens, and this is my wife, Amanda." The couple greeted him with a cordial nod. "Welcome to our gathering."

"I'm pleased to meet you both." He nervously expressed. "I saw your picture hanging in our dining room, sir," Jack added.

"I'm surprised it's still there." He chuckled.

The Captain looked at his daughter with an uneasy expression, and she reacted with a giggle.

"It's alright, father. Jack is a seer from 1971."

The Captain immediately transitioned to a demeanor of surprise, and excitement.

"Have that many seasons actually passed since 1927?" He shook his head. "Amazing!"

"I know," Bella added with exuberance. "The last seer visited us in the 1950s, before mother even rejoined us.

Amanda quickly jumped into the conversation.

"I've only been in spirit since 1961. Please tell me what has transpired in the years since."

"There's been quite a bit." Jack assuredly replied. "President Kennedy was assassinated in 1963. Then, we went to war in Southeast Asia, and we even put a man on the moon."

All listened with great interest and awe, "You mean to tell me that a man walked on the moon?" The Captain marveled.

"Yes sir!" Jack answered with a matter-of-fact nod. "And that's only part of what happened."

The spirits were stunned with surprise, and the Captain looked away in a moment of thought, "I knew of a Mendenhall family that lived in The Hamptons. They were fine people."

Jack nodded and smiled, "That would've been my grandparents. They had an advertising firm in New York City."

"Yes! I do remember now." The Captain replied.

Amanda eagerly broke into the conversation once more, "Those clothes you're wearing are very interesting." She commented. "Is that how people dress in the future?"

"Only in casual times." He answered. "I never realized that I'd be wandering into such a lavish party."

The Captain continued to quiz Jack with great interest, "Are you involved with your family's business, Jack?"

"No sir! I start my Freshman year at Princeton in the fall, and I have aspirations of being a writer."

"Then you must meet Samuel Clemens." He replied while glancing around him. "I'm sure he's milling about here somewhere in the crowd."

"Mark Twain?" Jack asked with great surprise.

"One in the same." The Captain replied in a matter-of-fact tone. "I do believe F. Scott Fitzgerald may be present as well."

"You'll just love his wife, Zelda," Amanda added. "She is quite the card."

Jack was rendered speechless, as he further surveyed the crowd, "Is that Nikola Tesla over there?" He asked, pointing with excitement.

"Yes, it sure is." The Captain laughed. "We have to make sure that he and Thomas Edison don't show up on the same nights."

"It wouldn't be proper," Amanda added in a discreet tone.

Jack was beyond amazed, while the Captain turned to his daughter who was still impatiently waiting off to the side and was giving her father a pouty face.

"Bella, my dear!" He addressed her with a smile. "You must take Jack, and mingle in the crowd. I'm sure everyone will be eager to meet him."

"Of course, father." She answered with a sly grin.

She eagerly seized Jack's hand, and pulled him away, while her parents joyfully watched. "What a charming young man," Amanda commented. "Do you suppose he's the seer that Lady Joy said would help us?"

"For Bella's sake, and the future of this estate, I certainly hope so." He answered in all seriousness.

Later that night, Bella and Jack sat on a bench near the merry-go-round, watching as the happy children went round and round on the carousel horses.

"This has been the most amazing night of my life." Jack proclaimed.

Bella took a deep breath as she rested her head against his shoulder.

"It's been very special for me as well." She turned and flashed a giddy smile. "Will you come here again tomorrow?

"Yes, I most certainly will," Jack replied. "And I promise that I'll dress appropriately."

They both laughed, and Bella then looked away in thought.

"You must promise me that you'll never tell another living mortal about the things you saw tonight." She stated with sober seriousness. "If anyone else were to ever find out, we would have to close the portal forever."

"I don't quite understand what you mean," Jack answered. "But I will promise you that I won't tell anyone."

"Thank you, Jack." She gratefully nodded. "And don't worry. In time, you'll understand everything."

The clock tower tolled at midnight, and all the spirits in the vicinity paused to take notice as it echoed throughout the property. Jack glanced down at his watch to verify the time, "I can't believe it's this late already." He mentioned.

"It's time for all of us to leave." Bella sadly replied.

A procession of spirits emptied onto the pathway from the lawn, and they quietly continued past the merry-go-round, and into the deep woods.

Bella smiled endearingly and kissed Jack on the cheek, "I'll see you tomorrow night." She whispered.

Jack watched as she joined the line with her parents, and the others. As the tower chimed for the 12th time, the last of the spirits disappeared into the woods, and Jack found himself alone in the dark. The path lights were gone, and the merry-go-round was once again a silent, dilapidated shell.

He glanced all around with confusion and hurried up the path toward the lawn. When he arrived, the guest house was gone, the clock tower was dark, and he found himself standing in waist-high grass. The sight caught him completely offguard, nothing made sense. It became hard to think, he almost felt dizzy. A few moments later, Jack wakened from his deep remembrance and opened his eyes to a darkened guest room. He was shocked to see a figure standing near his bed, watching him.

He could make out a light-colored dress, but the face was hidden in the dark shadows, "Who's there?" He whispered loudly.

The apparition quickly moved away when he spoke, and passed through the closed door, leaving Jack quite stunned. He looked down at the lighted face of the clock, which read 12:15. He then stared back toward the closed door with amazement, "Bella?" He quietly questioned.

The next morning, Jack joined Cecil and Sasha in the dining room for breakfast. As he sat down, he glanced up at the picture of Captain Brice, and couldn't help but break a smile.

"Good morning everyone." He joyfully stated.

"Good morning to you!" Cecil replied. "I hope you slept well."

"Go ahead, and help yourself, Jack." Sasha motioned to the hotplate at the center of the table. "I kept it warmed up for you."

Jack paused before serving himself, "Have either of you ever seen a ghost in the house?" He inquired.

The couple glanced at each other before answering. "Neither one of us, but others have told us that they had an encounter," Cecil answered.

"Did you see something last night?" Sasha asked.

"I thought I did," Jack replied. "Perhaps I was just dreaming."

The couple shared another glance before they all resumed eating. "Is the old library still down on Main Street?"

"They tore that one down, back in the '90s." Cecil answered. "They built a new one over near the community center."

"There's a high-rise office building where the old one used to be," Sasha added.

Jack sadly nodded, "If you can give me directions to the new one, I'd appreciate it. I need to do some research this morning."

Later that morning, Jack sat on a bench outside the office building where the old library used to be. As he sat there looking at the modern building, his mind drifted back to a different time, and he could almost envision the old library with its large Romanesque-style pillars.

In his imagination, he clearly saw himself entering the old library on that sunny day in the summer of 1971. He approached the front desk where the library aide sat reading a book. She was a woman that looked to be in her 70's. She had wire-frame glasses and snowy white hair. She glanced up at Jack with a smile.

"How can I help you, young man?"

"I was wondering where I might be able to find information about Brice Manor." He confidently replied.

"I can help you with that." She stated with exuberance. "I happen to be quite knowledgeable on the history of that property."

Jack leaned against the counter and continued to probe.

"Are there any old pictures of the property from back in the early 1900s?"

"Oh yes!" She exclaimed. We have quite a few in the archives upstairs." She smiled and motioned to Jack. "Follow me."

They both walked rapidly through the reading area, and up the carpeted stairs with the polished cherrywood banister. For a woman of her age, she was quite energetic, and even Jack found it hard to keep up with her gait.

"My name is Mrs. Wozniak." She announced. "I've never seen you around here before."

"I'm Jack Mendenhall. My family just moved into Brice Manor."

"Oh! So that's why you're so interested." She continued a few steps more, before turning with a mischievous grin. "You do know that it's haunted?"

Jack chuckled carrying the conversation as they entered the archive room, "Do you actually believe that's true?"

"If it were true, I doubt very much that you would have anything to be concerned about."

They continued, over to the book shelf, "You haven't seen anything out of the normal, have you?" She casually inquired.

"No ma'am!"

She grabbed hold of a very old, dusty scrapbook from the shelf, and laid it down on a nearby table. As she opened it, Jack looked curiously over her shoulder. The first pictures he saw were of Brice Manor while it was being built.

"These were taken during its' construction in 1896."
She explained. "It was quite a project for its' time." She
turned another page. "And this is the Captain himself,
standing in front of his finished home." She stated with a
fond grin. "He was very proud of that house."

"What can you tell me about him?" Jack asked.

She raised her eyes from the book and spoke as
though she had known him. "He was a kind and very
admirable man. He made the bulk of his money from the
shipping, and import industry, but he was also involved in
other ventures as well."

Jack listened with interest as she turned to the next
page. He was excited to see a picture, dated 1927, of the
Captain with his wife, and Bella, all proudly standing in
front of the clock tower, with the guest house in the
background. The image gave him the chills.

"I'm sure you recognize that tower." She pointed.
"That's his wife Amanda, and his daughter Bella in the
picture with him. They were both everything in the world

to him." Mrs. Wozniak sighed. "This is believed to have been taken shortly before Bella's death."

"How did she die?"

"It's been said that she was murdered." She answered with a sure nod. "She somehow fell from the cliff at Lookout Point. However, the person they believe pushed her, mysteriously disappeared, and was never found."

Tears appeared in her eyes, as she struggled to continue, "Bella was their only child."

Jack emotionally shut his eyes for a moment, before pointing to another picture, "What happened to the guest house?"

"The previous owner, Mr. Feldman, let the property fall into great disrepair. She stated with visible disdain. "The house somehow caught fire, and burned to the ground in the winter of 1965."

Jack pondered his next question for a moment, "Was there also a merry-go-round in the clearing of the woods?"

"There most certainly was." She replied with enthusiasm. "The Captain had it built for Bella, and he hired an Italian artist to paint the figures on the ceiling." She turned another page and pointed. "There it is in its' glory days. I remember it well as a young woman."

Jack marveled at the sight, as Mrs. Wozniak continued.

"Captain Stevens was quite the philanthropist, and he loved children." She beamed. "Even though his fortunes suffered greatly during the Great Depression, he still operated that carousel for all the children and people of the community. He did that right up until he died in 1938."

"Then what happened?" He asked.

His wife tried to continue operating it, just for special occasions. When she fell ill, she was forced to sell it." She looks off in deep thought. "I believe it was sold to an amusement park in Ohio, and all that remains here is the decaying shell."

Another assistant motioned to Mrs. Wozniak from outside the room.

"They need me at the front desk." She sighs. "But feel free to browse all you want, and you can also make Xerox copies of anything you might need."

She nodded to Jack, and turned to leave, but quickly turned back, "You know, I happened to be a personal friend of the Steven's family." She smiled. "Stop by anytime, and I'd be thrilled to talk to you some more."

Jack's daydream was interrupted by a man in a business suit, that leaned over to check on him.

"Excuse me, sir!" He announced with concern. "Are you alright?"

Snapping to his senses, Jack smiled gratefully, "I'm fine." He chuckled. "My mind was simply taking a short journey down Memory Lane."

The man simply responded with a cordial smile, before moving on.

Later that day, Jack typed away on his laptop in the guest room. He paused and took notice of the sunsets' golden glow that flowed in through the window.

"You made it through another day, Jack." He whispered to himself, with a smile.

He leaned back in his chair, while a gentle breeze drifted in from outside, and another memory swept into his mind.

On an evening similar to this, in that summer that seemed so long ago, a young Jack stood before his dresser mirror within this very room. He carefully adjusted his tie, and then put on a suit jacket. An R&B song played from the radio at the edge of the dresser, and he sang, and did a quick dance move, as he got into the beat.

He anxiously looked out the window, noticing that the warm glow from the sunset had now turned more of a red against the darkening skies. He quickly ran a comb through his thick mop of hair, turned the radio off, and left the room with a bounce in his step.

As he entered the hallway, his father was just coming up the stairs.

"Jack!" He called out. "I was just coming up to talk to you." He gave him the once over. "Why are you wearing a suit?"

"I was just trying it on to see if it still fits." Jack stammered.

"It fits great." Brad nodded his approval. "You look very professional."

Jack tried to shake off the awkwardness of the moment, while his father took a deep breath, and continued, "I just wanted to apologize for being so hard on you the other night at the dinner table."

"Did mom put you up to this?" He sighed.

Brad shook his head, "I only said those things because I'm concerned about you, and I want you to succeed in life."

"I will succeed." Jack proclaimed. "I have it in me."

"Somehow, I have to believe you're right," Brad answered with a sigh. "No matter what direction you choose in life, you'll always be my son, and I'll always love you."

"I love you too, dad."

Brad smiled and rested his hand firmly on his son's shoulder, "Just don't marry one of those hippy-dippy Liberal girls from Princeton. Please!"

They both laughed, and Jack quickly moved to another subject, "Hey, dad! Do you really plan on living in this house for the rest of your life?" He asked.

"Most definitely," Brad replied. "And, I hope to leave it to either you or Amy someday." He looked at Jack curiously. "Why do you ask?"
"Because I like it here too."

Brad answered with a pleasing grin and turned to go back downstairs. As he reached the first step, he turned back, "Columbo comes on at nine. You want to come down, and watch it with me in the den?"

Jack chuckled, "I'll have to pass tonight." He paused. "I really need to get some writing done." Brad gave him an assured wink.

As Jack snapped out of his memory trance, he now found himself alone, out in the darkened hall, still looking toward the stairway. While he focused his eyes on the diminished light, for one split moment, he could have sworn he still saw his father on the top landing, looking his way.

"Dad!" He called out.

"Jack!" A voice called out.

Jack waited, only to see Cecil, as he hobbled to the top landing, "I just wanted to come, and check on you." He looked around. "Were you talking to someone?"

"Just a ghost from my past, I guess." Jack chuckled.

Cecil motioned downstairs, "It was such a pleasant evening, I thought you might like to sit and chat on the back patio."

"That sounds like a good idea," Jack replied. "I just need to grab a jacket, and I'll meet you down there."

A short time later, the two men sat relaxed in Adirondack style chairs, looking out on the peaceful darkness of the backyard. A cool, brisk wind was blowing in from the Atlantic, reminding them both that summer had not completely arrived.

Jack lit up a joint, inhaled, and oppositely blew the smoke, away from Cecil.

"It's been quite a long since I smoked one of those." Cecil chuckles.

"I hope you don't mind," Jack replied. "It kind of dulls the pain a bit."

Jack offered the joint to Cecil, but he signaled refusal with his hand.

"I'll pass. You need it a lot more than I do."

Jack glanced up at the majestic clock tower and its'
lighted face.

"The tower looks like it's in great shape."

"Shortly after we bought this place, the Historic
Preservation Society deemed it an historical landmark." He
motioned to the tower. "They came in with grant money,
and updated all the mechanical parts of the clock."

The clock tolled at that moment, and its' chimes
echoed throughout the yard. Cecil shook his head and
cracked a pleasurable smile.

"I just love that sound."

Jack gave an agreeing nod, as he exhaled another
puff of smoke, "What kind of work do you do, Cecil?"

"I'm a network executive in New York, and my
wife is a fashion designer."

"I'm impressed." Jack nods. "You've both done
very well in your lives."

"I guess I didn't do too bad for a ghetto kid from Newark, New Jersey." He chuckled. "I was the first in my family to graduate from college."

"And from Princeton, no less," Jack added.

Jack's cell phone rang, and he looked down to see who it was, "Excuse me, Cecil. I have to take this call." He held the phone to his face, "Hello, Rosa." Jack listened instently, "Just settle down. It's alright! It's okay! Jack's eyes filled with tears as he listened. "Listen! Mr. Snagglepuss was fifteen years old. He lived a good, long life." Jack nodded as he listened more. "I'll call the vet tomorrow, and tell him where to send the ashes. Jack emotionally nodded. "Thank you, Rosa." Jack set his phone down on the arm of the chair and wiped the tears from his eyes.

"Is everything okay?' Cecil asked with great concern.

Jack sadly looked off in the darkness before he answered, "My cat died."

Later, as Jack knelt by his bedside, and prayed, his emotions overtook him, and he wept like a baby. He managed to get up and sit on the edge of the bed, quietly looking off into the corner of the room. It was as though a portal had opened there, and he could see through time, all the way back to that special summer.

Young Jack snuck out through the back door the night after his first encounter with Bella, and the other spirits. He paused at the patio and looked toward the glowing lights at the far end of the yard.

He proceeded on, past the clock tower, which now read 8:55. He got to the lawn just as a good number of the spirits were arriving. There was truly magic in the air on this pleasant summer evening. The spirits played croquet on the lawn outside the guest house, and Jack also took notice of the band, who were just setting up for the nights' entertainment.

Out of virtually nowhere, Bella approached from behind and tapped him on the shoulder.

"You really did come back." She stated with much joy.

"I wouldn't have missed it for the world." He replied with exuberance.

Bella noticed the suit and eyed him up and down with a sly grin.

"You look very nice tonight."
Jack looked at her admiringly as well.

"As do you." He slightly bowed. "I like the way you braided your hair."

Bella was very flattered and took Jack by the hand.

"Come on!" She said with a giddy laugh. "I want my parents to see you all dressed up."

She led him to her parents who were conversing with other guests, and her father quickly excused himself from the conversation when he saw them. "Now that's what

I call a properly dressed young man." The Captain announced as he approached the young couple.

"Thank you, sir!" Jack replied. "It's a bit modern for this period, but it's the only suit that I own."

The Captain turned to his daughter, and gave an approving wink, as his wife joined the trio. "Oh my!" Amanda exclaimed. "Jack certainly does clean up quite well." She and the Captain exchanged an approving nod that delighted Bella.

The Captain then placed a friendly hand on Jack's shoulder, "You're in for a special treat tonight, young man." He enthusiastically pointed toward the band. "Harry Bidgood and his orchestra are here from Great Britain."

"I have no idea who he is," Jack stated with a shrug. "But I'm sure I'll enjoy it."

The captain motioned, "Come! The band is starting." In a few seconds all the spirits began to dance to the upbeat, and happy music.

Jack turned to Bella, who was already swaying to the music and grabbed her hand, "Would you care to dance?" He asked.

"I'd love to." Jack took her hand, twirling her around. He reeled her in close, her carefree laughter filled the air.

Her parents, who were dancing at a much slower pace nearby, watched the young couple with pleasing smiles. As the song ended, the band quickly proceeded to their next song. Jack twirled her around once more and rested her body on his outstretched arm.

"You dance quite well," Bella remarked while trying to catch her breath. "I can't believe you know how to do the Charleston."

Jack laughed, "My parents made me learn how to dance when I was a kid. I guess the lessons paid off."

Bella's eyes sparkled as she looked admirably at Jack, and she enthusiastically grabbed his hand. "I want to take you somewhere very special."

They both hurried down the path, by the merry-go-round, and toward the bend that led into the woods. The happy music of the band carried from the lawn, and mingled with that of the carousel, to create a surrealistic feel in the night air.

Just past the bend, Bella led Jack into a grove of oaks, where the night was lit by a multitude of fireflies. Bella pulled Jack close, and passionately kissed him on the lips. Jack was immediately enraptured and could feel the magic tingle from the touch of her lips.

Whispers grew louder all around them, and Jack pulled away to look around at the giant oaks with awestruck wonder. "What is this place, and is that really the trees whispering?" He asked.

"This is the Whispering Grove." She giggled. "And yes, it is the trees that are talking." She pointed to a far end of the grove. "We enter, and leave each night, just beyond that tree line over there."

Jack shivered with exhilaration, "This place is electrified with magic."

"This is the place where dreams come true, Jack." She smiled. "And, it's even better on the other side."

A swift, sudden breeze blew through the grove, and a beautiful woman in a long, flowing white gown with blue and gold trim, stepped out of the nights' mist. She had radiant blonde hair and a heavenly glow.

As she sauntered closer, she displayed an endearing smile, "Hello, Miss Bella."

"Good evening, Lady Joy." She answered with a slight curtsie.

Lady Joy looked toward a befuddled Jack and nodded, "And of course, you must be Jack."

"How do you know me?" He asked.

"You're one of the seers that I knew would arrive here at some point in time."

"You mean there is someone else other than me?" Jack further probed with a perplexed expression.

"He will come in a future time." She calmly nodded. "The two of you will work together to save these woods and this grand estate."

"I don't understand all of this," Jack stated.

Bella turned to Jack and took hold of both his hands. "Lady Joy is the white sorceress of the Whispering Grove." She smiled sweetly. "She can see into the future."

"I can also turn wishes into reality." Lady Joy added.

Bella looked deep into Jack's eyes and nodded enthusiastically, "You were my wish, Jack."

"It's true, Jack." Lady Joy sighed. "Miss Bella and the others have waited many seasons for you to arrive. However…."

"Noooo!!!!!" A loud, angry cry coming from the direction of Lookout Point interrupted Lady Joy mid-sentence, and everyone looked in that direction.

Bella clung tightly to Jack, and cringed, as the deafening, and agonizing voice carried throughout the grove. "Don't be troubled dear. The scoundrel cannot harm you from where he is."

Jack looked seriously into Bella's eyes, "Who's trying to harm you, Bella?"

"Damien! The man who killed me."

Loud footsteps thundered quickly through the underbrush of the woods, and Jack turned to see a towering, muscular man, with wings, sword, and armor, swiftly heading their way.

"Miss Bella! Lady Joy!" The man exclaimed. "Is everything alright? I heard Damien scream."

"Yes." Bella calmly replied. "I'm just a bit shaken. Even still, after all of these seasons.

"Damien's spirit is not happy that Jack is here."

The large man re-holstered his sword, as he turned his attention toward Jack, who was totally awestruck, and a bit intimidated by his stature. Bella stepped between them and calmed the anxiety.

"This is Michael." She explained. "He's our protector, and the gatekeeper at the portal."

Michael gave a benevolent nod, "I've heard Lady Joy speak of you."

Lady Joy added an assured nod and a wink to his statement.

"If everything is fine here, I'll just return to the gateway." He grinned. "You never know when some nasty demon might try to sneak through."

Lady Joy took hold of Michael's muscular arm. "I'll walk back with you Michael." She turned to the young couple with a smirk. "We need to give these young souls some time to be together."

Michael and Lady Joy strolled off together into the woods, and disappeared in the mist, as a swift breeze rushed through the grove.

Jack was blown away by the whole ordeal, "Was I just speaking with an angel?" He asked. Bella nodded, "Outta site!" He exclaimed in response.

Bella looked at him with great confusion and giggled, "What do you mean by out of sight?"

"It's an expression that we use in the future when something is extraordinarily wonderful," Jack replied with an amused smile.

Bella giggled again, she flashed her radiant blue eyes at Jack. "People sure do talk funny in 1971."

Jack looked once again, with wonder, toward the misty fog where Michael and Lady Joy disappeared. "This gateway portal that exists out there. What's on the other side?"

"I can't tell you now." She reasoned. "But someday, when you're in spirit, you will know."

Jack gave an understanding smile, while Bella lightly placed her hand against the side of his face. She leaned in, closed her eyes, and once again, they engaged in a magical kiss.

"We should be getting back to the party." She stated with a clever smirk. "I wouldn't want my father to think we were being naughty."

As they sauntered down the path toward the lawn party, a calico cat strolled by them, and Jack turned to watch as the feline continued calmly on its' way.

"I've noticed that several dogs and cats are here as well," Jack commented. "Do they come with you through the portal?"

"Yes, they do." She replied with certainty. "In life, our pets are attached to us as family. So, it's only natural that their spirits would be here with us."

As they settled onto a park bench at the edge of the lawn, a gray cat jumped up onto Bella's lap, and she giggled.

"This is my little Esmerelda." She stroked the purring cat. "She was the first soul to greet me when I crossed over." She pointed over to where a dalmatian dog obediently stood sentry at the feet of the Captain. "That's my father's dog, Skipper."

Jack looked on with amazement, "So, when can I see you again?" Jack inquired.

"We're only permitted to come here on the weekends of the summer season." She forced a regretful smile. "It's only during those Friday and Saturday nights that we're able to step back into the spectrum of life, and time."

"What about this Damien." Jack sneered. "Why is he permitted to be here."

"He's confined to the perimeters of Lookout Point." Bella seriously answered. "None of us spirits, are permitted to go there."

"But it's such a beautiful place." Jack reasoned.

"Trust me, Jack. As long as his spirit inhabits those grounds, it will be a very dangerous place." She looked away with anxiety. "That's all I can tell you right now."

Questions flooded through Jack's mind as they sat there, "In other words. Everything other than the Point is like your private heaven?"

Bella nodded with a fond smile, "This is where we shared our happiest times in life, and it was there, at the Point that my life ended."

The cat jumped off of Bella's lap, and scurried into the bushes, while Jack continued to probe. "Why are the lawn parties constantly stuck in the summer of 1927?" Jack passionately asked. "Please tell me what happened, Bella."

"Okay. I'll tell you." She began. "It was during that summer that my parents first allowed me to be courted by young men." She paused as she painfully recalled. "Damien was the first to try, but I wasn't interested in him at all." She emotionally sighed. "When my father found out that he was pursuing me against my will, he forbade him from coming on the property." She visibly became upset. "Damien was infuriated."

"What happened then?" Jack asked with much interest.

"He snuck onto the grounds one night and tried to abduct me against my will. I got away. But he cornered me at Lookout Point." She shook her head with despair, and Jack slipped his arm around her shoulders to comfort her, while she continued. "All I can remember after that is falling."

Jack wiped a tear from her cheek, "I'm sorry that happened to you."

"When I died, my father ended the lawn parties." She closed her eyes. "For me, time forever stood still in that last wondrous summer."

Jack gave an all-knowing nod, "And, you and the other spirits have been caught in a continual time loop of that final summer."

Bella nodded, "I pleaded with Lady Joy to someday send me the love that I could not have in life, and she promised that some night he would come."

Jack gazed at the tear rolling down her cheek…. it tore at his heart. He reached up gently wiping her face. She lowered her head, pausing to gather her thoughts when she felt his warm lips press against her forehead. "You think it's me?"

"I know in my heart that it is." She stated with certainty.

Captain Stevens casually approached the couple and addressed his daughter.

"Bella!" He exclaimed with great authority. "I would like to have a word with Jack in private."

"Yes, of course, father." She stated with sober respect. "I'll go find mother."

Bella lightly kissed her father on the cheek before departing. The captain then sat down next to Jack and drew a deep breath. "She's very fond of you."

"I'm quite fond of her as well, sir."

The Captain raised his brow and sighed, "You are everything that Bella had hoped for in a young man, and my wife and I most certainly approve of you."

"Thank you, sir." Jack humbly replied.

The Captain took on a more serious tone, "However, we both know that true romance between the two of you is virtually impossible as long as you live." He paused to stress his point. "At least for the time being."

"Yes sir. I know." Jack sadly answered.

"Each season that you come back, you'll be another year older, but Bella will forever be seventeen." He paused.

"That wouldn't be fair to either one of you." He shook his head. "You have a life to live, Jack. You'll find another living woman, raise a family, and then someday, you'll pass into spirit."

Jack gave an agreeing nod, "Would you rather I didn't come here anymore?"

The Captain took another deep breath, "No. That wouldn't be fair either."

"What would become of Bella, if after a time, I never returned?"

The Captain looked downward, pondering Jacks' question for a moment, "I can only say that I waited 23 seasons for my wife to rejoin me here." He pondered another moment. "If Bella is truly the love of your life, then someday you'll return in spirit. You have to follow your heart, Jack."

The Captain smiled and gave Jack a friendly pat on the shoulder. "I can promise you this, Captain Stevens." Jack seriously stated. "Whether I return or not, I promise I will do everything I can to preserve this place for you, and the others."

"I believe you will." The Captain smiled. "For what it's worth, there will be another seer sometime in the future, who will help you accomplish just that."

Jack reacted with a raised eyebrow, "Do I know who it is?"

The Captain shook his head and grinned, "None of us know who it is, Jack. We'll just have to wait, and see." He stood up and beckoned for Jack to follow him. "Enough with the serious talk, young man. Midnight is closing fast, and we have two lovely ladies waiting."

Jack opened his eyes in the darkroom, and the afterglow of his memories made him smile. He first glanced at the clock on the nightstand and saw that it was just a hair before midnight. Then he glanced over toward the open window and saw a figure standing there. The apparition silently watched him for a few long moments, before quickly disappearing through the wall. The instance didn't even startle him. He already knew who it was that watched over him at night. The clock tower chimed at midnight, and he gazed upward with a grin.

"Goodnight Bella." He whispered.

Jack got up early the next morning and began typing away on his laptop. He could feel his health slowly failing with each passing day, and he knew that he had to put as much time as he could into finishing the novel. As he reached a certain part of the story, he had to pause to reminisce on how it took place. The thought of it still amazed him to this very day.

Young Jack arrived at Lookout Point with a pre-prepared lunch. It was a beautiful day, and the view out over the Atlantic Ocean was like something that would be seen on a picture postcard. As he took a satisfying bite from his bologna sandwich and soaked in the scenery, his thoughts were interrupted when another young man appeared, virtually out of nowhere, on the bench next to him.

The man looked to be in his early 20's and had straight dark hair. The clothes he wore were the style that would have been common in the 1920s. "Hello, sport!" He casually opened with a greeting.

Jack jumped up from the bench with surprise, "Where did you come from?" He moved back, "Don't you know this is private property?"

"I beg to differ on that." The young man chuckled. "I've been a permanent attachment on this spot of land for a very long time." He stood, and looked at Jack in a very peculiar sort of way. "So, you're the seer that they call Jack."

Jack took on an enlightened expression, "And, you must be Damien."

He arrogantly bowed toward Jack, "Damien Stone, to be precise." He grinned. To answer part of your question, I occupy this meager spot of land, and it is you sir who is trespassing in my domain."

Jack challenged him with a hard stare, "Why are you here in the daylight?" He asked. "I thought spirits only came out at night."

Damien let loose with a sinister laugh, "Unlike the other spirits, I'm not permitted to enter the gateway portal." He paused with his challenging stare. "Therefore, I maintain my presence here both day and night."

"So, in essence, this is your private hell," Jack stated.

"Ah! But such a lovely view." Damien sarcastically replied as he began to pace in front of Jack. "Let me explain everything in depth." He grunted. "Just like you, I was once very fond of Bella. I even asked for her hand in marriage." He frowned. But alas, her feelings weren't the same."

"But you didn't have to kill her." Jack sneered in anger.

"You're making a villain of me, Jack." He mockingly responded. "I simply backed her to the edge, and gave her an ultimatum." He pointed to the old oak tree. "It was the Elder Oaks fault that his branches could not reach her when she answered. No, never!"

Jack reacted with rising contempt but was diverted with surprise when the old oak tree opened its' eyes and sneered at Damien. He tried to ignore it as if it were a figment of his imagination.

"I heard that you disappeared without a trace." Jack further probed with much disdain. "What really happened?"

Damien continued to pace as he talked, "Many in town, speculated that Captain Stevens killed me, and buried my body somewhere on the estate." He arrogantly grunted. "But the Elder Oak and I know what really happened." He looked to the old tree. "Isn't that right, Mr. Oak."

The tree groaned, and its' leaves trembled, as Damien dramatically played out the scene.

"After I pushed Bella, I looked over the edge." He stated with a crazed smile. "It was then, that the old oak grabbed me with its' branches, and tightly crushed me against its' mighty trunk, until I was dead." He let out a maniacal laugh. "Then the old boy buried me beneath his vast root system."

"That's why you can't leave here." Jack stated.

Damien moved within inches of Jack's face, in an effort to intimidate him.

"So, you're a genius as well." He sarcastically answered. "If I were to ever attempt to wander beyond the perimeters of the Point, I'd be reduced to a pile of ashes."

"Why not just do it, and end your miserable reign?" Jack quipped with equal sarcasm.

Damien laughed, "Because, then I wouldn't have the joy of preventing you from accomplishing your divine mission."

"Is that so?" Jack stood his ground firmly. "Just what do you intend to do?"

"When my bones are eventually found, and moved from this place, I'll once again be free." He chuckled. "I'll return to destroy the portal, and Bella will be forever trapped in this realm along with me."

"I'll never let that happen." Jack angrily stated.

"Just as I expected." Damien sneered. "The spoken words of a foolish hero."

Damien faded and disappeared, but his maniacal laugh carried with the sea breeze and echoed throughout the grove.

The Elder Oak surprisingly spoke to an already baffled Jack.

"We must never let him carry out his plan or this place as we know it will cease to exist."

Jack felt a bit ridiculous, but still strolled closer to address the old tree.
"What can I do to prevent it from happening?"

"Just keep what you know a secret, and never let this property fall into the wrong hands." The tree's eyes widened. "That will ensure that his bones will never be discovered."

"I promise you that I'll do my best," Jack replied. "You have my word on that.

The old tree then peacefully shut its' eyes and spoke no further.

An old, weary Jack snapped out of his remembrance, and clenched his eyes shut, while he rested his fingers on the desk, at either side of his laptop.

"I let the spirits down." He sighed. "I only hope it's not too late."

Cecil peeked in the room and interrupted. "I don't mean to bother you, but Sasha was wondering if you'd be coming down for breakfast."

"I'll be down in just a few minutes." Jack chuckled. "As always, time kind of got away from me.

Cecil just smiled and turned away, but Jack called him back, "Cecil! Wait!"

He leaned back into the room to listen, "Is there a way that we could gain access to the woods without anyone knowing?" He inquired.

"It might be possible." Cecil nodded in thought. "Do you want to do it today?"

"I have somewhere I need to go today. Can we do it tomorrow?"

"Tomorrow it is," Cecil answered with an assured nod.

Later that day, Jack arrived at the local cemetery in Greenwich. Carrying a lawn chair in one hand, and a single rose in the other, he slowly walked from his car, weaving through the well-kept gravesites, until he reached his destination. He paused in front of a large monument of a muscular angel that towered over a marble top covering. At the base of it was an inscription that read STEVENS.

He stood for a moment, observing the beautifully carved sculpture, and it brought a sense of peace to his soul, "It's been a long time. Hasn't it, Michael?" He smiled.

He glanced beyond the monument to a large headstone that read, MENDENHALL. It was an ironic coincidence that his family plot was only a short distance away from the Stevens plot. It was as if by grand design, the two families were eternally connected. He unsteadily strolled over to the humble marker and placed his hand on the marble face.

"Hi, mom and dad." He forced a weak smile. "I guess I'll be joining you here pretty soon."

He set up the lawn chair, and comfortably settled into it. He sat soaking in the peaceful silence, that was only occasionally interrupted by chirping birds, and the distant sound of a lawnmower. He adjusted his fedora hat, and leaned back, feeling the warmth of the sun on his face. It was the perfect moment to reminisce about his parents.

He drifted back to a beautiful Sunday morning in that summer of 1971. He and his father were enjoying breakfast on the back patio and looking at the photocopies that Jack had made at the library.

Brad looked up from one of the pictures and glanced to the far end of the yard.

"That was quite an elaborate guest house that once stood there." He commented.

He looked back down, and casually viewed the other photos with amazement.

"It's hard to believe that old structure in the woods used to be a merry-go-round." He chuckled.

He took one long look at a particular photo, before handing them all back to Jack.

"The Captain's wife and daughter were very attractive women." He stated with a grin.

Jack couldn't help but smile himself.
"Yes! They most certainly were."

Jack put the photo neatly back into the folder and looked to his father once again.

"Now that you've seen the pictures, do you think we could ever restore this place to its' original glory?"

Brad stared straight ahead and pointed toward the clock tower.

"It's going to cost nearly five thousand dollars to fix the clock tower." He sighed. "I'm getting an estimate next week for clearing the brush, and power washing the statues." He shook his head with doubt. "As far as everything else is concerned, the upkeep alone would be too astronomical."

He laughed and looked toward Jack, "Besides, what in the world would your mother and I do with a merry-go-round?"

Maureen peeked out of one of the French doors and spoke with urgency, "Come on you guys. We don't want to be late for church."

Brad gestured toward Jack with a glint of mischievous humor, "The boss hath spoken."

His mind raced ahead to later that day. He and his mother were waiting in line at the grocery store, with a basket full of items. "I'm glad you came in with me, Jack"

Maureen stated. "Your father always wants to stay in the car to listen to his Sinatra 8 tracks."

"I know." He replied with a laugh. "And he's always the first to scold you if you forget anything."

"Jack! Jack Mendenhall." A familiar voice called out.

He turned to see Mrs. Wozniak walking their way, "Mrs. Wozniak! What a pleasant surprise." He paused for a moment, before gesturing toward his mother. "Mom, this is Mrs. Wozniak. She's the woman at the library that helped me research the property."

The two women shared a friendly nod "I'm pleased to meet you, Mrs. Mendenhall." She smiled. "Your son is a fine young man."

"Thank you," Maureen replied as she glanced toward Jack. "We are quite proud of him."

Jack quickly intervened in the exchange, "Mrs. Wozniak, I was wondering if you could tell me anything about the summer lawn parties that the Steven's used to have?"

"Oh yes!" She answered with great enthusiasm. "My first husband and I used to attend them. They were elaborate affairs that were attended by many of the famous people of that era."

"How interesting," Maureen commented.

"In fact, the Captain wrote about those parties in his daily journals." She added. "If you stop by the library this week, I'll show them to you."

"I can stop by tomorrow afternoon." Jack replied with excitement."

"I'll be looking for you then." She beamed with exuberance. "I'll have a cold glass of sun tea waiting for you."

"Great!" He exclaimed. "I'll be there."

The line moved forward, and Maureen gestured toward her, "It was a pleasure meeting you, Mrs. Wozniak."

"As well, Mrs. Mendenhall." She cordially smiled, before continuing on her way.

Maureen glanced back at Jack as she placed the items in the cart onto the conveyor belt.
"What a fascinating woman" She commented with an impressed nod.

Jack smiled at the memory, and slowly lifted himself from the chair. He looked one final time at the marker which included his name, and birthdate of 1954. He knew that soon his death would be recorded on it as well.

With a sigh, he folded the chair and made his way back to the Stevens plot. Resting the chair against an adjacent tombstone, he approached the marker and whispered what was written on it. "Captain Brice M. Stevens, March 28, 1870 - February 2, 1938."

His eyes wandered respectfully to the next name, "Amanda Halsey Stevens, July 22, 1885 – January 26, 1961."

Tears welled in his eyes as he read the next name, "Isabelle A. Bella Stevens, August 16, 1909 – July 16, 1927."

A gentle breeze swept through the cemetery at that moment, and he closed his eyes to savor it. He then placed the rose over Bella's nameplate and rested his hand against the cold marble next to it.

"I'll see you soon, sweetheart."

After breakfast the next morning, Jack and Cecil made their way out to the backyard and strolled along the perimeter of the cyclone fence that divided the properties. Cecil carried a large bolt cutter in one hand, as he hobbled along in his brace. Jack paused at the point where the yard used to merge with the walking path, and both men looked to the other side.

"Are you sure this is the spot?" Cecil asked.

"I'm certain of it," Jack replied with vigor. "It doesn't look like they've done much to that side for quite some time."

"It looks like somebody drove back in there recently." Cecil pointed. "Those tire tracks in the weeds look rather fresh."

Cecil then gripped the bolt cutters and steadied them against the fence wire, "I can't believe I'm doing this, but here goes."

He clipped the fencing, bent it back, and held it for Jack to squeeze through. Once he was on the other side, Jack took a deep breath and suffered a brief coughing spell that Cecil observed with great concern. After a few more heavy breaths, Jack looked to Cecil with confidence.

"Are you coming along?" He asked.

"I can't take a chance in those high weeds with my knee," Cecil replied while shaking his head. "Are you sure you'll be okay?"

"I'll be fine, Cecil." He answered in a calming tone.

Cecil looked at him with a worried expression, "If you get in trouble, call me on your cell phone."

Jack gave a confident nod, and wave as he waded through the high grass, and made his way along the overgrown path. He paused at the clearing where there was now not a single shred of evidence that a merry-go-round had once existed there. He continued to the curve, where he immediately heard the loud whispers of the oaks in the grove. He paused once more to curiously look deep into the woods, as though hoping to catch a glimpse of Lady Joy.

As he walked closer toward Lookout Point, he could see a pickup truck parked there. Two workers were sizing up, and preparing to cut down the Elder Oak with a chainsaw.

Jack panicked, and hurried toward the scene, "Hey! He yelled. Stop!"

The men stopped and watched Jack as he ambled toward them as fast as he could. "What are you doing here, mister?" One worker asked. "Don't you know this is private property?"

"As we speak, my attorney is negotiating to buy the property," Jack answered. "My family used to own it."

The worker walked closer to Jack, and looked at him with great curiosity, while the other, holding the chain saw remained in place. "You're Jack Mendenhall." He said with amazement. "I heard on the TV that you've been quite ill."

Jack gave a reluctant nod and pointed toward the old tree. "Why are you cutting down the old oak?"

"The owner hired us to come in, and clear the property." He answered with a glance back at the tree. "That old tree's half-dead, and it's blocking the view of the ocean."

A loud buzz of whispers bellowed from the grove, and both workers looked in that direction. "What the hell was that?" The other worker yelled.

The first worker shrugged it off. "Just the wind blowing through the trees." He waved back at him. "Let's get this done?"

"The sooner the better. This place gives me the creeps." The other worker yelled back.

"You know. People always said these woods were haunted." Jack commented, rather jokingly.

"That's just an urban legend." The other worker laughed.

Damien's maniacal laugh suddenly echoed throughout the point, and both workers paused to look around with anxious expressions, while Jack remained calm. "You don't own this property yet, Mr. Mendenhall, and you sure don't look like you're in the condition to be out here." The worker nervously warned. "You really should leave."

He motioned to the other worker, "Cut it down."

The other worker fired up the chain saw, and set the blade to the large trunk, while Jack cringed. The tree suddenly groaned loudly and shifted hard away from the saw. The worker dropped the chain saw and jumped back with fear.

"That damn tree is moving away from me." He yelled out.

The tree groaned once more, as it shifted back. In the process, part of its' root system pulled up from the ground, and along with it, a human skull popped out of the soil.

Jack looked on in dread, knowing that Damien's bones had been discovered. The worker closest to the tree screamed and took off running toward the truck, while the other worker walked cautiously closer, and saw the rest of the bones exposed in the broken ground.

Damien's maniacal laugh echoed out again; the worker ran toward the truck in anxious fear. The truck sped away along the pathway, as Damien appeared, still laughing. "I just love scaring the hell out of people." He announced, still chuckling.

In a flash, Damien appeared just inches from Jack's face, "Hello there, Jack." He spoke while surveying him head to toe. "Time has definitely not been kind to you."

Jack stared at him, as he tried to catch his breath, and Damien joyfully pointed toward the skull, "Look what the earth revealed, Jack." He spoke with intimidation. "In just a short while, the authorities will come to retrieve my bones, and I'll be free from this solitary confinement forever."

"I told you that someday I'd come back, and make sure that never happened." Jack intently stated.

"You're a sick, dying man." He replied with a sinister laugh. "I seriously doubt that you'll make it to the first Friday of summer. That means you'll never see your precious Bella, or have your wish fulfilled by Lady Joy." He stepped menacingly closer to Jack. "There's not a thing you can do to stop me."

"Maybe he can't, but I can." A voice bellowed from behind them.

They both turned to see the Elder Oak with its' eyes wide open. Damien immediately buckled over in extreme pain, as he watched in horror at the tree frantically gathering up his bones with its' withered branches, and stuffing them into its' large mouth.

"No, you blasted deadwood! Not my bones!"

Jack also watched with surprised shock, as the tree shoved the last of the bones down its' gullet, and Damien's spirit was consumed with flame. Within seconds, he was completely incinerated, and his ashes scattered in the wind. "It's over!" The Elder Oak announced with a huge sigh.

The tree's branches fell limp, and its' eyes drooped. As Jack moved closer, he was quite baffled over what had just transpired. "I don't understand what just took place. He said, addressing the tree directly.

The tree glanced up with its' sick, weary eyes, "I had to devour his bones, so they could never be found." It let out a dying groan. "But the evil in those bones is toxic, and will kill me."

Jack laid a trembling hand on the old tree, "You sacrificed your life over this."

The tree looked to Jack with ever-weakening eyes, "Alas, I lived a good long life, as you have, Jack." Its' mouth formed a weak smile. "I'll be dead to this world, but I'll dwell with you and the others in another realm."

"So, it's true that trees also have souls?"

The tree answered with a weak glance. It then let out one final, mournful groan. Its' eyes shut tightly, and it withered in death. Jack emotionally embraced the tree with his arms. "Thank you!" He exclaimed.

Sirens could be heard approaching in the distance, and Jack hurried from the scene as fast as his sick body could carry him.

Jack struggled to make it to the French doors of the house. He stumbled into the house in an exhaustive state and collapsed in a chair. Cecil hurried into the room when he heard him enter.

"Jack!" He exclaimed. "Thank God you're okay." He rushed to check on him, showing great concern. "I heard sirens. What happened?"

"Some workers were clearing the land." He struggled to catch his breath. "I think they might have seen me, and called the cops."

"You're not looking well," Cecil commented with concern.

Jack tried to stand but still struggled to catch his breath, "I have so many things I need to do."

"Just sit here, and rest for a minute," Cecil ordered. "What can I do to help?"

Cecil sat down in a nearby chair, while Jack leaned forward, and took a deep breath. "I gave my attorney your email address," Jack replied. "He should be sending over the finalized sale papers for me to sign."

"I didn't even realize you started the process." He shook his head with amazement. "I can't believe you closed the deal that quick."

"It's amazing how much quicker you can get things done when you pay in cash." He laughed. "When those papers come across, I need to get them down to the clerk of courts to sign."

"I can drive you there" Cecil replied.

"My sister is trying to assume power of attorney over my estate, because of my failing health." He grunted. "I have to make sure the property is signed over to the Historical Society before she has a chance to legally contest the sale."

"I can help you there, Jack." He paused with emphasis. "I know those people at the Historical Society, and I can get this thing done quick."

"Okay!" He nodded with renewed energy. Let's take this thing, and run with it."

"That's what I'm talking about," Cecil replied with exuberance. "We'll work this thing like a well-oiled machine." Both men let out a laugh and exchanged a high five.

Later, as Cecil hobbled down the stairs, and entered into the grand entranceway, the doorbell rang. He called out to Sasha who was in an adjacent room, "Sasha! Didn't you close the gates when you came home?"

"Yes. I'm certain I did." She answered back.

The doorbell rang again, and Cecil turned to answer the door with a sigh. When he opened it, he saw a stocky-built man in his mid-fifties standing there. The man held up a badge for him to see.

"Mr. Duncan." He began. "I'm Detective Murphy from the Greenwich police department."

"How did you get through the gate?"

Murphy glanced in that direction. "I used the emergency code that we have on file at the station. I hope you don't mind."

"There's no emergency here." Cecil protested. "How can I help you?"

"Do you have time for me to ask you a few questions?" Murphy asked.

"Yeah! Sure!" He cluelessly shrugged.

Both Cecil and the Detective noticed a FedEx package by the door, and Cecil alertly scooped it up, making sure to conceal the name it was addressed to. "The FedEx driver must have that same code," Murphy commented with a raised brow.

"Yes, he does," Cecil answered in a guarded tone. "Please come in."

Murphy gave a quick sweep of the interior with his eyes as he entered. "We had an issue on the adjoining property earlier today." He announced.

"I heard the sirens," Cecil replied. "What was the nature of the issue?"

"Two workers claim they uncovered some human remains out at Lookout Point." The detective shrugged.

"Problem is, there were no bones to be found when we got there."

"I hope you're not insinuating that I had anything to do with it." Cecil retorted in a defiant tone.

"Not at all, Mr. Duncan." He looked to his braced knee. "I don't think a man in your condition would be mobile enough to maneuver the rough conditions of that property."

Cecil calmed a bit, and Murphy continued, "The workers claim they saw Jack Mendenhall out there, at the same time they found the bones." He paused to gauge Cecil's reaction. "Have you seen Mr. Mendenhall?"

Cecil simply shook his head with a clueless expression. He gripped the FedEx package tighter and held it close to his body. Murphy stared at Cecil for a long moment, and rapidly nodded his head in calculating thought, before handing over his business card. "If by chance, Mr. Mendenhall happens to come around, would you mind giving me a call?" He asked. "His sister is quite concerned with his well-being. He is a very sick man."

"Of course," Cecil assured.

Before heading to the door, Murphy turned with one more question, "By the way, Mr. Duncan. We noticed that the fence on the property line had been cut."

He stared as though interrogating. "Did you know about that?"

"No," Cecil answered cluelessly. "I did not."

Murphy nodded, never breaking eye contact, "I'll make sure the owners have it repaired." He pointed with his finger. "But keep an eye out for any unusual activity. There's been a rash of break-ins throughout the neighborhood."

"Thanks for the heads up, detective."

Murphy took another glance around the room Then gave a friendly nod, as he moved toward the door, "Have a good day, Mr. Duncan."

"You as well, detective."

Cecil shut the door and watched through the side window until his car drove away. Sasha, who had been listening in, entered from an adjoining room. "Something tells me that we haven't seen the last of him." She stated.

"That means we have to kick this transfer of the property into high gear." He nodded. "I may need your help. Jack is getting weaker by the day."

"My assistant, Chantelle can take care of things in the city this week."

"Good!" Cecil exclaimed with an added sigh. "Like you, I have a feeling that Detective Murphy suspects something. The last thing we needed was to have him snooping around."

"What do you think he knows about those bones?"

"There's no bones out there." He laughed. "It's just someone's imagination running wild." He chuckled again. "Even if there were bones, how would Jack be able to get rid of them so fast. He can't walk five feet without being winded."

"I suppose you're right about that." She replied with a pondering thought.

Meanwhile, Jack worked diligently on his novel in the upstairs guest room. He paused from his work when he heard a light knock on the partially closed door.

"Come on in." He called out.

Cecil slowly hobbled in and laid the FedEx box on the desk in front of Jack. He then wearily sat down at the edge of the bed and propped his leg up.

"I need to get off this leg for a while." He announced with a deep breath. "You certainly look a lot more energetic than you did earlier."

"I'm burning through these final chapters," Jack replied with a smile.

"If you don't mind me asking, what's the book about?"

"I'm not going to tell you that." Jack chuckled. "You'll just have to buy, and read it after I'm dead, and gone."

Both men laughed, and Cecil moved the conversation ahead.

"Sasha typed up those stipulations on the property transfer. Barring any complications, we should be able to close the deal sometime tomorrow."

"Great!" Jack replied with enthusiasm.

"Speaking of complications. A detective came by here looking for you."

"I'd imagine my sister sent him. Hopefully, you didn't tell him I was here."

Cecil shook his head no and continued.
"It was about the incident this morning." He grunted. "Something about bones out at Lookout Point."

Jack's eyes wandered off to the corner of the room, as he shrugged.

"I wouldn't have a clue as to what he's talking about."

Cecil leaned back and took a deep breath, "I'm just curious. Why did you ever let your sister sell this house?"

Jack shook his head with disgust, "I didn't." He leaned forward and rubbed his hands together. "My sister took over the family business when my father retired." He grunted. "She ran that into the ground, and ended up selling out to a larger firm." He shook his head again and continued. "After my mother died, my dad went downhill very quickly, and Amy assumed power of attorney for the estate." He sighed. "She and her good-for-nothing husband Philip, sold the place while he was losing his mind in a nursing home."

"You don't have to tell me anything more unless you want to, Jack."

Jack wiped a tear and shut his eyes, "It's okay! It's therapy for the soul." He looked upward and forced a smile.

"My dad loved this place. When he found out they sold it, I think he may have died of a broken heart."

"I'm sorry," Cecil replied with sympathy. "I can understand how he must've felt."

Jack drew a deep breath and continued the story, "At the time, I was in New Zealand on a movie shoot for three months. I never knew about all that had taken place until I got back." He shook his head. "They never even had the decency to notify me of my father's death."

Cecil rolled his eyes in disbelief, "Wow! That sucks."

"Yeah!" Jack chuckled. "They burned through all that money, and now, they want to get their greedy hands on my fortune."

"Well! We won't let that happen, Jack." He assured.

Cecil struggled to his feet, and pointed toward the package, "I know those are your cats' ashes. If you want to spread them in the backyard, I don't have a problem with it."

Jack smiled with gratitude, "Thank you, Cecil."

Jack worked on his novel until the late-night hours. He struggled to sit up straight in his chair as he typed the last words, "All finished, and ready to go." He whispered to himself.

Taking another deep breath, he hit save, and then keyed in the command to send the file.
"Off it goes to the publisher." He smiled.

Jack reached up and switched off the lamp, and then gently dropped his head onto the desktop in exhaustion. He rested there, and thought back to the last time he saw Brice Manor, and the spirits on the lawn. It was the beginning of the summer of 1975.

Jack pulled up to the Brice Manor gates in his Mustang convertible. He paused to admire the Brice Manor sign with a smile before he continued to the house.

He opened the front door with excitement and saw his parents waiting there for him.

There's our college grad." Brad proudly announced, while his mother hurried to hug him.

"Oh, sweetheart!" She exclaimed. "It's so good to finally have you home." She sighed. "I only wish you could stay just a bit longer."

"I know." Jack sadly replied. "I have to pack whatever I can get in the car, and be in LA by Wednesday morning."

Brad shook his head with disbelief, "You already have two best-selling novels, and now a job with MGM." He gave Jack a nod of approval. "I'm very proud of you, son."

"I'm sure Jack is very tired from the drive," Maureen added. "You two guys go sit down, and I'll make some coffee."

Jack and his father made their way to the adjacent Sitting Room and settled comfortably into chairs. "I wish you could stay for another week or more," Brad stated with a grin. "I could sure use a conservative ally, while your sister is here with her Leftist Commie husband."

They both laughed, "I can't believe Amy married that idiot," Jack remarked. "She'll be supporting him for the rest of her life."

They laughed again before Brad moved on to a more serious subject, "I thought you should know this." He began. "Last fall, I had to have what remained of the merry-go-round structure torn down."

Jack only replied with a sad nod, as Brad continued, "Most of it was either eaten away by termites or dry rotted."

Brad stood up and grabbed hold of a four-foot by two-foot object with wrapping paper on it. He handed it to Jack, who appeared clueless. "Shortly after you left for college, I was able to salvage something that miraculously wasn't too far gone."

Jack slowly tore the wrapping paper from the object, and his eyes grew wide, "One of the tigers." He shook his head with disbelief and held it up. "I'll cherish this for the rest of my life."

Brad responded with a pleased smile, "I had the wood treated and sealed, and I touched up some of the faded colors." He looked emotionally to his son. "You can frame it, and hang it on the wall of your home in California. It will always remind you of home."

"Thank you, dad." He looked at the panel again with excitement. "I need to take this down to the library, and show it to Mrs. Wozniak."

"Before you go and runoff, there's something else I need to talk with you about."

Brad took on a more serious tone, and Jack listened attentively, "The city agreed to work with me on restoring the woods if I would let them make it into a public park." He stated, and Jack quickly raised concerns.

"Would it mean that we'd have to give up total control of the land?"

"No way!" Brad exclaimed. "I would never agree to that." He paused with great emphasis, before continuing. "They'll restore the walking path, lighting, benches, and they'll even maintain the grounds."

"What do we get in return?" Jack further inquired.

"We'll pay no taxes on it," Brad explained. After fifteen years, we can either take the land back or sign a new contract."

"It sounds fair." He replied. "But did you give them a list of stipulations?"

"Of course!" Brad answered with great assurance. "There won't be a playground or construction of any kind. It can only be open during the summer months, and the gates need to be closed at sunset. It's simply a place to walk, and enjoy a great view of the ocean."

Jack gave a slight sigh of relief and pondered the information for a moment.

"You need to add that under no circumstances should the grounds be dug up or disturbed at Lookout Point." He nodded with certainty. "You need to get that in writing."

Brad gave a clueless shrug, "What would the reason be for that?"

Jack had to think quickly for an answer, "Bella Stevens died there." He stated. "Out of respect for her, everything should be left as it is."

Brad answered with an assuring nod, "The bench will have to be restored, and probably a fence to keep people from meeting the same fate as Bella did."

"That's fine! But no trees are to be cut down, and no excavation."

Brad looked a bit perplexed but gestured his agreement, "I'll add that in, and I also think a memorial plaque would be an appropriate addition."

"Thanks, dad!"

A short time later, Jack enthusiastically marched into the library with the wood panel his father had given him. He went to the front desk, where a dark-haired library assistant greeted him with a smile. "Can I help you?" She asked.

"Is Mrs. Wozniak here today?"

The librarian reacted rather uneasily, and lowered her voice, "I'm sorry, but Mrs. Wozniak passed away back in February."

Jack lowered his head in sorrow, "Was she a friend of yours?" The librarian asked.

"Yes." He answered sorrowfully. "She was a very good friend of mine." Jack slowly turned and left without another word. As he walked to the car, fighting back tears, the first raindrops began to fall on that overcast day.

Later, as he sat near the French doors of Brice Manor, he watched as the rains came down heavily outside. His mother slowly approached and laid her hand on the back of his shoulder. "I'm sorry about Mrs. Wozniak." She sighed. "Your father and I didn't know that she had passed either."

Jack closed his eyes as she continued, "The last time we saw her, she mentioned that she had read your novels, and was very proud of you."

Jack looked up at her with great emotion, "Thanks, mom."

"I made a pot roast for supper." She smiled. "Let me know when you're ready to eat."
Jack gave her a nod, and a forced smile as she departed, leaving him alone once again with his thoughts and memories.

After supper that night, Jack returned to his vigil at the French doors and waited patiently for nightfall. The torrential rains had never let up since they began that afternoon.

He stepped out onto the patio shortly after dark, and noticed the glow of lights on the far end of the lawn, but heard no music. He just had to go see if Bella and the spirits were there. He adjusted the hood on his rain poncho, and set across the yard, against the heavy deluge.

When he arrived at the far end of the lawn, hardly a spirit could be found. There were a few canopied tents set up along the perimeter, but most of the activity seemed to center around the guesthouse.

Just then, a familiar voice called to him from beneath one of the tents, "Jack! You're really here."

He raised the tip of his hood to see Bella running across the lawn toward him, dressed in an oversized rain slicker. She crashed against him, and her energy nearly knocked him over. She embraced him tightly, and Jack could feel the love radiating from her being. "Come on" She motioned. "Let's get under a canopy."

They ran to one of the tents where her parents and a few other spirits were waiting.

"Welcome, Jack!" The Captain announced. "You've matured quite a bit since we saw you last season."

He and his wife gave Jack a long look, "How old are you now?" Amanda asked.

"I'll be twenty-two in August," Jack answered.

Bella eyed him with great infatuation, "He continues to get more handsome with age."

The Captain gestured toward the rain, "It's a shame that the weather isn't cooperating for the first night of the season.

Jack took notice, as the rains seemed to be falling even harder, "I'm surprised all of you are even here."

The Captain joyfully laughed off the comment, "As hosts of these grand affairs, we're here every weekend evening, whether it be rain or not."

"This is the heaviest rain we've had in five seasons," Amanda added with a laugh. "You know what they say, Jack. In every life, a little rain must fall."

"I guess that's true for the spirit world as well," Jack commented jokingly.

"We can only hope it clears by tomorrow night." The Captain emphasized. "We invited Benny Goodman and his Orchestra to join us."

Jack chuckled, "I wish I could be here for that."

Bella looked toward him with an extremely hurtful expression, "Why can't you be here?"

"I took a job with MGM Studios in California." He took a deep breath. "I have to leave tomorrow."

The Captain chimed in, and tried to steer the conversation from the inevitable, "Ahh! Sam Goldwyn and Louie Mayer's company." He smiled. "Congratulations, Jack."

Bella continued to emotionally focus only on Jack. "California is a long way from here. When will I see you again?"

Jack became rather uneasy, and the Captain took notice. He cleared his throat and placed his hand on the small of his wife's back. "Perhaps we should wander over to the guest house, and leave these young people to talk, Amanda."

"Yes." She answered with a raised brow. "That's a very good idea, Brice." They both pulled the hoods of their rain slickers over their heads and hurried away in the pouring rain.

Once they were far enough away, Jack took a deep breath, and tenderly wiped the wet hair from Bella's face. "Bella. I made a promise to your father, and I'll make the same promise to you." He forced a smile. "I have to go away for a long time, but I promise that someday I will return."

Jack emotionally paused, while Bella waited, hanging on every word, "For you, and the others, that time will seem like a blink of an eye." He looked away. "But for me, it will seem more like an eternity."

"But it's not fair." Bella protested. "I know you're the one that Lady Joy said would come to me. You're the only one I've ever loved."

Jack gently placed his hands on her tiny waist, "I love you too, Bella. But I'm a mortal, not a spirit." He smiled sympathetically. "Each season, I grow older, while you always remain young." He sighed. "If you truly love me, you'll wait until it's time for me to pass into your world."

Jack cradled her face in his hands and wiped her tears away, "Lady Joy will someday grant me a final wish, and I think you already know what it is."

Bella forced a smile, and Jack tried to lighten the conversation, "You know. We can still ride the merry-go-round in the rain." He stated with a sly grin.

Bella laughed through her tears, "Yes, we can." The two young lovers pulled their hoods over their heads, and ran hand in hand, out into the rain.

A short time later, as they rode the carousel horses, Jack glanced up at the endless circle of tigers along the perimeter of the ceiling and smiled. The swirl of the lights as they spun round and round, only added to the magic of the moment. A moment he knew he would carry in his heart for a lifetime.

The rains eventually transitioned into a light sprinkle, and more spirits began to arrive through the portal. While Jack and Bella strolled along the path, arm in arm, another young couple in their mid-twenties approached.

The eyes of the pretty brunette lit up with excitement when she saw them. "Bella!" She called out.

Bella immediately broke into a smile, and the two women embraced. "Florence Johnson!" Bella exclaimed. "When did you arrive here?"

"This is my first season." She replied with exuberance. "I passed into spirit just this past winter."

Bella glanced at her husband, who was dressed in formal military attire, "I know Ronald here, has waited a very long time for you."

Ronald sighed, and gave an agreeing nod, while Florence turned to Jack with a friendly smile. "It's so good to see you again, Jack."

Jack was quite baffled by her greeting, "I'm sorry. Do you and I know each other?"

She seemed quite amused by his question, "We knew each other well at one time. But I certainly looked a lot different then."

Jack was still stymied, and Ronald stepped in cordially, "Hello Jack." He smiled. "It's a pleasure to meet you."

Jack shook hands with him and gave him a nod of respect, "I see you were a soldier."

"Yes, I was." Ronald proudly answered. "I died in World War I, shortly after Florry and I were married."

"I'm sorry," Jack replied.

Ronald took a quick glance around, "We used to come to these parties quite often back in the day."

Florence turned an adoring glance toward her husband, "That was many seasons ago, but he was well worth the wait." She smiled. "I loved my second husband as well, but Ronald was always my true soul mate."

They affectionately pulled each other closer, and it brought warm smiles to the faces of Bella and Jack. "I know you two lovebirds have a lot of catching up to do," Bella stated while turning her glance to Florence. "I look forward to talking with you more, my dear."

"As well," Florence replied. "I hope you both have a wonderful evening."

As Jack and Bella watched them walk away, Jack was still perplexed over the encounter.

"Florence seems so familiar to me. But I just can't place who she is."

Bella calmly smiled and took hold of his hand. "You'll know in time." She replied.

Later, a small group of musicians played, as the crowd began to thin. Jack and Bella danced barefooted in the wet grass, holding each other close, with their eyes shut tight.

"I wish this night would never end." Bella sadly stated.

Jack nodded in somber agreement and glanced at his wristwatch, "It's seven minutes to midnight." He sighed. "you and the others will be going back to the portal soon, and I'm not quite sure when I'll see you again."

Bella gazed dreamily into his eyes, "I love you, Jack." She paused as tears welled in her eyes. "Wherever life takes you, always know that I'm watching, and listening to you from a distance."

"I love you too, Bella." He forced a smile. "I'll never forget you."

They kissed one final time before Jack slowly pulled away, "I'll see you again, someday." He assured.

"I'll be waiting." She replied. Jack walked away slowly, just as the clock tower tolled at midnight. He couldn't bear to look back.

Captain Stevens, who had been watching from the guest house steps, strolled over to comfort his grieving daughter. Bella buried her head against her father's chest and cried uncontrollably.

The Captain's eyes filled with tears, as he embraced his daughter, and watched Jack walk away into the dark. "He'll be back, sweetheart." He assured. "I know he will."

As the clocktower tolled for the final time, Jack turned to the now dark, and quiet lawn.
"Goodnight, Bella." He emotionally whispered. "I promise that I'll say that every night until the day I die."

In the darkness of the guest room, Jack was too exhausted to raise his head from the desk. He rested in the conclusion of his memories, knowing that soon, he too would be a part of that same spirit world.

An apparition gracefully moved across the room and stood sentry behind the desk chair he sat in. She gently rested her hand on the back of his shoulder. A peaceful smile appeared on his face, but he barely stirred at the touch. There was no need for him to look. He already knew who it was.

Morning came quick, and much had to be done. Jack was now the sole owner of the property, and it was time to transfer it over to the Historical Society. Time was of the essence. Though Jack had grown so weak, that he could barely stand on his own for 5 minutes, he soldiered on to complete his mission.

For most of that morning he, along with Cecil and Sasha, negotiated and closed the deal. It was finally finished. They returned triumphantly to Brice Manor and congregated in the kitchen area. "I'll put the coffee on," Cecil announced with a sigh.

"Forget that!" Sasha laughed. "Break out the wine, baby. This occasion calls for a celebration."

"Yes indeed!" Cecil exclaimed. "After a long seventeen-year fight, that property is finally back in rightful hands."

"And we owe it all to our good friend Jack." She happily commented.

Jack leaned, and steadied himself on a stool at the kitchen island, while Cecil strolled over to the Alexa unit on the counter. "Alexa! Play Earth, Wind, and Fire." He stated.

"Good choice," Jack commented.

"That's what I'm talking about," Sasha added jokingly, as she pointed to the two men.

Jack stood and took Sasha by the hand. They did a few dance steps, and he twirled her around, before sitting back down and breathing heavily. "You must've been quite the dancer back in the day." Sasha quipped with a smile.

"I used to love dancing," Jack replied. "Even still, I can't resist a few steps when there's a lovely woman in the room, and good music."

"Oh! And the man is a real charmer too, Cecil."

They all shared a pleasant laugh, and then Cecil caught the eye of the newspaper that he had brought in, and laid on the counter. 'Oh no!" He exclaimed as he picked it up for a closer look. "This is not good."

"What's not good?" Jack cluelessly asked.

Cecil held the paper up and pointed to the headline. "Did you realize you were missing?"

Jack grabbed hold of the paper to check it out himself. "I got so busy trying to finish the book, and take care of everything else that I forgot to check in with the caseworker that my doctor assigned to me."

He read a little further and rolled his eyes. "Leave it to my sister. She's trying to claim that I'm mentally incompetent."

Jack stood up and placed the paper on the counter. He paced a few steps and looked very worried. "If they find me, it's all over."

Cecil and Sasha shrugged and exchanged a clueless glance. "What do you mean, Jack?" Cecil asked. "We got everything done, and finished."

Jack acted as though he hadn't heard a word. His mind was definitely somewhere else.

"This just really took the wind out of my sails." He emotionally paused. "I really should go rest."

"I'll come up later, and check on you," Cecil stated with concern.

Later that night, Jack sat in one of the Adirondack chairs on the patio and stared out at the dark lawn beyond the clock tower

Cecil quietly exited the house and sat in the chair next to him. "You couldn't ask for a more perfect evening."

Jack took in a deep breath, "I just love the smell of freshly mown grass on a summer night."

"The landscaper was here all afternoon while you slept."

Jack shifted in his chair, and groaned from the pain in his stomach, "I forgot to formally thank you and Sasha for everything you've done so far."

"No need." Cecil shook his head. "We were just glad to be a part of the journey."

"Now, if I can just make it to tomorrow night. He nodded. "Everything will be fine."

"What's so special about tomorrow night?"

"That's a secret, Cecil," Jack stated with a straight face. "If I told you, I'd have to kill you."

Cecil looked at him with disbelief. Then Jack cracked a smile, and they both burst into laughter. "You're one crazy dude, Jack."

Cecil took on a sober expression and gestured out toward the lawn. "Is your cat out there?"

Jack sadly nodded, "I spread the ashes on the far lawn at sundown."

"You got any other family or special people you want me to notify?"

"I already said my goodbyes to the people that count." He sighed. "Just make sure no one knows I'm here until after I've passed. I don't want to die in a hospital."

An uneasy silence fell between both men, and Jack changed the subject, "Do you and Sasha have any kids?"

"One." He answered with little enthusiasm. "Her name is Lesa. She goes to NYU."

"What's her major?"

"Social activism." He replied in a disgruntled manner. "She hasn't figured out yet that the only activism that counts is when you get off your butt and make something out of yourself."

"Sounds a lot like my sisters' husband." Jack chuckled.

"What about you, Jack? Did you ever get married, and have any kids?"

Jack smiled shaking his head, "Women came, and went. But I guess my life was just too full to have anyone else in it." He shrugged. "I regret that sometimes. But then again, perhaps it just wasn't meant to be."

Cecil leaned forward in his seat and stared at Jack with disbelief, "You mean to tell me that there wasn't one woman in all those years, who might've captured your heart?"

Jack looked back into the darkness of the yard and pondered the question. "Actually, there was someone a very long time ago." Jack nodded in reflection. "I never met anyone else that could quite measure up to her."

Jack's eyes filled with tears, "She must've been a special lady," Cecil remarked.

"Oh yeah!" He smiled. "She sure was."

Cecil glanced up at the clock tower, "It's almost midnight. You ready to pack it in?"

"I think I'll stay out here until the clock tolls."

"I get you on that." He understood, "Let me know when you're ready to come in, and I'll help you up the stairs."

"I think we both have an issue with those stairs." Jack laughed. Cecil chuckled as he stood. He patted Jack on the shoulder, and then hobbled his way into the house.

The clock tolled, and for that solitary moment, Jack closed his eyes. When the 12th chime struck, he opened them once again, and peacefully smiled to himself. "Goodnight, Bella." He whispered.

The next morning, Cecil hobbled into the dining room to find Sasha sitting at the table with Detective Murphy. "Good morning, Mr. Duncan." He spoke in a commanding tone. "Have a seat."

Cecil shot a tense glance toward Sasha as he settled into a chair. "I have a lot to cover with you two," Murphy stated, pausing with emphasis. "First of all, I'll ask you the same question I just asked your wife. Where is Jack Mendenhall?"

Cecil took a deep breath as he shot another glance toward Sasha, who reacted by nervously closing her eyes. "He's upstairs, in the guest room," Cecil answered with a sigh.

"Why couldn't you tell me that, Mrs. Duncan?"

"He didn't want to be found." She shrugged. "He should be coming down any time now for his morning coffee."

Murphy nodded rapidly and looked to Cecil, "Is that the same reason you lied to me the other day?"

"I was only trying to protect him." Cecil rolled his eyes. "He's a very sick man, who just wanted to come back here to die." The detective slammed the tabletop with his hand.

"There are laws here that need to be followed." He paused and stared at both of them. "If a person is gravely ill, they need to be under the constant care of a licensed worker, or in a hospital." He shook his head in disbelief. "If the two of you knowingly deny him that care, you're breaking the law."

They both gave an understanding nod and continued to listen. "Secondly. Don't think for a moment that the sale and transfer of that property will stop our investigation. He grunted. "As we speak, my people are out there combing those woods for any sign of those bones."

Murphy's eyes dart between the couple. If anything is found, both of you could be viewed as suspects, or accessories to the crime." He paused. "If you know anything, it would be in your best interest to tell me now."

Cecil took a deep breath before beginning, "There's a legend that Captain Stevens may have killed his daughters' murderer, and buried him somewhere out there."

"I've heard that story over the years as well," Murphy commented while glancing up at the painting of the Captain.

"All of the Steven's family have been dead for years," Sasha stated. "There's no way of validating if it's true or not."

The couple both drew a stressful sigh, as Murphy pondered in thought, then continued, "Lastly, I'll ask this. Have you looked out your front window this morning?"

Cecil and Sasha exchanged a clueless glance and shook their heads. "The street out there is lined with tabloid vultures, who are all waiting on news of Mr. Mendenhall's death."

Cecil rolled his eyes in disbelief, as Murphy continued, "They all know he's here, and our department doesn't have the available staff to chase them all away."

"So, what do we need to do?" Cecil asked.

"Well, I need to take Mr. Mendenhall with me. That is if he's physically able. Murphy stated. "If not, then I'll have to call an ambulance."

"The man just wants to die here in peace, detective," Cecil replied with impatience.

Sasha held her hand up before another word could be said, "Wait just a minute!" She exclaimed. "I think I have an idea."

Both Murphy and Cecil paused to listen, "I know a licensed nurse who also volunteers for home hospice cases." She paused to see their reactions. "If we brought her in to take care of Jack, would you allow him to stay?"

"I suppose that would be acceptable." Murphy pondered. "But we need to have a doctor look at him first, and then we'd need to get it cleared with his Oncologist in California."

"I understand that," Sasha replied. "I can make those arrangements as soon as possible."

"We can also pay a cop to keep the paparazzi away," Cecil added. "I'm sure some of your people would appreciate the extra work."

"Fair enough!" Murphy nodded. "But this all needs to be taken care of by this afternoon, or the deals off.

"Trust me. I'm on it right away." Sasha assured.

Later that day, when things settled down a bit, Cecil limped through the open door of the guest room. The hospice worker, Jana Wilson was already there, trying to comfort Jack in any way she could. Jack rested weakly against the headboard of the bed, and stared off into a corner of the room. It was evident to all that the end was near.

Sasha peeked in behind Cecil. She was almost afraid of what she would inevitably witness. She glanced at Cecil with great concern, and they both moved closer to his bedside. Jana maintained her vigil and held Jack's weak hand within hers. "I missed our coffee chat today," Cecil mentioned in a low voice.

Jack managed to look his way with glassed-over eyes and forced a weak smile. "Too weak to get up." He answered in a shrill voice.

"You can go anytime you want, Jack." He emotionally stated. "We'll be right here with you."

Sasha turned away to hide her tears, "I don't want to die here." Jack replied. "That would mean I'd have to come back and haunt the place."

Cecil forced a smile, "You, and your odd sense of humor." He shook his head in amazement. "So, just where do you want to take your last breath?"

Jack's eyes gestured toward the window, "Out there? Out in the yard?" Cecil questioned.

Jack nodded, looking straight ahead, then urgently turned his eyes back to Cecil, "I have to be there by sundown."

Everyone exchanged a clueless glance, "Sundown? Why sundown? Cecil further quizzed.

Jack simply shook his head and looked away, "He's determined to hang on until then, Cecil." Jana commented. "He keeps on telling me that over and over."

Cecil looked toward Sasha as if pondering a profound thought, "Baby! What's the date today? He asked.

"June 22." Sasha shrugged. "Why?"

"It's the first Friday of the summer season." He answered with enlightenment.

Cecil turned his attention back toward Jack, "I know you love the summers here at Brice Manor as much as I do." He paused. "Does that have anything to do with it, Jack?"

Jack weakly stared at Cecil and shook his head, "I can't tell you."

"He's a stubborn one." Jana chuckled. "I've been trying to get an answer out of him all afternoon."

Cecil pondered for another moment and then motioned Sasha out to the hallway. They walked a short distance down the hall, and out of earshot of the room. "I got the issue outside with the paparazzi under control," Cecil stated. "Those people are like vultures ready to pounce on a dead carcass."

"I know," Sasha answered with disgust. "They have absolutely no respect."

"Get this!" Cecil continued. "I spoke to his attorney, and he told me that his sister indeed tried to contest his will."

"Can she do it?" Sasha gasped.

"No way!" He laughed. "Jack was one smart cookie. He put everything in a trust to go toward the philanthropy, and charities of his choice. The only person who got anything was his housekeeper."

"I'm happy about that." She acknowledged.

"What do you think about him wanting to die out there on the lawn, and wanting to wait until sundown?" Cecil curiously asked.

"I don't know." She shrugged. "I think he might be to the point of being delusional." They both sighed. "What's all this about with the first Friday of summer? Do you know something I don't?"

"It was just a hunch." He shook his head dismissively. "All I do know is that he's intent on holding on until after sunset, and we have to help him make it."

Sasha gave an agreeing nod, and they both headed back toward the guest room. They re-entered the room just as Jack motioned for Jana to come closer. "What time is it?" Jack weakly whispered.

Jana checked her wristwatch, "It's 6:40 in the evening, Mr. Mendenhall."

"Could you help me get dressed, so I can go downstairs, and sit on the porch?"

Jana looked to Cecil, who calmly nodded his approval.

A short time later, Jack sat in the Adirondack chair, dressed in a neatly pressed blue Oxford shirt, khaki pants, and casual loafers. Jana carefully placed a light blanket over him to ward off the evening chill. She then settled into the chair next to him and took hold of his hand. All the while, his eyes were fixed on the clock tower, as if waiting for the inevitable moment.

The clock chimed at 8:00, and Jack weakly glanced to see how far down the sun was in the sky.

Cecil and Sasha watched from behind the French doors, inside the house, "I think he's going to make it," Cecil commented. "He definitely dressed sharply for the occasion."

"He'll make it." Sasha confidently stated.

The sun was now setting, and it cast a golden glow onto the yard, "What a beautiful sunset, Mr. Mendenhall." Jana spoke with a comforting smile, while gently squeezing his hand.

Jack turned his head to watch it as it slowly slid below the horizon, and he managed a weak, peaceful smile, "Now, don't you go anywhere, Jack." Jana ordered in a soothing voice. "I have to pay a visit to the lady's room, and I'll be back in a flash."

Jana got up and exited into the house. It was now dark enough that the lights appeared at the far end of the lawn, and he could hear the first notes of music echo throughout the yard. His heart raced with anticipation. His eyes widened, and though weak beyond measure, he was able to lift himself from the chair. He stumbled into the yard, barely able to walk.

Just before he reached the clock tower, he fell in the dew-covered grass and laid there for several moments.

With ambition, he looked up at the glow of the lights once again and somehow found the inspiration to get up, and continue.

Just as he was making his way to the far end of the lawn, Jana came back out, accompanied by Cecil and Sasha. "Where on earth is he going?" Sasha inquired.

Cecil glanced to the far end of the yard, and an expression of enlightenment appeared on his face. "I think I might know," Cecil answered with a confident grin.

Sasha and Jana looked at each other, clueless as to what he meant. "Just go back in the house, and wait." He calmly stated. "I'll stay out here with him for as long as it takes." Without another word, Cecil set out, hobbling in pursuit.

Jack reached the lawn party and desperately searched for Bella among the gathering of spirits. His sight was failing him, as everything seemed out of focus, and spinning. The Captain turned from where he and his wife were conversing with guests and quickly reacted when he saw Jack stumbling his way across the yard.

"Good Lord, Amanda! I do believe that's Jack." He gently took hold of his wife's arm. "Go find Bella." He ordered. "We need to get him to the Whispering Grove, and Lady Joy as soon as possible." Amanda nodded with urgency, and swiftly took off in one direction, while the Captain hurried toward a struggling Jack.

Jack fell and was desperately trying to stand up as the Captain reached him. Cecil hobbled onto the scene, and the Captain looked at him with surprise. "Cecil! I haven't seen you in quite some time."

"So, Jack was the other seer that you told me about."

The Captain answered with a quick nod, while Jack let out an agonizing groan. "We have to hurry. He's dying." Cecil and the Captain supported Jack so that he wouldn't fall, and other spirits rushed to the scene to help.

The spirits lifted Jack's limp body and carried him toward the pathway. Jack could feel the life energy slowly draining from his body as they continued on the path. Through barely open eyes, he could see the merry-go-round as they passed. Children rotated in slow motion atop the carousel horses, all looking on with curiosity and concern. It all merged in a blur of lights, and disjointed music.

"Hang in there, Jack." The Captain urged. "We're almost there."

Jack widened his eyes enough to see the bend in the pathway that led into the Whispering Grove. The spirits carried him in that direction, while Cecil hobbled along behind as fast as he could.

Lady Joy stood amid the grove and beckoned toward a place she had prepared beneath one of the oaks. A swarm of fireflies hovered above that area like a large mass of blinking lights. The trees whispered loudly to each other and created a huge buzz.

Bella ran into the grove and fell to her knees beside Jack's dying body. She cradled his face and kissed his forehead. "Oh, Jack!" She cried. "You're so cold, and sick."

He opened his glassy eyes and forced a faint smile, "I came back, just as I promised."

"I know," Bella replied. "But it seemed like an eternity. We're both very old now."

A spark ignited in Jack's eyes in that single moment, as he forced himself to speak. "You're the most beautiful 108-year-old woman that I've ever seen."

At that comment, light laughter filled the grove among the onlooking spirits, and Bella cracked a hurtful smile. "You've maintained your sense of humor, right up to the bitter end."

Lady Joy stepped forward and nodded to Bella, who promptly stood, and backed away. Lady Joy then knelt and supported his head within her hands. "Hello, Jack." She whispered. "I know it's been a long journey to get back here."

Jack answered with his eyes, and the grove suddenly got still and silent. "I know the desires of your heart." She continued. "But you must try to speak them to me."

Jack gently whispered with all the breath he had left, "I wish to have my youth restored so that I can spend eternity with Bella, and the other spirits on the lawn."

Lady Joy closed her eyes, and caressed his face with her gentle hands, before raising them to the air. "So, it shall be!" She exclaimed.

Jack looked upward with wide eyes, as though the sky had opened before him. He gasped, and then breathed his last breath of life. Lady Joy respectfully closed his eyelids, then stood and stepped away. She couldn't help noticing the peaceful smile that was still fixed upon his face.

The fireflies then descended on Jack's body until it too became a large, glowing mass of blinking light. All watched with amazement, as they slowly ascended upward, carrying his spirit high above the canopy of the grove. Within moments, it disappeared, and all that was left was solemn silence.

A few long seconds passed before a sudden gust of wind blew throughout the grove, and Lady Joy pointed toward beyond the tree line. Michael appeared out of the mist, escorting a now young spirit being of Jack. "My kindred spirits of the lawn." She announced. "I now present, and welcome our new member, Jack Mendenhall."

Cheers erupted throughout the grove, and the trees whispered loudly. Bella could not contain her enthusiasm and ran to greet and embrace him. "Oh, Jack!" She happily exclaimed. "I can hardly believe that we're finally together."

"I missed you so much." Jack emotionally expressed. "I spoke to you every night of my life."

"I know," Bella replied. "I could hear you, and I watched over you the whole while."

"I'll never say goodbye again." He assured. "I promise."

Jack embraced her tightly and lifted her off her feet as they kissed. The onlookers erupted into even louder applause, mixed with joyful cheers.

Cecil shook his head in amazement as he approached the old shell that Jack formerly inhabited. He looked down with a smile, "Goodbye, my friend." He motioned around with his hands. "You too, are now a permanent part of this place."

He gave one final long look, before moving on toward the congregation of spirits that were gathered around Jack and Bella. As he approached, a young and energetic Jack, he greeted him with a brotherly hug.

"You were certainly a handsome young guy." Cecil joked.

"Unlike the broken-down old man you knew." Jack countered with a grin. "Thank you for everything, Cecil."

"It was my pleasure, brother." He smiled. "You and I were part of the plan all along."

"We were all a great team," Jack replied before he gestured toward Bella who was conversing nearby. "That was the special woman I told you about."

Cecil expressed his approval, "The spirits often spoke about another seer that she was in love with, and anticipated that one day he would return." He shook his head with amazement. "I knew for sure that it was you when I saw you struggling across the lawn tonight."

Jack smiled with amusement, "Hopefully, you'll come and visit us once in a while."

"Absolutely!" He assured. "On pleasant summer evenings like this, I'll go out for a stroll, and I'll find my way here."

"I'd guess that Sasha doesn't know about all this."

Cecil shook his head no, "Like you, this is a secret that I have to keep until I die." He motioned all around. "This place must always be protected."

"And when it's time for you to transition, I hope you'll be here with us," Jack stated with great emphasis.

"Absolutely!" Cecil once again exclaimed, then pondered in thought for a moment. "By the way. What's the name of your novel? I'd like to get a copy when it comes out."

Jack cracked a wide smile and gestured to their surroundings, "The Spirits on the Lawn." He chuckled. "What else would you expect?" Cecil smiled, as well, and gave a definite nod of approval.

Captain Stevens approached the two with a sigh, "Cecil, my good friend." He announced in a greeting, followed by a firm handshake.

"It's good to visit for another season, Captain."

The Captain gave him a friendly nudge with his elbow, "Fred Douglas and Harriet Stowe were looking for you earlier." He glanced out over the crowd. "I'm sure they're still milling about."

"Give them my regards." He replied, "My wife is waiting for me at the main house, and I really should be getting back."

With a wave, Cecil departed from the crowd to return to the world of the living. The Captain placed his arm across Jack's shoulders as they watched him walk away. "You should know that we weren't the only ones who were waiting for you to return." The Captain slyly remarked.

Jack was perplexed by his statement, and the Captain gestured for him to turn around.
"I believe you might know these people."

Jack turned around, and there stood his parents, along with Florence Johnson. Jack was quick to embrace both his mother and father at the same time. "I missed you both so much." Jack emotionally stated. "I'm sorry I didn't come back to visit more often."

"It's okay, Jack." His mother assured. "We're all together now, and that's all that matters."

"I'm so proud of the man you became." His father proclaimed with a beaming smile.

Jack then turned to Florence, who was waiting patiently, "I still can't place who you are, but I somehow recognize your spirit."

"Perhaps you'll remember me better this way." She quipped with a grin.

With a flick of her wrist, she transformed into the much older version of herself, and Jack quickly recognized her. "Mrs. Wozniak!" He exclaimed with excitement.

"Yes, it really is me." She happily announced.

Her husband, Ron stepped forward and placed his arms around her. "Young or old, she's still just as beautiful."

Jack gave an enthusiastic nod of agreement, while Bella strolled over, holding a big orange Tabby cat. "And last, but certainly not least." The Captain announced. "This little fellow wandered onto our lawn tonight as well."

"Mr. Snagglepuss!" Jack exclaimed with childlike joy.

Bella carefully handed the purring cat over to Jack, and it began affectionately licking his face, causing everyone observing to chuckle. Esmerelda circled Bella's feet, meowing, and begging for equal attention. She scooped the cat up into her arms and cradled it closely.

The Captain strolled over next to Jack's parents, as they all joyfully viewed the happy reunion. He turned to both with a cordial nod. His faithful dalmatian followed closely by his side. "I think we did quite well at raising our children." He proclaimed.

"We most certainly did," Brad replied, while Maureen gestured her unanimous agreement as well.

As the night progressed, Jack and Bella managed to get off to themselves. They strolled hand in hand along the pathway and came within eyesight of Lookout Point before Bella froze with fear and anxiety. "I can't go any further." She fearfully stated, while clinging tightly to Jack's arm.

"It's okay," Jack assured. "Damien's not there anymore."

"I know." She replied. "The trees told us all about it." But it's still very hard to visit the place where I died."

"We can claim it as our special place now, and nobody can take it away from us." Jack smiled. "Cecil and I made sure of that before I died."

Jack slowly urged her on, and they stood in the moment, viewing a calm ocean on a moonlit night. "It's so beautiful, and peaceful here," Bella stated.

Much to their surprise, they noticed a beautiful, healthy tree where the Elder Oak once stood. "The Elder Oak came back!" She enthusiastically exclaimed. "I thought he was gone forever."

The tree suddenly opened its' eyes and sprung to life, "I came back, just as I told Jack I would." He winked at Bella. "There is one catch though. You all must now refer to me as the Young Oak."

They all shared a hearty laugh, and Jack shook his head with amazement, "I still can't believe I'm conversing and laughing with a tree."

"I told you there was magic here." Bella grinned.

The tree motioned with its' branch, and continued, "There's one more thing you should know." He announced. The other trees and I decided to change the name of this place. He paused, and his large mouth formed a grin. "How does the name Bella's Point sound."

Bella clutched Jack's arm with excitement as the tree waited for a reaction, "I'd have to say that it was out of sight."

"I haven't heard, or used that term in years." Jack laughed. "But I'd have to wholeheartedly agree."

The clock tower tolled at midnight, and all the spirits paused to take heed of it.

"It's time for us to go, Jack." She squeezed his hand tightly. "Are you ready?"

"I've been ready for this since the first night we met." They kissed, before joining the procession of the spirits who wandered toward the portal. As they slowly strolled into the grove, hand in hand, Mr. Snagglepuss and Esmerelda followed close behind.

Cecil waited until after midnight to alert the authorities of Jacks' death. He had never really left the lawn party as he said he would. He found a bench on the far end of the yard and observed the happy scene from a distance. He couldn't risk the questions he knew Sasha and Jana would have. He also wanted to make sure that the spirits were not disturbed until after they had reentered the portal.

An hour later, police cars and an ambulance were parked at the entrance to the woods, as the attendants carried Jacks' covered body from the grove. Detective Murphy and Cecil followed close behind. "So, you're telling me that he wandered from the house late tonight, and you found him just before the time he died, under that old oak tree. Is that right?"

"That's where he wanted to be," Cecil answered. "I stayed with him until he passed."

"Normally, I'd take issue with that." He looked away in thought. "But considering the circumstances, I think we can write it off as a man's dying wish."

"I appreciate that, detective."

"I can tell he went peaceful," Murphy commented. "He actually had a smile on his face."

The detective then motioned toward the paparazzi who waited behind the taped-off barrier. "I'm sure you'll get a hundred questions from them." He sarcastically stated.

"It will all pass in a few days, and be old news," Cecil answered. "Famous people die every day."

Murphy further pondered the situation, "What do you think about those bones, Mr. Duncan? He probed. "Those workers seemed pretty certain that they were there."

Cecil gave a carefree shrug, If there indeed are any bones out in that woods, I'm sure there isn't anyone alive that knows anything about it."

"You do understand that I need to keep the case open until my people can thoroughly canvass the area?"

Cecil nodded, and the detective studied his face for a moment before continuing.

"Is there anyone else we need to contact about his death?"

Cecil shook his head, "He left me instructions on what to do. I can take care of it."

"What kind of plans does the Historical Society have for this property?"

"We plan to restore it to its' original glory."

Murphy gave a nod of approval, "I can't wait to see it when it's done." He exchanged a firm handshake with

Cecil. "We'll get in touch with you when the medical examiner is through with the body."

"Thank you, Detective."

Several days later, Cecil, Sasha, and Jana all stood at Jack's gravesite to pay their respects. The grave diggers left the trio alone with the casket before they started their work. In the distance, the chapel bell was the only sound, besides the chirping birds, to interrupt the silence. All three laid their hands atop the casket to bid their final farewell.

"Such a shame," Jana commented with a shake of her head. "With all of his fame and fortune, we were the only ones here to say goodbye."

A warm smile graced Cecil's face as he replied, "I truly believe that Jack is in a better place, and he certainly isn't alone anymore."

"I say amen to that!" Sasha exclaimed.

They all turned away and proceeded back to the car, but Cecil paused at the Stevens monument. He respectfully glanced up at the muscular likeness of Michael, who watched over their resting place. He saw a now withered rose resting above Bella's name, and it brought a peaceful smile to his face.

He bent over, and touched the marble next to her name, and whispered, "Take good care of him, Bella."

Days later, Cecil sat at the Dining Room table, looking over old maps, and photos of the property. He glanced up at the photo of Captain Stevens, who appeared to be watching his every move. For a moment, as he gazed at the picture, he could've sworn he saw the Captain smiled.

Sasha strolled into the room, carrying an item wrapped in brown paper, with an envelope attached, "What are you doing Cecil?" She asked.

"Jack wanted me to oversee the renovation of Stevens Park for the Historical Society." He explained. I'm just looking these over to get some ideas."

Sasha handed him the package, "The maid and I found this in Jack's room when we were clearing out his things." She smiled. "That envelope has your name on it."

Cecil waited for Sasha to leave the room before he removed the envelope, and tore the wrapping paper off. He held the framed wood panel up to look at it, and he shook his head with amazement. "Would you look at that?" He chuckled. "One of the tigers."

He eagerly removed the letter from the envelope, and as he read it, he could hear Jack's voice in his mind, "Cecil!" It began. "I can't think of anyone else that I'd rather pass this on to. Be a good caretaker. Always know that when you look to the far lawn on summer evenings, I'll always be there."

Tears welled in Cecil's eyes as he once again glanced upward toward the ever-watching portrait of the Captain.

The next Friday evening, Cecil and Sasha relaxed on the patio, enjoying the sunset. "The end of another wonderful day at Brice Manor," Sasha commented.

Cecil nodded, as he glanced out toward the far end of the yard, "I miss Jack already."

Sasha placed a comforting hand over his, "I do too."

They both looked out at the yard in deep thought, "I have to ask this." Sasha stated. "What was the reason for Jack wanting to wait until sundown before he passed?"

"I can't tell you." He replied with a matter-of-fact expression. "It's a secret between him and me."

"Oh, come on, baby!" She jokingly answered. "You can tell Sasha."

Cecil pondered for a few moments before responding, "What would you say if I told you that on summer nights like this, spirits gather for grand parties on the far end of the lawn?

"I'd say you're crazy." She laughed. "I think Jack's wild imagination must've rubbed off on you."

He glanced over toward her and smiled, while she shook her head with amusement. She then stood up, as she prepared to go inside. "Where do you think you're going, woman?

She leaned over and kissed him on the cheek. "Oh, baby!" She explained. "I have that big fashion show in New York tomorrow. I have to get some sleep."

Cecil playfully pouted, and she sighed, "Are you coming in too?" She asked.

Cecil shook his head, as he glanced back out over the ever-darkening yard, "I think I'll stay out here for a while." He grinned. "I might even take a little stroll."

"Just don't you go dancing with any spirits now." She playfully warned. "I wouldn't want you to re-injure that knee."

"Yes ma'am!" Cecil nodded with amusement. He waited until Sasha was well into the house, before leaning forward in his chair with anticipation. He could hear the first note of music sound out in the night air, and he saw the glow from the party lights on the far end of the lawn.

He looked back toward the house to make sure Sasha wasn't watching him. Then he stood up, looking back at the yard with pondering thought. "Oh! What the heck!" He stepped down from the patio, and hobbled across the yard with great determination, to join the magical festivities with the wondrous spirits on the lawn.

Tale Two:

The Summerland

All evil that hides within the shadows shall be revealed by the light of righteousness and justice…

In a high-rise office building in downtown Atlanta, Mitch Grant casually strolled through the office area of the investment firm that he built from the ground up. Workers glanced up from their work spaces as the dignified, middle-aged man walked by. Although well-liked by his employees, Mitch was not considered very outgoing. He had a quietness about him that many perceived as snobbery. But in reality, he was a humble and very generous man. It was as though a quiet storm brewed within him, that he tactfully contained.

Rinaldo Perez, a young executive with the firm waved him down and pursued him, "Mr. Grant!" He called out. "I need you to sign off on this check for your wife's charity."

"Is it for the women's shelter?" He asked.

"Yes sir! It's her monthly contribution."

Mitch looked at the check and reacted with a wide-eyed sigh. "They seem to be the only charity that doesn't send a receipt of acknowledgment." He paused. "I'll sign this, but we need that proof to claim it as a write-off."

"I'll look into it right away, Mr. Grant."

Mitch marched on toward his office without further word, and on the way, he was joined in step by his long-time business partner, Ron Baumgartner. Ron was a rather portly, and balding man that Mitch had known since college. They both started with nothing, and together they built a business empire. Where Mitch was normally of a calm demeanor, Ron was the total opposite. Even the smallest issues were a crisis. But he was best at calculating deals, and the two personalities made for a well-balanced partnership.

He followed into Mitch's office at a quickened pace and began speaking his purpose before either could settle into a chair. "They're finally ready to close that big deal in Toronto. I booked you a flight for tomorrow morning at 10:00." He spoke rapidly as he sat down in a chair opposite Mitch. "That should give you a little time to recover from tonight's festivities."

"I can't believe they haggled over a mere $50,000. That's pocket change for those people." Mitch sarcastically stated.

"Who knows?" Ron shrugged. "Maybe someone needed to buy their girlfriend a new car."

Mitch leaned back in his chair and chuckled at the comment. Then he cupped his hands together and peered at Ron with all seriousness. "Lakewood Heights Women's Shelter." He paused. "What do you know about it?"

Ron shrugged cluelessly, "All I know is it's a charity that April is pretty passionate about. Why?"

"I'm just curious." He pondered in thought for a moment. "Never mind. Is all the legal paperwork finished?"

"I'll have it on your desk by the end of the day." Ron shifted in his chair and looked suspiciously at Mitch. "What's wrong, Mitch? Your mind is on another planet today."

Mitch sighed with much emotion and glanced out the window at the Atlanta skyline. "I was watching the news this morning, and it left me wondering what happened to the world we used to know."

"We got old." Ron joked. "But seriously, I do know what you mean. Nothing seems to be as good as it once was."

"I feel guilty about getting this damn award tonight." He voiced with frustration. "I don't give to charities for the recognition. I do it out of the goodness in my heart."

Ron stood up and gave him a friendly pat on the shoulder. "We both know that, and that's all that matters." He smiled. "Just roll with it."

Ron went to depart the office, but turned with pondering thought, and pointed to Mitch. "We sure had some good times when we were young."

Mitch's face lit up with a sentimental smile, We certainly did, buddy."

Later, at Mitch's residence, he stood before the mirror, trying to perfectly position the tie on his tux. April Grant, his much younger wife, and an attractive blonde in her late 30's, sauntered up from behind, dressed only in a slip.

"No! No! You got it all wrong." She scolded. "Let me help you with that."

Mitch reacted with frustration and turned around to let her do it for him, "This is why I don't wear a tie unless I absolutely have to."

April undoes the tie and patiently starts over. "Just settle down." She further scolded. "We have to make sure you look the part of the successful entrepreneur that you are."

Mitch reacts with an annoyed sigh, as she finished, and gave it a light tap. "There you go. Now you look the part."

"While I remember it, can you have the bookkeeper at the women's shelter send us verification for the donation money they received?"

"I assumed Rinaldo had taken care of that." She replied. "I'll be sure to take care of it tomorrow."

The grandfather clock chimed in an adjacent room, and Mitch quickly checked his wristwatch.

"We have to get going, and you're not even dressed."

April reacted with frenzied anxiety, "Oh, Mitch! I'm sorry! Time just got away from me." She paused. "You go ahead, and drive the BMW. I'll take the Land Rover, and get there when I can."

Mitch reacted with reluctance, "Okay! But hurry!" He exclaimed. I wouldn't want people to think I didn't have a supportive wife."

"I'll be there before the ceremony begins. I promise." He kissed April on the cheek and hustled out the door.

April waited a few moments, and then peeked out the window to watch him depart. She turned around with a confident smirk and picked up her cell phone, "План сработал. Пора двигаться. (The plan worked. It's time to move), translated, in Russian,

Later, At the award ceremony in the Grand Ballroom of the Hilton, the mayor of Atlanta spoke from the podium while she held a plaque in one hand. As she began the presentation, April slipped in the back door just in time and quietly made her way to the front table, where Mitch held her seat. "Without further ado." The mayor announced. "I gladly present this year's community humanitarian award to the CEO of Grant Investments, Mitchell Grant."

Everyone stood with applause, as Mitch made his way to the stage. He graciously accepted the award and waited patiently for everyone to settle back in their seats. "Thank you, Mayor." He nodded and turned to the audience. "Thank you, citizens, of Atlanta."

He paused to make eye contact with April, who urged him on, "The last thing I want to do is bore everyone to death with a long speech, so I promise I'll keep it short."

A mild buzz of laughter filtered through the crowd but quickly dissipated as he continued. "My grandfather used to tell me to always work hard, strive to be as successful as possible, but never forget where you started."

He smiled and gave an intent nod toward the crowd as he continued. "We're living in times when we could all use a little more kindness, goodwill, and respect toward others. I enjoy giving back to the community that helped fuel my successes, and I plan to continue giving back for as long as I possibly can."

He raised the plaque toward the audience, "Once again, I thank you."

The crowd erupted in a thunderous ovation as he made his way back to his table.

Afterward, Mitch mingled with the attendees. April slipped her arm around him and gave him a quick kiss, "I am so very proud of you darling.

Ron approached, and couldn't help but make light of the tender moment. "Hey, April! Can you spare one of those kisses for an old fat guy?"

Those nearby took the comment with straight-faced indignance, but despite the embarrassment, Mitch greeted him with a brotherly hug, "Great speech, buddy!" Ron exclaimed.

Rinaldo Perez struggled through the well-wishers and reached in for a handshake "Congratulations boss! Great speech!"

With an assuring smile, Rinaldo quickly slipped away through the crowd.

"It should be against the law to be that handsome." Ron quipped while enviously shaking his head.

April became somewhat restless and lightly tugged on the arm of Mitch's tux. "You two gentlemen will have to excuse me. I need to use the ladies' room."

Both men watched admirably as April sashayed away, "She's quite a gal." Ron commented, while Mitch gave a nod of agreement.

Ron downed the last of his drink and jiggled his empty glass. "I need another martini. Can I get you something from the bar?"

"Please!" Mitch exclaimed. "Get me whatever pilsener they have on draft."

While Ron made his way toward the bar, a well-dressed older woman shuffled Mitch off to the side to chat. Mitch glanced up while conversing, and took notice of a young Black man that was observing from a distance. He stood off to himself with a gray tailored suit, white open-collar shirt, and held a trumpet in one hand. Those around him were almost oblivious to his presence. For some strange reason, Mitch was intrigued by his sober appearance while also wondering why he carried a musical instrument at such a formal affair.

The socialite woman continued to chat up a storm, while Mitch simply nodded, and listened politely. When he glanced up again, the young man was gone. At the bar, Ron stood waiting and took notice of April and Rinaldo at the other end. They seemed a lot more friendly with one another than one would expect. Especially with her husband in the next room.

The bartender called out, diverting his attention, and Ron responded awkwardly. He held his glass up and pointed. "I'll take a martini, and a pilsener draft."

He looked back toward April and Rinaldo, but both of them were now gone. He passed a large bill to the bartender, as he took the drinks, and slowly headed back to the Ballroom, with a pondering expression of concern on his face.

When the night was over, Mitch and Ron strolled along in discussion as they made their way back to their cars. "Where's April?" Ron inquired.

"She and I came in separate cars. She had a headache, and decided to leave early."

Ron carefully measured his words in careful thought, "Is everything okay with you two?"

"Yeah!" Mitch shrugged cluelessly. "Why do you ask?

"You're my best friend." He sighed. "I'm just concerned. That's all."

"I assure you that everything is just fine." He chuckled." Right now, my hand is a little numb from all the glad-handing I did in there, but…"

"Maybe you should run for politics." Ron joked.

"I actually had someone else suggest that to me tonight." He replied with a laugh.

"You know, it's been some time since you and April had a vacation."

"Since our honeymoon to be exact." Mitch agreed. "It's long overdue."

"You two should get away, and spend some time at one of our resorts."

Mitch shrugged and thought about it for a moment. "That's a good suggestion. I could look into the issues we've been having with that property in the Virgin Islands."

"Why not?" Ron agreed. "Mix a little business with pleasure."

Ron went to shake Mitch's hand but tapped him on the shoulder instead. "I'll give your hand a rest." He joked. "We'll talk more when you get back from Toronto."

"I'll give you a call when I get there, and fill you in on what's going on." He paused and pointed to Ron. "And thanks for your concern."

The same young Black man that Mitch saw earlier, strolled from the shadows and weaved between the parked cars. He paused to blow a few blue notes into the trumpet he was carrying and then continued on his way. Mitch looked in that direction. But when Ron turned around, he saw nothing.

"Did you see something over there?" He asked.

Mitch slowly shook his head, "Just someone else getting into their car that I thought I knew." He smiled. "Have a good night, Ron."

Despite being curious, and a bit perplexed, Ron simply waved, and went on his way, while Mitch got into his car. Mitch started the engine and turned on the radio that was playing 80's rock n' roll. He smiled to himself, as he accelerated to leave the parking lot. As he turned onto the street, his car hit a large pothole with a jarring impact.

"Damn!" He cursed. "I'll have to speak to the mayor about fixing some of these potholes."

He turned up the music and began to sing along with the tune. As he approached a busy intersection, he applied the brakes as the traffic light turned to red. His foot went to the floor, but the car would not stop. In that split second, he panicked, and fear ceased his entire body. As the car entered the cross-traffic, he closed his eyes. Horns blared, brakes squealed, and then a loud crash. All went dark, and silent at first, followed by bright white light.

Mitch slowly opened his eyes and squinted eyes against the bright sun that peeked through the curtains of an open window. He rolled over and was startled to find himself in bed with strange surroundings.

He sat straight up, trying to snap to his senses, "April! Honey! Are you here?" He called out.

In the silence, he waited for a response. The birds chirped outside, and dogs barked in the distance. Mitch pushed aside the plush royal and white sheets and kicked his feet on the floor. A few seconds later it dawned on him he was naked…. *Where in the hell am I?*

A pleasant breeze blew in the open window, catching his attention. He glanced across the room at the rustling curtains. *I can't leave this room naked,* he chuckled. *Where are my damn clothes?*

He noticed that the door to the room was slightly ajar, and his eyes then moved to the four drawer dresser near the bed, *I hope there are some clothes in that dresser.* Inside the top drawer were neatly folded garments. The whole scene had him stunned…. He chose a pair of jeans and strolled toward the closet, noticing it was also fully stocked with mens clothes and shoes. *Somebody has good taste...., * he thought as he sorted through the garments.

Mitch took a shirt from a hanger, and checked the collar tag, *same size that I wear.* He shrugged, *what are the odds?* One specific detail caught his attention, n*o women's clothes. I guess April's out of luck.*

As he studied the whole scene more closely, and placed the clothes he had chosen, neatly on top of the bed, he took notice of his own body odor, *whew! I need a shower.* He glanced to the adjacent bathroom, and went to investigate. It was stocked with all the items he'd need to freshen himself up.

In no time at all, he was showered, shaved, and fully dressed. Now it was time to explore the rest of his surroundings, *I wish I knew what I did with my cell phone*, he muttered as he pushed the bedroom door open, and entered into the living room. He slowly wandered toward the large bay window, taking note of the retro-style furniture around him. It was a bit rustic, but comfortable and homey just the same.

Mitch's thoughts continued to run wild, *this is crazy!* He exclaimed. *I don't even see a landline phone in this place.*

A pleasant breeze drifted through the open window, and brought the smell of fresh-cut grass along with it. *What a beautiful view.* He thought out loud as he looked out into the spacious lawn with a serene lake in the backdrop. *Where in the hell is everybody?* He expressed with mild anxiety.

"April!" He called out. *Where is that woman?*

Mitch finally decided to explore the rest of the cottage. He wandered into the adjoining kitchen, and curiously winced, *I need to get rid of this pounding headache. I have to get a cup of coffee.*

The pantry looked appealing, and he opened the doors to scan the shelves. *Oh, chock full of o' nuts.....* it put a smile on his face. *How lucky can I get? Somebody actually drinks the same brand of coffee that I do.*

A short time later, Mitch ventured outside with a cup of coffee in hand. A stone path followed across the fresh mown lawn that was still glistening with morning dew. He looked ahead to the lake, which was as blue as the sky above it, *this is like paradise.*

As he strolled toward the lake, he noticed several frolicking orange Tabby cats on the lawn around him. The sight, made him giggle. He scanned the shoreline and caught sight of the young Black man he'd seen at the awards banquet. Mitch paused for a second to enjoy the sweet tune he was playing with his horn before trying to get his attention.

He called out to him just as he began to stroll away, "Hey, you there! Wait!" However, his address went unheeded, and the man carried on along the shoreline.

In the distance, he heard the engines of an incoming boat on the lake. It diverted his attention from the man with the horn, as the outboard slowed in its approach to the pier. The boat throttled down gliding to a resting spot near the dock.

Mitch curiously watched as a balding young man in his early twenties tied the line of the vintage Chris-Craft to one of the pier posts. His attire matched the early 20th century, including his round horn-rimmed glasses. Mitch set his coffee down on the path, and desperately hurried toward him, waving his arms, "Hey there!"

When the man saw Mitch, he calmly, but eagerly marched to greet him, "Mitch!" He called out. "It's good to see you've finally made it."

As the two men came to a halt, Mitch appeared to be totally perplexed, "Do you and I know each other?" He asked while accepting his firm handshake.

"Yeah! I guess you could say that." The man stated with a grin, "It's been some time since we last saw each other, but I knew right away it was you."

Mitch motioned to everything around them, "I can't seem to figure out how I got here or where I'm at."

"That's understandable." The man smiled, "It took me a while to figure it out as well."

Mitch gazed oddly at him, but then turned his attention once again to the scenery, "There was a Black guy with a horn walking along the shore just as you arrived. I tried to talk to him, but he ignored me."

The man looked in the direction Mitch was pointing, but there was no one in sight. "I didn't see him, but it sounds like you're talking about Gabriel."

Mitch hesitated, in pondering thought; he was even more perplexed than before, "Have you by chance seen my wife April? I can't seem to find her"

"Unless she was walking on the water, there's no way of me knowing her." He chuckled. "What does she look like?"

"She's a good-looking blonde with a descent set of assets." Mitch explained with his hands.

"Believe me!" The man laughed. "If there was a woman around here that fit that description, I'm sure I wouldn't have missed her."

Mitch couldn't help but laugh along with him, and he settled into a calmer demeanor. "This is a beautiful place you have here," Mitch stated, as he motioned all around them. "It's the type of place that I always dreamed of having for myself."

"I'm glad you like it, Mitch." He chuckled, "But needless to say, I'm just the caretaker..."

"If you don't own it, then who does?"

"You do, Mitch." The man replied matter-of-factly.

Mitch turned perturbed, trying to hold his rage, "Okay! This joke has gone far enough." Mitch fumed. "It's obvious that someone must've drugged me, and brought me here. Who exactly are you, and where are we?"

The man motioned with his hands, trying to calm Mitch down, "You really don't know who I am. Do you?" He asked.

"No!" Mitch impatiently exclaimed. "I've never seen you before in my life."

"I wouldn't exactly say that." The man answered. "Let's just say you knew me when I was much older." He paused. "I'm your grandfather, Harry Grant."

Mitch sarcastically laughed, and shook his head, "And I suppose this place must be heaven."

"Close!" Harry responded with a slow, thoughtful nod. "We call this place the Summerland. People come here to recover from the traumas of life, before either moving on to eternal rest, or reincarnation."

Mitch defiantly shook his head, "You expect me to believe that?"

Harry looked away with frustration and pondered the situation for a moment, "Okay! Let's try this." He stated. "I had a blue 1968 Chrysler Imperial convertible. I used to take you downtown with me when I played the numbers. We'd always stop on the way home, and get an ice cream cone from France's Dairy."

Mitch listened with amazement, "And, I promised to never tell grandma where we went."

"That was always our little secret." Harry chuckled. "But I think Tilly always knew."

Mitch was rendered speechless….. Harry motioned toward two Adirondack chairs in the yard.

"Maybe you and I better sit down." As they both settled comfortably in their chairs, one of the Tabby cats eagerly jumped into Mitch's lap and settled comfortably.

Harry motioned toward it with a warm smile, "Do you remember that little guy?"

Mitch looked closely at the cat, and shrugged, "He looks a lot like the first of the many orange Tabby's I've had throughout the years."

Harry motioned to all the other cats who settled closely around them on the lawn. "And every one of those cats were named Thomas." He chuckled. "There were six to be exact."

Mitch took the time to eye every one of them, and took on a more serious demeanor, "So, if this all isn't a dream or some cruel joke. Am I really dead?"

Harry answered with a matter-of-fact nod, "It must've happened rather suddenly. Otherwise, you would've known."

Mitch pondered his predicament for a quick moment, "It must've been the accident. I heard the crash, and felt the impact." He paused "Before that, I remember listening to big hair music on the radio, and then my brakes wouldn't work."

"What in the hell is big hair music?" Harry sarcastically asked.

Mitch couldn't help but chuckle at his reaction, "It was a style of music that was popular in the 80s." He answered. "They called it big hair because the musicians had very long hair, used lots of hairspray to make it stand up, and they wore skin-tight spandex pants."

"In other words, they were what we called fairies back in the day," Harry stated with an odd expression.

Mitch emphatically shook his head and laughed with amusement, "No grandpa!" Actually, the chicks went crazy over those guys." He paused. "I should know. I played in one of those bands."

Harry looked straight at Mitch with near shock, "My Lord! I'm certainly glad you came to your senses."

"I did what I had to do back then to help pay the bills." Mitch reached over, and patted his grandfather on the arm, "I suppose we have quite a bit to talk about." He smiled. "But then again, I guess we have an eternity for that."

Mitch grabbed hold of his head with both hands, and cringed, "This damn headache!" Mitch cried with frustration.

"You must've had some serious head trauma," Harry stated with sober concern. "It'll heal in time." Harry gave an anxious gesture toward the boat, "How would you like to take a ride, and go see your grandmother, and your parents?

Mitch lifted his hands and shrugged, "Sure! I can't wait to see them again, and it's not like I have anywhere else I need to be."

"Just don't be too shocked by what you see." Harry quipped with a grin.

A short time later, Harry and Mitch were cruising across the lake in the boat. The cool mist from the wake felt soothing against Mitch's skin, as he took in all the beautiful scenery along the shoreline, and absorbed the warmth of the sun. They conversed with each other loudly over the pleasant hum of the inboard twin engines that sounded like an amplified swarm of bees around a hive. "I love this boat, grandpa. What kind is it?"

"It's a sixteen-foot, mahogany Chris-Craft, Special Runabout." He let out a joyful laugh. "I always wanted one of these baby's when I was still alive, but I just couldn't afford it."

Mitch glanced over at Harry, and replied without words, but with just a pleasing smile.

April sat calmly reading an entertainment magazine, while Ron leaned forward in his chair, and nervously stared at the clock on the wall of the hospital waiting room. Ron had been there for most of the night, while April only arrived about a half-hour before. Doctor Howell, a dignified man in his early 60's entered, and motioned to them in a rather grim, and apprehensive demeanor.

They both stood up, expecting the worst, "Is he…?

The doctor shook his head before she could finish her question, "Mr. Grant had a very severe head trauma, among other internal injuries." He paused. "We had to put him into an induced coma so that we could relieve the pressure on his brain."

Ron reacted with great distress, while April simply stared blank-faced at the doctor, "What are his chances for recovery?" Ron asked.

"Very slim" the doctor took a deep breath. "We have him stabilized for now, but only time will tell."

"I don't want to see him suffer like that." April glanced away momentarily in frustration. "If it looks like there's no hope, I would rather we pulled the plug, and let him die with dignity."

Both the doctor and Ron reacted awkwardly to her request, "With all due respect, Mrs. Grant, it's a bit early in the process for that sort of decision." He exchanged a quick, wide-eyed glance with Ron. "Do you know if Mr. Grant has a do not resuscitate order in his will?"

April turned her attention to Ron in a somewhat state of annoyance, "You're the executor of his will. Does he have that clause in it?"

"Not that I'm aware of, April." Ron slowly shook his head.

"He's being prepped in the ICU unit as we speak." The doctor concluded. "Mrs. Grant should be able to see him in about an hour or so."

"What about me?" Ron asked.

"Are you family?"

"Close." He smiled. "I'm his business partner and best friend."

"It'd be best if you waited a few days." The doctor advised. "He's in pretty rough shape." Ron reacted with great disappointment, while April simply returned to her seat without further word.

In a much happier place, Harry's 1957 Ford Sunliner convertible pulled into the driveway of a two-story Craftsman-style home. The yard of the home was well maintained, and an American flag waved proudly from one of the support posts on the front porch.

Mitch got out of the car and looked around with wonder and awe. Harry chuckled with amusement as he watched his reaction. "This is amazing, grandpa. This is exactly the way I remember your old house" He surveyed the area further. "Even the neighborhood looks the same."

"We were quite happy in that old neighborhood," Harry stated. "Come on! Let's go inside."

Every step that Mitch took brought him further back to a time that he thought he'd never see again. As they entered the house, he took note of every detail from the dark woodwork, the varnished hardwood floors, and the décor from an era gone by.

"Tilly!" Harry called out. "We have company."

Mitch's grandmother entered from the kitchen wearing a summer dress, and apron. She looked as she did in her mid-20s. A likeness that Mitch had never seen. "Our little Mitch!" She rushed to hug and kiss him. "You grew up to be such a handsome man."

"Grandma!" Mitch exclaimed with surprise. "I never saw you when you were young. You are one hot-looking lady."

"Oh my!" She backed away with embarrassment. "Am I sweating that bad? I have been working over the stove."

"No! No!" Mitch laughed. "That came out wrong. I was trying to say that you were very pretty."

"Really, Mitch!" Harry joked. "Surely you didn't think that your grandpa would ever marry an ugly woman."

"Oh, Harry!" Tilly blushed. "He probably just remembers me when I was a fat old lady."

Much to Mitch's surprise, two small children that he couldn't recognize rushed into the room. The boy, who was dressed in brown knickers, a white button-up shirt, and a flat cap spoke first.
"There's my boy, Mitch."

The little girl, who wore a gray dress, and had a pink ribbon in her blonde hair, ran and embraced Mitch around his knees. "Ohhh! My baby!" It's so good to see you again."

Mitch was flabbergasted, "Mom?... Dad? No! It can't be. They're kids...."

Harry and Tilly had to cup their hands over their mouths to contain their amusement, while the little boy jokingly elbowed Harry in the hip, "I told you he wouldn't recognize us, dad."

Harry cleared his throat and tried to maintain a straight face. "These are really your parents, but they prefer to be addressed as Bobby and Doris."

"But they're children!" Mitch stated with disbelief.

"This is how they chose to be in the Summerland," Harry explained. "They spent an adult life together, and now they're sharing the joys of childhood."

Doris stood and examined Mitch for a long moment with her bright blue eyes. "You've aged quite well."

"I never expected to see you two as children." He rolled his eyes. "This is all rather bizarre, to say the least."

Mitch tried to process the moment and turned to Harry with a perplexed expression, "I don't quite understand all of this." He paused. "How is it that you and grandma are young, mom and dad are even younger, but I'm the same age as I was when I died?"

"Let me ask you this, Mitch." He grinned. "If you could go back to the happiest years of your life, where would you most like to be?"

"That's easy," he replied. "I'd like to be in my early twenties again."

Harry gave him an assured nod, "Just close your eyes for a moment, and imagine it."

Mitch clenched his eyes shut, and concentrated, while Harry continued speaking in a calm tone.
"Now, open your eyes, walk over to that mirror, and take a look."

Mitch opened his eyes to see everyone watching him with brimming exuberance. He walked over to the wall mirror in the foyer and began laughing, "It worked! I'm really young again."

"Where's all that long hair you had back then?" Doris asked.

"That was an aspect of my life that I chose to leave back in the 1980s, mom."

Harry laughed and rested his hand firmly on Mitch's shoulder. "Here in the Summerland, you can be anything, or have anything that you want." He chuckled. "all you have to do is imagine it."

"So, the boat, the car, and everything else here is just a manifest of our imaginations?" Mitch asked.

"And, also a re-enactment of the most cherished memories of our lives," Harry answered with an assured nod.

Mitch glanced at all the smiling faces before him, and let out a laugh, "This place is amazing!" He declared. "It's where all dreams come true." Harry replied.

A short time later, they all sat around the dining table to eat lunch. Tilly glanced up at Mitch, who was delightfully devouring the food on his plate. "I bet it's been a while since you had a home-cooked meal."

Mitch nodded with his mouth full, "This is delicious."

Bobby shot a stern look in his direction, "Don't talk with your mouth full, young man."

"Yes sir!" Mitch answered with a sober glance.

There was a short pause of silence, as everyone continued eating their meal. Tilly was persistent in continuing the conversation with her grandson. "How do you like your cottage, dear?" She asked with a sly grin. "All of us spent a lot of time preparing it for you."

"It couldn't be more perfect, grandma." Mitch quickly glanced at every face at the table. "Thank you all."

After a few more moments, Doris spoke up with the expected exuberance of a child.
"Would you like your dad and me to take you to the amusement park, Mitch?"

Mitch burst out laughing, nearly choking on his food, "Shouldn't I be asking you two that? You're the only kids in the room."

Bobby pointed a scolding finger at Mitch, accompanied by a scornful expression. "Watch your attitude, young man. We're still your parents."

"I'll try to remember that dad. It's not that easy."

Harry finally chimed in, addressing Bobby and Doris, "You two kids need to settle down." He scolded. "Mitch hasn't even been here for a day. The amusement park can wait." They both pouted as children would, while the three adults exchanged glancing smirks.

Suddenly, without warning, Mitch dropped his fork onto his plate, and clutched his head, groaning with excruciating pain. Everyone at the table immediately rushed to his side with much concern. "We need to get him over to the couch," Harry ordered. "He's having some kind of a seizure."

At the hospital, a nurse ushered April into the ICU, and April strutted on ahead like she owned the place, "I'll give you a few moments, Mrs. Grant."

April turned her nose up and said nothing as she left the room. She gazed down with emotionless disdain at Mitch, whose entire head was bandaged. He had a large breathing tube leading into his mouth and monitors constantly measuring all of his vitals.

"You stupid, stubborn idiot!" She exclaimed with venom in her voice. "Why couldn't you have just died the way you were supposed to." She grunted. "Now you've gone, and complicated everything for me." She shook her head with frustration. "I should've just killed you myself."

Back in the Summerland, Mitch laid sleeping on the living room couch. Doris had placed a cold wash cloth across his forehead and sat holding his hand. He woke with a sudden startle and looked all around him. "Are you okay, honey?" His mother asked.

He looked at her with a puzzled expression, "Did you just hear that voice, mom?" The rest of the family entered from an adjacent room.

She shook her head and turned to the others, "Mitch is hearing voices."

"What did the voices say?" Bobby asked.

"It was my wife April." He stared off with a hurtful expression, "She asked me why I couldn't have just died."

"That doesn't make any sense," Harry stated. "You're already dead, Mitch."

"Perhaps you were just having a dream, sweetheart," Tilly suggested.

He removed the washcloth from his head, and slowly sat up. "What happened to me?"

"You fainted at the dinner table," Doris replied. "You've been sleeping for over an hour."

Mitch continued in distress, "I think I know how I died."

"From the way you described it, you were obviously in an accident," Harry stated.

Mitch subtly shook his head, "I think my wife had me killed."

Everyone exchanged a quick, concerning glance, while Mitch sat trying to make sense of it all. Bobby walked over and gave him a light hand tap to the side of his face, "It's all done, and over." He assured. "Everything is okay now, son."

"You went through something very traumatic, Mitch," Harry added. "We'll do our best to help you recover."

Everyone else remained quiet but showed extreme concern with their expressions. "Maybe we should just let Mitch rest awhile," Harry suggested before turning his attention back toward him. "I'll get you back to the cottage before sundown."

"That sounds like a good plan, grandpa." Mitch smiled. "I'm really tired."

At a police station in Atlanta, a uniformed cop strolled over to the desk of Detective LeVonte Clark with a file in his hand. "We got the report back on that accident investigation where the garbage truck creamed that BMW last night."

LeVonte, who was a sober-faced detective with a tough demeanor, gazed up at his fellow cop as he handed off the file. "That was Mitchell Grant in that Beamer." He remarked.

The other cop answered with a quick nod and an urgent expression. "They mentioned down in the lab that you might want to look this over right away."

LeVonte looked at the file with pondering thought, and waited for the officer to depart, before opening it. He studied the content quickly, but carefully. He then flipped to the last page to view the conclusion.

As he closed the file, he leaned back in his chair with an intense, thoughtful expression, "I'll be damned!" He whispered to himself.

Later that day, Mitch woke up on the couch, feeling quite rested. He threw aside the crotched blanket that was covering him, sat up, and stretched.

After a few moments, he got up and paced through the quiet, and seemingly empty house. "Grandma! Grampa!" He called out and waited for an answer. "Mom! Dad! Anyone?" He questioned with a subtle laugh. *I sure hope I'm not all alone again.*

Mitch strolled outside onto the porch and decided to take a walk in the neighborhood. He admired all the beautifully kept properties and gardens along the street. It was very peaceful....

As he meandered along, the sound of harmonious music could be heard in the air, coming from some unknown destination. Curiosity got the best of him, and he decided to follow in the direction that it seemed to be originating. At the end of the street, near the lake, the young black man sat at the end of a pier, belting out a tune on his horn. He was lost, almost enraptured with his music, while his bare feet dangled in the water below. Mitch smiled as he approached, and the man quit playing when he saw him. "Please don't quit playing because of me," Mitch stated. "I was enjoying it." Mitch extended his hand. "I'm Mitch! I'm new here."

The man soberly shook Mitch's hand, "I know all about you. You're Harry's grandson." He looked up, shielding his eyes from the late day sun. "My name's Gabriel."

Mitch sat down on the pier next to him, "You're pretty good on that horn." He nodded. "I play the guitar. Maybe we can jam sometime?"

"Yeah! That'd be cool!" Gabriel smiled. "I jam out with your grandparents once in a while." He studied Mitch for a moment. "How do you like it here?"

"It's great!" Mitch exclaimed. "It's just hard getting adjusted and understanding everything.

"You'll get used to it." He laughed.

"I guess I have eternity to figure it all out."

Gabriel paused for a moment, looking outward, as if listening to an invisible voice on the gentle breeze that blew in from the lake. "I'm being summoned. But I'll definitely see you around, Mitch."

"I'll look forward to it, Gabriel."

A stiff breeze suddenly blew in from the lake, and Gabriel disappeared into thin air. Mitch was quite startled by his exit and looked all around with confusion.

At Grant Investments, Ron sat at his desk, sifting through a stack of documents. The door slowly opened, and his secretary peeked in, "There's a Detective Clark here, that would like to have a word with you."

Ron appeared a bit perplexed at first but then nodded to her, "Sure. Send him right on in."

She ushered LeVonte in, and Ron immediately pointed to a chair on the opposite side of the desk, "Please have a seat, Detective." He sighed. "As you can guess, it's been a very tough day for all of us here."

LeVonte gave an understanding nod as he sat down, "How can I help you?" Ron asked.

"I'm the lead investigator on Mr. Grants' accident." He paused with a deep breath. "We have reason to believe that someone may have tampered with the brakes on his car."

Ron replied with a shocked look of disbelief, "Are you saying that someone attempted to kill Mitch?"

"Possibly." He cautiously stated. "With you being his business partner, I was hoping you could shed some light on why someone would want him dead."

Ron nervously shook his head, in search of an answer, "I seriously don't know. Everyone loves Mitch." He paused to reflect for a moment. "He's the last person you'd expect to be a rich entrepreneur. He's just a down-to-earth, all-around great guy."

LeVonte shifted in his seat and looked off into the corner, "You should know up front that you're considered a prime suspect, because of your business relationship, Mr. Baumgartner."

Ron became cautiously defensive, "Listen, detective. Mitch has been my best friend since college." He paused. "I love the guy like a brother, and I would never do anything to harm him."

LeVonte glanced downward in thought. Then he grabbed a notepad and pen from his pocket and looked back toward Ron. "What can you tell me about his wife, April?"

"Her maiden name was Anderson, and I know she was originally from Wisconsin." He paused in thought. "Madison, if I remember right. She and Mitch met at a trade show in New York."

LeVonte quickly jotted down notes, "How long have they been married?"

"Just over two years," Ron replied. "I was the best man at their wedding."

Ron pointed to a photo of a small wedding party that sat on a corner of his desk. LeVonte picked it up to look at it. "Mrs. Grant is a very beautiful woman." He commented.

Ron gave an accentuated nod of agreement, "Any problems in their marriage that you might know of?"

Ron hesitated before deciding to answer the question, "Look!" He leaned in. "I'm not certain about this, but I suspect she may be having an affair with one of our employees."

LeVonte also leaned forward with sparked interest, "What makes you think that, Mr. Baumgartner?"

Ron took a deep, thought-filled breath before continuing, "Last night at the awards ceremony, I saw her, and the mentioned employee having a close and a rather intimate discussion at the bar." He paused. "April and Mitch drove separate cars, and she left the party early."

"Interesting!" He jotted further notes. "Anything else?"

"Well!" Ron continued. "I can't say I'd fault April for falling for this guy. If I were a woman, I'd want to hook up with him too."

LeVonte looked away, and chuckled, "He must be a real stud."

Ron reacted with amusement, while LeVonte rose from his seat, "Do you have that employee's contact info?" He asked. "We may need to question him about his relationship with Mrs. Grant."

"Yeah!" Ron answered. "His name is Rinaldo Perez. His office is to the left of mine, but he's not here today."

Ron quickly checked the contact list on his phone. He then jotted down the info and handed it to the detective, "This is his phone number, and address."

"Okay!" LeVonte exclaimed as he placed the info in with his notes. "Thank you for your time, Mr. Baumgartner."

He paused as he stood up, "I'd appreciate it if you kept everything we discussed confidential."

"Of course, detective."

LeVonte handed him a business card, "If you can think of anything else that could help, don't hesitate to call me."

"I'll do that," Ron assured.

LeVonte departed with a half-grin, while Ron settled back in his chair with an expression of deep concern.

At the Grant residence, April paced, pondering her next move. She grabbed the phone, dialed, and began a conversation in Russian, "I want to know who bungled the hit. They must pay for their mistake." Her expression turned cold, "why did the device not detonate?" The trembling contempt spread throughout her body, "this fool has left me in a complicated situation." She yelled. "Since your people can't get anything right, I'll take matters into my own hands." April rolled her eyes and abruptly ended the call.

As April stormed across the room she noticed a picture of her and Mitch on the end table. The sight made her stomach turn, and she slammed it down on her way past.

In a happier place, Mitch returned from his walk and sauntered up the front steps of the porch to join Harry and Tilly, who were sitting in rocking chairs. "Where was everyone when I woke up?" Mitch asked.

"There's a pond a few streets over," Tilly replied. "We took Bobby and Doris to feed the ducks."

"They're settled in for their afternoon naps," Harry added.

"I met Gabriel on my walk."

"Was he playing that horn of his?" Harry asked as Mitch settled into one of the other rockers.

"Oh yeah!" Mitch exclaimed. "He can really lay down a tune on that thing." He paused. "It was kind of a strange encounter. I was talking to him, and he suddenly got called away for some reason."

"He has a habit of doing that." Harry chuckled. "He can be a rather odd fellow at times." He sat forward in his chair. "Are you ready for me to take you home? Tilly doesn't like me to be on the lake after dark."

Mitch took a deep breath and stood up, "Sure! I'm ready to call it a day."

A short while later, Harry pulled the boat to the docking post, while Mitch jumped onto the wood-planked pier. The orange Tabby's were all there to greet him with enthusiastic, and loud meows.

"You better feed those little guys," Harry suggested. "There's plenty of cat food in the kitchen pantry closet."

The late-day sun filtered through the trees, casting long shadows across the lawn. "Do you want to stay and talk for a while, grandpa?"

"I should really get home." Harry gestured toward the Adirondack chairs with a sly grin, "Besides, there's someone over there that's been waiting for a very long time to see you."

Mitch squinted his eyes against the bright sun, and could only make out a lone figure sitting in one of the high back chairs. He looked back toward Harry with a puzzled expression, and his grandfather answered with an assured wink and nod, "Enjoy your visit. I'll see you tomorrow, Mitch."

As Harry fired up the engines and departed, Mitch set his sights on the figure in the chair and began striding that way, with the cats following close behind. "Hello there!" Mitch called out.

A striking brunette in her early 20's stood up and slowly turned toward him. Her face immediately lit up with a smile when she saw him. "I've waited a very long time for you, mister. She emotionally stated while Mitch was awe stricken.

"Chris! Is it really you?"

She nodded with tears escaping her eyes and moved closer to greet him. Memories of a long-lost love flooded Mitch's mind, and drowned out any feeling for April that remained. They stood for a long, awkward moment, gazing at each other. "I hardly recognized you with your hair cut short." She humorously commented, breaking the silence.

Mitch was speechless, and they embraced each other tightly, "I've been waiting here every evening for what seems like an eternity." She smiled. "I was beginning to think you stood me up again."

He stroked her hair lovingly with his hand and looked directly into her light brown eyes. "No! Don't say that!" He emotionally shook his head. "It didn't happen that way."

Chris took hold of his hand, "Come on! Let's go sit and talk."

They both sat down in the high back chairs, but they never let go of each other's hand, "I didn't stand you up that night." Mitch stated with frustration. "My stupid old car broke down, and when I tried to call the Beachcomber, they said they were too busy to have you paged." He shook his head with obvious frustration. "Unfortunately, we didn't have cell phones back then."

Chris's eyes wandered to the lake, as Harry's boat picked up speed, and moved away across the water. "Your grandfather's a good man."

Mitch nodded as she continued, "He has a lot of the same qualities that I remember seeing in you."

"I had a good teacher," Mitch replied.

Mitch looked at her with great curiosity, "You said you come here every evening. Do you have a place here on the lake?"

"It's close by." Chris nodded. "Your family helped me get settled."

"What about your family?"

"My mom is still alive, but my dad's here." She paused. He has his own special place with the rest of the family, and they visit once in a while."

"Why aren't you with them?" Mitch asked.

Chris stared straight into his eyes, and her answer touched his soul, "Because I only wanted to be with you." She replied.

Mitch searched for the right words to say next. There were so many answers to unresolved issues between the two of them that he had long pondered. "I've waited for the answer to this question for most of my life." He paused. "Why were you in Jim Davidson's car that night?"

Chris leaned forward, and gently gripped both of his hands tighter, "Oh, Mitch!" She sighed. "I waited until closing time, and it was too late to get a cab. Jim offered me a ride, and I accepted.

"If you only would've waited a little longer. I borrowed Steve DeMarco's car, and eventually got there." Mitch stated out of frustration.

"If I had the chance to do it all again, I would've waited there for you until the sun came up," Chris replied with great remorse.

"How did the accident happen?" Mitch asked.

"I didn't realize Jim was so drunk, and he was driving like an idiot." She wiped a tear from her eye and continued. All I can remember was the car drifting over the center line, and then a set of headlights coming toward us."

Mitch looked away, and clenched his eyes shut, while Chris gently placed her hand against the side of his face. "I'm so sorry that for all those years you thought I was with him that night for the wrong reason."

Mitch gave an understanding nod, while Chris forced a painful smile, "You have to believe me when I say this. I was so in love with you that I could never bring myself to be with anyone else." She emotionally stated.

"I loved you too, and I never wanted to doubt you. But there were so many rumors about that night, and no one around to dispute them."

"I'm sorry." She looked downward for a moment, before continuing. "How did your life turn out after I was gone?"

"I started a business with my buddy, Ron Baumgartner. I became a billionaire, and ironically, I died in an accident as well."

"Wow! That's pretty impressive and quite ironic." She smiled. "I should've known that you would've done something great with your life."

"I owe quite a bit to Ron." Mitch nodded. "Life was really hard for a long time after I lost you. But he was a good friend, and helped me through it."

"Did you ever get married?"

"I never thought I would, but I did." He sighed regretfully. "I think my wife was responsible for my death."

"Did you love her?"

"I thought I did until I saw you again."

They looked dreamily at each other, and gently kissed, "Maybe we should go inside before the mosquitos start biting." Mitch suggested.

"There are no mosquitos here," Chris laughed. "Not in the Summerland."

Mitch leaned back in his chair and listened to the haunting calls of the loons, and whippoorwills that carried through the evening air. The golden sun sank quickly on the horizon over the lake, and the crickets made the perfect soundtrack to usher in the first fireflies of nightfall. "That's quite a symphony. Isn't it?" He stated with a satisfied grin.

"It's absolutely perfect." Chris proclaimed. "Even still, I think we should go inside, and snuggle just like we used to."

"I was hoping you'd suggest that." He grinned.

They both stood, and romantically draped their arms around each other, as they began a stroll toward the cottage. The cats all hurried along close behind, "I'm really curious, Mitch. "What's a cell phone?"

Mitch laughed at the question and shook his head with amazement, "You and I have about 32 years of catching up to do, sweetheart."

In an Atlanta police precinct, LeVonte was preparing to leave after a long shift when a female officer swiftly entered his workspace with a file in hand, "You might not want to leave just yet, LeVonte." She gestured toward the file, as she handed it off to him.

"This better be good." He replied with sarcasm. "I've only had a short nap in the last 24 hours."

"Oh! You're going to want to see this. She stated as he opened the file. "We ran a background on April Anderson like you requested, and found no proof of her existence before 2013."

LeVonte removed his suit jacket and placed it on the back of his chair. He looked inquisitively at the officer with renewed vigor, as he tapped his finger on the file. "Are you sure you checked everything, Darcy?"

She responded with a confident nod, "We ran a search on every April Anderson from Madison Wisconsin, and only came up with two." She paused. "One is 84, and the other is 15."

"That definitely doesn't fit our girl's description." He chuckled, as he skimmed over the report, "I see you ran a DMV search."

"We found a match for April Anderson in New York for 2013, and then April Grant here in Georgia for 2015."

"That checks out, but did you match the social security number associated with her records."

"Keep reading. This is where it really gets interesting." She shook her head with disbelief. "The number she listed matches up to a Daniel Piersal in the state of Indiana. He's been dead since 1976."

LeVonte looked up in a huff of frustration, "You mean to tell me that the DMV in two separate states never caught that?"

Darcy responded with a clueless shrug, 'We can try to run a facial recognition from her license, and see if we get a match in the crime database. We could do that now on your computer."

"Let's do it!"

Darcy settled into LeVonte's chair and began to access the program on his desktop, while he looked over her shoulder. They both watched with heightened suspense, as the matching process began. After a few short minutes, they both responded with a disappointed sigh, as the screen signaled NO MATCHES.

"We came up empty on this one." Darcy declared.

"She has to have a true identity." He paced, "April Grant just didn't appear out of nowhere."

He cupped his hand over his mouth and looked upward in deep thought. "You know, Darcy." He paused. "I have a wild hunch about something."

Darcy swiveled her chair around to listen, "A few years back, I had a case where we couldn't ID a murder suspect." He paced as he talked. "I ran his facial image on the Interpol database and got a hit. Maybe we'll get lucky with her."

"We can try. It may take a little longer."

"Great!" He exclaimed with urgency in his voice. "We also need to have a protection detail placed on Mitch Grant at the hospital, and also Ron Baumgartner." He nervously paused. "He may be in danger as well."

"I can get that done with one phone call." She replied. "Do we need anything else?"

LeVonte pondered in desperate thought, "Notify Mitch Grant's doctor, and tell him if he wakes up, he's not to notify anyone but me." He nervously nodded. "Especially not April Grant."

"I'll make that priority." She replied.

"How long do you think it will take to make all this happen?" He inquired.

"I'll need to link up with the NSA data base. It shouldn't take any more than an hour."

"Good!" He sighed. "That'll give me time to get a good cup of coffee, and something to eat."

"Make sure it's something healthy." She quipped humorously.

LeVonte responded with a wink, and a smile as he put on his suit jacket, and prepared to leave once more. He paused and halted her before departing, "And, Darcy!" He added. "Make sure none of this has a chance to leak out to April Grant. If she finds out we're on to her, she could be gone with the wind."

"I love how you always quote old movies titles." She joked. "You know you can count on me."

Darcy swiftly departed the room with the confidential file in hand, while LeVonte stood for a moment, analyzing the scenario in his mind, "One way or the other, we're going to get you, April Grant." He whispered to himself.

In the Cottage bedroom, a cool breeze blew through the open window, and into the darkened room. Mitch laid awake, with Chris quietly snuggled at his side. She opened her eyes and looked up at him with a smile, "What are you thinking about?"

I'm thinking about how happy I am right now." He pulled her closer. "All I ever truly wanted was to be with you in a place like this."

Chris glanced at him curiously, "With all of your money, you could've had anything you wanted. Weren't you happy?"

Mitch shook his head, "I would've given it all up for moments like this."

"I wish I could've been there in life with you." Chris sadly stated.

"We're together now, and that's all that matters." Chris looked dreamily into his eyes, and the two long-lost lovers kissed passionately.

Nearly two hours had passed when a very weary LeVonte re-entered the precinct. Officer Darcy jumped up from behind her desk holding the folder, "I got a hit while you were gone." She opened the folder with enthusiasm and showed it to him. "Meet Ludvina Cherakova. AKA April Anderson, and April Grant."

LeVonte's eyes widened as he looked at the mug shot, "I'll be damned!" He replied with much emphasis.

"Oh! Wait until you read up on her." Darcy stated. "She's far from being the sweet little housewife that she's trying to portray."

LeVonte read a few lines and looked to Darcy with urgency, "We need to notify the NSA office in Washington as soon as possible."

"Already done." She replied. "They said their agent would be here first thing in the morning to assist in the case."

He pumped his fist in jubilant victory, "Excellent!" He exclaimed. "You did a great job, Darcy."

"All in a day's work, LeVonte." She smiled.

"I'll have Officer Stuart pick up Ron Baumgartner, and Rinaldo Perez in the morning." He paused. "I want them here when that Federal Agent arrives."

"Do you need me to do anything else?" She asked.

"You've done enough." He grinned. "Thanks to you, I think we'll be able to nail this bitch."

"We will" She assured, before leaving his work area.

LeVonte let out a stressful sigh and tapped the folder on the desk with great thought. "It's going to be another long night." He commented to himself.

Harry and Tilly sat at their dining room table, playing a late-night game of poker. Harry's mind seemed to be drifting elsewhere, and he nervously drummed the fingers of his free hand on the tabletop. "Harry!" Tilly yelled. "Quit with the fingers! You're driving me nuts."

He set his card hand face down on the table and stared across the table, "Something's bothering me, sweetheart."

Tilly set her card hand down as well, and listened, "Do you remember when Mitch heard his wife's voice this afternoon?

Tilly nodded yes, and Harry continued, "On the boat ride home, he also mentioned that he heard the voices of doctors and nurses that seemed to be discussing his vitals."

He propped his chin up with his hands as he pondered, "What if Mitch isn't dead?" He suggested. "What if he's suspended between two worlds while he's in a coma?"

"Oh my God!" She exclaimed, "What kind of consequences would that have?"

Harry leaned back in his chair and folded his arms in front of him to further ponder the situation.

"I'd have to assume that if he were to ever wake up again, he'd no longer be here with us." Tilly reached across the table, and Harry affectionately placed his hand over hers, as they both felt anxiety at the thought of losing Mitch.

The morning sun peeked through the curtains in the cottage bedroom. Mitch opened his eyes when one of the Tabby cats affectionately licked his face. He looked to the foot of the bed and was startled to see Bobby and Doris standing there, watching as he and Chris slept. "We thought you'd never wake up," Bobby complained.

Chris stirred, and opened her eyes. Startled at seeing the children, she pulled the covers up around her. "What in the world are you two doing here so early?" Mitch asked.

"We're taking you to the amusement park today," Doris announced with excitement. "We know how much you used to love to go."

"That sounds like a lot of fun," Chris stated. "Can I go too?"

Doris answered with a sober, and serious nod, while Mitch looked over at Chris with groggy eyes, "I assume you know my parents?"

"Oh yes!" She answered with an amused grin. "We're all very well acquainted."

"We're so happy that you and Mitch are finally together." Doris proclaimed.

"I'll tell you this, son. You're not going to find a peach any better than this young lady." Bobby commented with a wink.

Chris had to cup her hand over her mouth to keep from laughing. Mitch glanced over at her with an amused smile, "Well, dad!" I'd certainly have to agree with you on that."

"If you two give us time to get ready, we'll all go after breakfast," Chris suggested.

Both children gave an enthusiastic nod, "I'll go fix some bacon and eggs," Doris stated.

"Just be careful around that stove," Mitch warned.

Doris rolled her eyes, "In case you forgot, young man. I am your mother, and I do know how to cook."

It was all Chris could do to hold back from laughing once again, as the two children hurried from the room. "They are so cute, Mitch." She giggled, "I guess we'll get an idea of what it would have been like to have our own kids."

"I swear those two are doing this to get back at me."

"Were you a bratty kid?" She jokingly asked.

Mitch just rolled his eyes, and then looked at her rather inquisitively, "Was I dreaming, or did I hear it raining last night?"

"It rains here every night between 3 and 5 in the morning." She answered in a matter-of-fact tone.

"Never during the day?"

"Only when someone's leaving the Summerland."

"Why in the world would anyone want to leave here?" He sarcastically asked.

"A time will come for all of us to either move on to the next level or return to the cycle of life." She smiled. "But don't worry, it's usually equal to hundred years in our time."

"I can tell you this." Mitch shook his head. "I would never want to go back to the world I just left."

At the police precinct, LeVonte entered into his workspace, holding a cup of coffee, and his laptop. Another officer immediately flagged him down from a nearby desk. "Hey, Vonte! That Fed guy is waiting for you in the interrogation room."

"Did you offer him some coffee?"

"Said he didn't drink coffee." The officer laughed. "Prepare yourself! This guy's a real stone face."

LeVonte proceeded to the interrogation room, where the agent was already hard at work, with opened files, and papers scattered on the tabletop. He was a broad-shouldered man in his early 40's who resembled more of a professional bodybuilder than a Federal Agent.

He glanced up and greeted LeVonte with a rough, gravelly voice, "Detective Clark." He nodded.

"Agent Nuccio. Pleased to meet you."

LeVonte extended a greeting hand, that Nuccio accepted without standing up, "That's quite a grip you got there." LeVonte quipped.

Nuccio showed no expression as he quickly turned his attention back to the files in front of him.

"Let's get this thing underway. Shall we?"

LeVonte sat down on the opposite side of the table and listened attentively as Nuccio slid a file across for him to view. "Our suspect, Ludvina Cherakova has operated under other aliases over the years." He pointed to another picture, "In 2005, under the alias of Lauren Elias, she married this man in Athens." Nuccio paused, "Constantine Kostopoulos was a rich shipping magnate who mysteriously drowned in 2009, while his yacht was anchored in the Aegean Sea." He flipped a page and continued. "Later in 2009, she surfaced again in Copenhagen under the name of Ula Levencko, where she married this man, Lars Frederickson." He glanced at LeVonte with a raised brow. "He was a rich entrepreneur. I'm sure you can see a pattern here."

LeVonte reacted with widened eyes, as Nuccio continued, "Frederickson disappeared in 2012 while hiking near the French Alps. Only traces of his torn clothes and a backpack were ever found."

"This bitch sounds like a real black widow." LeVonte proclaimed.

Nuccio answered with a hardened glare and continued, "After inheriting millions from Frederickson's estate, she disappeared again. We now know that she surfaced again as April Anderson here in the U.S."

"Aliases aside, who exactly is Ludvina Cherakova?

Nuccio answered with a sarcastic grunt, as he flipped to another page, "Ludvina started her career working for the Russian Secret Service. She went deep cover, and is believed to be working closely with this man, Sergei Sachovsky." He pointed to his picture.

"So, what exactly is their game?" LeVonte probed.

"They target rich bachelors, kill them, and make it appear to be an accident." He paused with emphasis. "Then, Ludvina inherits their fortune, and they funnel the assets into a shell corporation that launders the money into a Swiss bank account tied to the Kremlin."

LeVonte sat back in his chair and stared straight ahead with amazement, "So, we're basically dealing with the Russian mafia?" Nuccio answered with a definitive nod and continued,

"Now, according to your report, the brakes on Grant's car were tampered with." He took on a clever grin. "I think there's something more to all of this."

"What's your take on it?" LeVonte asked with heightened curiosity.

"Ludvina is way too smart." He leaned forward and animated with his hands. "She would've known there would be a 50/50 chance that Grant would've survived the wreck. Do you have the security cam footage from that intersection?"

"I've got it right here on my laptop."

LeVonte opened it and pulled up the footage. He then positioned the screen so both of them could watch, and walked Nuccio through every step of the footage.

"This is where his car enters the intersection. It then gets clipped by the first car, spins around, and finally gets hit by the garbage truck, and the car traveling in the lane next to it."

"Jesus, Mother Mary!" Nuccio exclaimed as he blessed himself.

"The rest is just the aftermath. Do you want to see that too?"

"Yeah! Keep it rolling."

They continued watching, and Nuccio caught something.

"Wait! Stop it right there. He pointed. "What in the hell is that guy doing?" He shook his head. "Back it up just a bit."

Both watched with intensified interest, "He stopped his car, got out, looked around, and then slid under the backside of Grant's car." LeVonte called it like a play-by-play announcer.

"Back it up to just before the accident."

They both watched, and Nuccio pointed to the screen with excitement, "Right there! That car was parked on the other side of the street." He looked up at LeVonte. "That bastard was waiting to make sure everything went as planned.

They continued watching, "There!" Le Vonte pointed. "He pulled into the intersection shortly after impact."

Nuccio slapped the tabletop with his hand, "We need to work on getting a closeup of that guy. Maybe we can pull up a facial ID."

The door to the interrogation room opened, and Officer Darcy peeked in, "Ron Baumgartner and Rinaldo Perez are here."

Nuccio looked up from the laptop screen, "Send them in!"

Both men were ushered into the room, and Nuccio motioned for them to sit down. Before either could get settled in their chairs, Nuccio began without a pause, "Mr. Baumgartner!" He grinned. "I stayed at your company's resort on St. Croix a few years back. Enjoyed my stay."

He quickly shifted his attention to Rinaldo, "Mr. Perez! We understand that you may be having an affair with Mrs. Grant." Rinaldo reacted nervously, shifting his eyes to each person at the table, and hesitating to answer.

Nuccio impatiently slammed his fist on the tabletop, startling everyone including LeVonte, "I need an answer here! Are you having an affair with April Grant?"

He answered with a quick, reluctant nod, as Nuccio continued his stern interrogation, "Were you also aware that somebody tried to have Mitchell Grant killed?"

Rinaldo raised both of his hands, to quickly plead his innocence, "Look! I'll admit I was banging his wife. But I swear, I had no part in an attempted murder."

"We know that," Nuccio assured. "So, just settle down."

Rinaldo breathed a sigh of relief, and continued in his own defense, "She's the one that seduced me."

"Mr. Perez!" He seethed with frustration, "I couldn't give a damn about who seduced who, or if it was the best sex you ever had. I just want to know when the last time was that you were with her."

"Last night." He answered sheepishly.

Nuccio looked upward and shook his head with disbelief, while LeVonte had to cup his hand over his mouth to hide the amusement, "What is your job title, Mr. Perez?" He further probed.

"I'm the company accountant."

Nuccio and LeVonte exchanged a quick, serious glance, "So, would I be correct in assuming that you oversee all the money that comes in, and goes out?"

Rinaldo answered with a matter-of-fact nod, and Nuccio quickly glanced back at LeVonte.

"This investigation just got a lot more interesting, Detective Clark."

Nuccio stood up and paced in thought for a moment. Then he walked around the table and stood over Rinaldo in a very intimidating way, "Have you ever transferred money at the request of Mrs. Grant?"

"Yes! Many times." Rinaldo answered, "That's how she and I became acquainted."

Once again, he reacted very sheepishly to a hard look from Ron, and an intimidating stare from Nuccio, "Her charity of choice is the Lakewood Heights Women's Shelter." He added.

Nuccio shifted his glare to Ron, "And, were you aware of this as well, Mr. Baumgartner?"

"Yes!" He answered. "Mitch and I both approved the allocations."

"I'd be willing to wager that the money never even went to its' intended purpose," Nuccio replied sarcastically.

Ron and Rinaldo both exchanged a nervous glance before Nuccio turned his attention to LeVonte. "Both of these men are now in my protective custody until further notice, detective."

"What else do you need from me?" LeVonte asked.

"I need your people to get a search warrant for the bank where that money was deposited, and I also want to find out more about this Lakeview Heights Women's Shelter." He sighed. "Lastly, I'm having my crew transport, Mr. Grant, to a secure, undisclosed medical facility for his own protection."

Nuccio then paced slowly toward the door and turned back toward LeVonte with urgency.

"Get off your keister, detective. We need to get all this arranged, and then you and I need to revisit that crash scene."

Simultaneously, April entered the back room of a restaurant lounge. She glanced around the dimly lit room, then strolled over to a corner booth where a large-framed man with gray, slicked-back hair was waiting. As she sat down, they greeted each other and began conversing in Russian. "Did you make sure you weren't followed?" He asked with heightened concern.

April nodded, and quickly got to the point, "With circumstances being as they are, should we abort the mission?"

He glared at her with intense eyes, "No! There is too much here at stake."

"But we won't be able to negotiate a sale of his partners' share until he's dead."

He downs a final slug of his vodka drink, and peers across the table with a sinister smile, "That problem is being taken care of as we speak."

Just then, his cell phone rang, and he quickly answered it with an arrogant smirk. That smirk erupted into an expression of anger as he listened, "What do you mean, he is gone? He inquired with rage.

He glanced across at April, as he continued to listen, "Absolutely not! Leave there immediately!" He ordered. "We'll have to let Ludvina handle things from here."

He hung up and took a deep sigh, "It appears that Mr. Grant is missing from his room. I need you to find out where he is."

"I'll take care of this." She confidently stated.

Later, at the accident scene, LeVonte and Nuccio backtracked on foot from the intersection to where Mitch had left the hotel parking lot. They conversed as they walked, looking for any clues that may have been initially missed, "According to your report, Mitchell Grant left the hotel at roughly 11 pm. The time seal on the intersection feed read 11:13 at the time of impact."

"So, what exactly are we looking for, Agent Nuccio?"

"The same thing that guy was looking for under Grant's car." He grunted, "I have a hunch it may have fell off before impact."

A short distance from the hotel lot, LeVonte spotted something in the street, close to the curb, and moved in for a closer look, "What have you got there?" Nuccio asked as he approached.

"Not sure. It looks like a cell phone that's been run over quite a few times."

Both men went down on one knee to examine it further, "Bingo!" Nuccio exclaimed. "This was a cell phone." He points while pulling an evidence bag from his jacket. "See those wires sticking out from it? That was once hooked up to some type of explosive device. I've seen many detonators like this in my career." He glanced at Le Vonte as he carefully bagged the evidence with a gloved hand. "I'll bet you this was originally under Mitch Grants' car.

Le Vonte pointed to a large pothole just a short distance away, and near the entrance to the parking lot, "Look at the size of that pothole. If Grant hit that on his way out of the parking lot, I can guarantee it would've jarred that device loose."

"And, the killer grabbed the failed plastic explosive, that was probably situated near the gas tank of the car," Nuccio added.

"If that was the case, that pothole saved Mitchell Grants' life."

Nuccio looked around to the surrounding buildings, and pointed, "We need to get the surveillance feed from that building over there. Then we'll get this phone to the lab, and try to lift some prints."

"Maybe we can recover info from the SIM card as well," LeVonte added.

Nuccio's cell phone rang, and he quickly answered it. LeVonte listened as he talked to the agent on the other end, "Yeah! Perfect!" He paused. "Now, I want you to obtain a bogus death certificate from Dr. Howell. Detective Clark and I will meet up with you at the hospice location."

Nuccio ended the call, and Le Vonte cluelessly peered at him, "A death certificate?"

"We're going to make April Grant think her husband is dead," Nuccio replied with a sly smirk.

In the hospital morgue, Agent Sadler, a rugged-looking man in his early 30's, stormed into the room with Ron Baumgartner hustling close behind, "What's the status down here?" He demanded with urgency.

A female agent posing as a nurse motioned to the real body of Mitch, that was on a gurney, and hooked up to life-sustaining devices, "We have him all prepped, and ready for transport." She replied.

He motioned to the Medical Examiner next, who was carefully bandaging the face of a decoy cadaver. The agent answered Sadler before he could ask the question, "That's the stiff we're using to convince Mrs. Grant."

Ron looked over to the medical staff who were ready to wheel Mitch from the room, "Wait!" He nervously interrupted. "Before you move him out, I just want to have a few moments with him."

They all looked to Sadler, who granted a sober-faced gesture of agreement. "Make it quick, Mr. Baumgartner."

Ron hurried over to Mitch's body and awkwardly began, "Hi buddy!" He painfully paused. "I don't know if you can hear me, but I want you to know that none of us will let April get away with this. As always, I got you covered."

Ron gently patted Mitch's hand with assurance, "That's enough!" Sadler impatiently ordered. "We got to move, people!"

The phone in the morgue rang, just as the medical staff departed with Mitch. While the Medical Examiner answered it, Sadler addressed Ron, "Remember everything I told you to do."

Ron eagerly nodded as the Examiner hung up the landline, "It's showtime!" He announced. "Mrs. Grant is on her way down." Sadler gave Ron the thumbs up as he exited the room.

At the amusement park in the Summerland, Mitch sat on a park bench with his head in his hands. Chris sat next to him, and the children stood around them with concern. Chris tried to talk to him, but his mind was somewhere else, "Mitch! Talk to me! What's wrong?"

She shook him, and he finally came to his senses, "I'm sorry! I must've blacked out for a few minutes."

"I'd have to say so. You practically collapsed onto the bench." Chris stated.

"Did you hear the voices again?" Doris asked.

Her question was only answered with a desperately perplexed expression, "Well! Did you?" Bobby impatiently probed.

Mitch answered with a quick nod, "It was Ron's voice. I could hear him as clearly as I can hear all of you, and I could even feel him patting me on the hand."

"We can talk about it later." Chris said. "I can tell you're upset over it."

"You don't look so good, Mitch. Maybe we should take you home." Bobby suggested.

Chris gently cradled the side of Mitch's face with her hand, "Your dad is right. Perhaps you should get some rest. We've all been pushing you a bit too hard."

Mitch pondered for a moment, then defiantly stood to his feet, "No! I'll tell you what we're going to do." He glanced at all three of them, "We're going to ride that merry-go-round at least three more times, and then we're going somewhere for ice cream."

The kids cheered and happily ran ahead toward the carousel. Chris took hold of Mitch's hand and gently squeezed it, as they continued to stroll along. Even still, it was obvious that Mitch was preoccupied by what he had heard Ron say, and Chris tried to change the subject. "You would've made a good father." Mitch answered only with a smile, and leaned in to kiss her on the cheek.

April was escorted into the morgue by a hospital security guard, who held the door open for her, then promptly left without a word. She shivered as she sauntered across the unwelcoming room to where Ron held a reverent vigil in front of a covered gurney.

The Medical Examiner and the undercover agent busied themselves nearby, as she took her place next to Ron. "I can't believe he's really gone." She stated.

Ron only replied with a cold, sideways glance, before she stepped forward, and pulled the sheet back, "Why is his face still bandaged?" She asked.

The Medical Examiner solemnly stepped forward to answer, "We can't remove them until we perform the autopsy, ma'am." He sighed. "I'm not sure you'd want to see the condition of his face."

"Very well then. I suppose there's nothing more for me to see here."

She glanced back at Ron, and succeeded in mustering up some fake tears, "This is all so emotional, and surreal. I honestly don't know what to say."

Ron stared at her rather soberly, "I know this may be a bad time to mention this, but I have some very pressing issues that I need to discuss with you." He paused, while the agent listened with raised brow from a distance. "Perhaps we could go to the cafeteria, and discuss it over coffee."

"Yes! Of course!" April cautiously answered, before turning back toward the Examiner. "When will his ashes be ready?"

"In a day or so. We'll call you, ma'am."

April gave an understanding nod, and the undercover agent quickly interjected herself into the conversation, "I'll escort you two out of here." She smiled. "I desperately need to grab a coffee as well." April only answered her with a haughty, half-grin, as the agent lead the way through the swinging doors.

LeVonte drove along, with Nuccio in the passenger seat, as they headed toward the hospital. He had the sleeves of his dress shirt rolled up, revealing a military tattoo on his forearm. "I see you're an Army man." Nuccio grinned.

"I did a stint in the Iraq war, but didn't re-enlist when my tour was finished."

"Can't say I blame you," Nuccio grunted. "I was with the Marines in Iraq and Afghanistan. Saw things I wish I'd never seen."

"How ironic!" LeVonte chuckled. We both came home, but now we're fighting a different war here."

"The life of a dedicated soldier, I guess," Nuccio answered while gazing out the window. "Do you have a wife and kids, Detective Clark?"

"I'm divorced. We have a seven-year-old daughter." He paused to glance over to his passenger, "What about you, Agent Nuccio?"

Nuccio shook his head, "I'm married to the job." He looked away. "I'm sure you know how that goes."

April and Ron chose a table at the far end of the hospital cafeteria, while the undercover agent chose a table across the room. She seemed rather cool, as she sipped on her coffee, oblivious to the listening device planted under Ron's suit jacket.

"I suppose we'll need to make funeral arrangements." She sighed.

"Absolutely not!" Ron emphatically shook his head. "Mitch was very specific about what he wanted in his will. He didn't want a service, and he wanted his ashes spread by the lake in his hometown."

"That sounds easy enough."

There was an awkward moment where Ron nervously fidgeted with his clasped fingers before he finally spoke. "Let me just get to the point here, April."

She tilted her head with curiosity and leaned into the conversation, "I had wanted to talk this over with Mitch before the accident, but I never got the chance." He began.

April set her coffee down and listened with renewed interest, "There are other ventures that I'd like to pursue at this stage of my life, and I wondered if you might be interested in buying out my half of the business?

She was taken back with surprise, and it was hard for Ron to maintain a sober face. "Believe it or not, I had intended on asking you the very same question when the time was appropriate." She paused to take note of Ron's reaction. "I have a group of investors who would be more than interested in putting up the money to buy your portion."

He shook his head trying to appear amazed, "When would you be ready to start the process?" He asked.

"The sooner, the better…" she quipped with a pleasing smile.

"Very well then." Ron gave a thoughtful nod to her answer. "I'll let Rinaldo, and our attorney knows about this, and we'll get the wheels in motion."

"I'll do the same." She tipped her coffee cup toward Ron.

They both stared at each other for an uncomfortable moment, before April glanced down at her watch. "Oh my! I really should be going. As simple as they are, I still have arrangements to finalize."

"I understand." He replied with assurance.

April wasted no time in standing up, and Ron courteously stood as well.

"I'll be in touch, Ron." She smiled sweetly, before swiftly exiting. When she was completely out of sight, Ron gave the thumbs up to the agent sitting across the room.

In the Summerland, Harry and Tilly sat in their rockers on the front porch, sipping on mint iced tea, and enjoying the beautiful day. Gabriel came casually strolling down the street, carrying his horn, and sauntered up the walkway toward the porch. "Good afternoon, Gabriel," Harry announced.

Gabriel cordially nodded and took a seat atop one of the concrete pedestals at the top of the steps. "I have something I need to talk over with you, Harry." He uneasily glanced toward Tilly, and she immediately found it best leaving the men to talk. "It's getting on into the afternoon. I'll go in, and start dinner while you two talk."

Tilly exited into the house, and Gabriel waited a few moments before almost reluctantly continuing, "It's about Mitch."

Harry gave an all-knowing nod looking toward Gabriel with a raised brow, "I was afraid you'd say that."

At a private Hospice outside of Atlanta, LeVonte and Nuccio watched from across the room as medical workers tended to Mitch. "You ever wonder where a person's mind goes while they're in a coma?" LeVonte casually asked.

"I'd like to believe it's a pleasant place," Nuccio replied, never making eye contact. "Hopefully better than the world we live in."

They both pondered in thought for a long moment, before Nuccio continued, "That phone call that I took a few minutes ago was one of my agents." He paused, glancing toward LeVonte. "That bank account for Mrs. Grant's charity only had two hundred dollars in it, and the Lakeview Heights Women's Shelter doesn't even exist."

"So where is she funneling all that money?"

"My team is working on that answer as we speak," Nuccio replied confidently.

"We have to make sure we build a good case," LeVonte stressed. "I want to make sure we shut down Ludvina's cartel permanently."

"We will!" Nuccio assured. "You should go home, and get some rest, Detective Clark. I'll stay here for a while."

"Thanks." He sighed. "I'll see you first thing in the morning."

"I'll be raring to go." Levonte departed, while Nuccio settled comfortably in a chair, and stared off into the corner of the room, in deep, contemplative thought.

Harry remained sitting on the porch, long after Gabriel departed. The smell of Tilly's cooking wafted through the screened door and brought a much-needed smile to his face. His attention was diverted by the sound of loud rock music, and he looked up the street to see a dark blue 1963 T-Bird convertible cruising that way. As it got closer, he realized it was Mitch driving it, with Chris in the seat next to him, and Bobby and Doris in the back seat.

They pulled to a stop in the driveway, and Mitch lowered the music, as Harry strolled down from the porch to greet them and check out the car. "That's some car you got there." Harry proclaimed. "It looks just like the Matchbox toy used to play with as a kid."

"Amazing! Isn't it?" Mitch beamed.

Bobby and Doris quickly got out of the car and ran toward the house.

"I'm glad we're home," Bobby yelled. "That darn rock n' roll music was driving me bonkers."

Mitch chuckled as he got out of the car, and leaned back against the door. Chris strolled around to his side of the car and slipped her arm around him as he continued conversing with Harry. Mitch gestured toward the kids, who were now ambitiously rocking back and forth on the porch swing.

"Do those two ever take the form of their adult selves?"

"Once in a great while." Harry chuckled, "But most of the time, they just prefer to be kids."

"With all of that excess energy, I can't say I blame them." Chris laughed.

They all slowly proceeded up to the porch, where Tilly was now outside waiting.

"Did everyone have a good time?" She asked.

"We had a wonderful time, Mrs. Grant," Chris replied.

"We rode the merry-go-round seven times." Doris enthusiastically stated.

"My goodness! Seven times?" Tilly beamed with amusement.

"Hey, dad! Can you play us a tune on the banjo?" Bobby asked.

"I'll tell you what." Harry paused. "How would it be if Tilly and I did a song with Mitch?"

"That sounds like fun," Doris stated with excitement in her voice.

Harry looked to Mitch, "Are you up for it?"

"Sure! Do you have a guitar?"

"I got a special one inside, just for you." Harry chuckled. "Wait until you see it." They all filed through the door, and into the house, as the late day sun filtered through the large oaks in the front yard, casting long shadows on the quaint porch.

Once inside, they all made their way to the large living room, where Tilly took her place at the Baldwin piano. Harry and Mitch placed fold-down chairs on either side of her, while the children sat lotus-style on the floor. Chris settled comfortably into a chair nearby.

Harry grabbed his banjo and then pointed to a near corner of the room, "That's yours over there, Mitch."

His face lit up with surprise when he saw the pristine, blonde wood, Martin acoustic guitar. He picked it up as though he were handling a newborn baby, "This is beautiful! I always wanted one of these."

"Well! Now you have one." Harry beamed, as he turned his attention to Tilly. "Pick us a song, and we'll join in."

She shuffled through her sheet music, and pulled out a selection, "I used to play this one for the silent films down at the Shea's Theater. Let's see if you remember it."

Tilly elaborately opened the tune on the piano, and Harry and Mitch joined in. The second time around, they all began to sing the lyrics to the chorus. As Tilly subtly played the last keys of the song, everyone clapped, and she turned to Mitch with amazement. "I can't believe you remembered that song. You were just a little boy when we used to play it."

Mitch emotionally chuckled, "I remember it like it was yesterday. Those were the best years of my life." He paused with further emotion. "I missed you all so very much."

Chris quickly stood up and placed a supporting hand on Mitch's back, and Harry wiped a tear from his eye, "We all missed you too, Mitch." Harry smiled. "In fact, we're having a big picnic in your honor at the cottage tomorrow."

"Just like the ones we used to have?" Bobby asked with excitement.

"Just like the good old days. The rest of the family, and a lot of old friends are going to be there too." Tilly added.

Mitch shook his head with amazement, as he exchanged a loving glance with Chris, "I can hardly wait."

After dinner that night, Mitch and Harry sat peacefully on the porch, while the crickets and cicadas chirped loudly, "Another beautiful summer evening." Harry sighed. "I've been here 44 years now, and I haven't gotten tired of it yet."

"There's so much I don't understand," Mitch stated. "How can such a perfect place exist outside of an imperfect world?"

"I suppose you could say that this is a reward for those who lived life without evil intent. Just as it was in life, this place has different levels. I'd like to think this is the pinnacle." He chuckled. "Obviously, you must've lived a righteous life to make it here."

"I did my best."

Harry pointed to all the houses in the neighborhood, "In all of these houses you see, and everywhere else around the lake, each person is experiencing the life, and moments they either cherished or couldn't have in their previous life. This is their private heaven."

"How long did it take for you to figure it all out?"

Harry glanced over at him with a calming smile, "Even in life, the answers were always there. But we were too busy to realize it." He gazed out into the darkness and continued. "In quiet moments when you're looking out over the lake, watching the sun rise or set, looking at the stars, or just sitting like we are now, it will all start to make sense."

"I can see that." Mitch paused. "I don't know why anyone would ever want to go back after being here"

"I suppose it depends on what level you occupy in the afterlife. When people realize they could've done better, some decide to go back, and take another shot at it."

Mitch leaned back, and looked out into the dark, "The real world as it is now, is a rotten place to be, grandpa. If you went back, you might end up leading a worse life than you previously had."

"I hear that from a lot of the newcomers," Harry answered.

"Knowing what you know now, would you ever go back?"

"I could never build a better life than the one I had." He shook his head. I married the woman I loved, had great memories, and the perfect family. I have all that, and so much more here."

"That's all I ever wanted from life." Mitch chuckled. "All the money in the world could never buy what I have here with all of you."

"You learned your life lessons quite well, Mitch." Harry smiled. "I'm very proud of you."

Mitch glanced over and calmly smiled as well, "I guess I had good teachers."

A peaceful silence fell between the two men, while Harry contemplated, but didn't have the heart to bring up what he and Gabriel had discussed earlier that day. Mitch got up and filled his lungs with the fresh night air, "I suppose I'll go in, and see if Chris is ready to go home."

"It's a long ride to the other side of the lake. We have a couple of spare beds if you two want to stay the night."

"Thanks, grandpa." Mitch grinned. "But I'll have to take a pass this time. It's a beautiful night in the Summerland, I have a convertible, and I'm finally with the woman I love." He winked. "What would you do?"

"I see your point, kiddo." Harry joked, and rolled his eyes. "We'll just leave it at that"

In her residence, April Grant paced with excitement, as she conversed on her cell phone in Russian. "The fat man was much easier to deal with than I originally thought." She grinned, "He actually offered to sell his half of the business before I could even ask." April paused, listening to the chatter on the other end with enthusiasm. "Yes, I know. The acquisition of all the holdings will greatly add to our international portfolio." She paused, "I understand. I will stay in touch."

Meanwhile, Mitch and Chris laid side by side in the T-Bird, with the seats fully reclined, gazing up at the vast canopy of stars. They lit up the night like tiny diamonds casting a subtle light across the calm lake surface.

"This is so romantic!" Chris enthusiastically proclaimed, "Seeing all of these stars makes me realize what a small part of the universe we actually are."

"It's crazy!" Mitch smiled. "I never shared moments like this with my wife, April." He sighed. "I somehow lost sight of all the simple elements of romance that you and I used to share. Until now, I never realized how much I missed it."

Chris also smiled, and snuggled closer, as Mitch continued to speak his mind, "Once you arrived here, did you ever think you might want to go back, and live another lifetime?"

Chris pondered the question for a moment, "I had the opportunity to go back sooner, because I was young, and lost my life unexpectedly."

"Why didn't you do it?"

"Because I didn't wait for you that night, and I lost you." She paused, as tears welled in her eyes. "I didn't want to make that same mistake twice."

Mitch reached over and took hold of her hand, "I'm glad you waited. I know now that you were the only true love of my life."

They cuddled closer and kissed passionately. Chris opened her eyes and paused with a mischievous smile. She subtly gestured toward the lake, "Do you want to go skinny dipping?"

"Lady! I would have to be crazy to say no to that offer."

They both giggled, and affectionately rubbed noses, "I'll race you to the water, mister." She jokingly stated.

"I'll give you a head start." Mitch laughed.

Later that night, Mitch laid awake in the cottage bedroom. Chris slept contently, snuggled beside him. A distant flash of lightning lit up the room, and a gentle rain began to fall outside. It was a comforting sound that filtered through the screen of the open window and put his busy mind to rest. He lightly kissed Chris on her forehead, closed his eyes, and fell into a peaceful sleep.

Mitch woke up to a sun-lit room, and a gentle morning breeze blowing through the open window. He was alone, except three of his orange Tabby's who rested on the bed as well. Mitch looked around in a slight panic. "Chris!" He yelled and waited for an answer. "Chris!"

Chris came rushing into the room a few moments later, and he gave a huge sigh of relief, as she hurried to his side, embracing him with concern, "Are you okay, honey? What's the matter?"

"I just can't bear the thought of waking up, and you not being there." He replied emotionally, embracing her tightly. "I never want to lose you again."

Chris kissed him on the forehead and held him securely in her arms, "I'm not going anywhere, sweetie." She looked at him with tear-filled eyes. "You need to get up. Your grandparents are already here, getting the yard ready for the picnic."

Mitch glanced at the clock on the dresser, "Why didn't you wake me up earlier?"

"Because you were sleeping so good. I wanted you to get rested."

Mitch gently cradled her face in his hands, "I love you so much."

"Oh, Mitch!" She giggled with joy. "I love you too."

LeVonte entered the police precinct early that morning, holding a cup of coffee in one hand, and a newspaper in the other. The policeman at one of the desks greeted him with a quick gesture. "Nuccio's been here for over an hour."

"Doesn't that guy ever sleep?" Le Vonte jokingly asked.

"The media is pushing hard for a statement on Grant's death. What do you want me to tell them?"

"Just tell them he's dead, and we can't say any more until the investigation is complete."

He plopped the newspaper down on the officers' desk, "You might as well read this." He grunted. "I got the feeling I won't have the chance."

LeVonte continued into the interrogation room, where Nuccio already had his shirt sleeves rolled up, and was deep into his work. He just briefly glanced up, as LeVonte set his coffee on the table, and settled into a chair, "It's about time you got here. We have a lot of new developments, Detective Clark."

"Fill me in…."

"We got word this morning that the Georgia State Police found a body just off I-95 near the Florida line."

"What does that have to do with our investigation?" He shrugged.

"Plenty!" Nuccio exclaimed. "They identified him as Leonid Prevscho."

He opened a file and pointed to his picture, "Prevscho was a known hitman for the Russian crime syndicate in Miami. Somebody put a bullet in his head."

LeVonte casually examined the picture, "He must've pissed somebody off."

"Yeah!" Nuccio chuckled. "That somebody would be Ludvina. Prevscho fits the description of the guy we caught on camera going under Grant's car."

LeVonte leaned back in his chair with renewed enlightenment, as Nuccio continued, "Do you have any idea who the head of the Russian mob is in Miami?

LeVonte shrugged, and took a wild guess, "Sergei Sachovsky?"

Nuccio pointed across the table with exuberance and gave him an assured nod.

"What else have we got?"

Nuccio turned his attention to his laptop, "I got the feed from that other camera, and enhanced it." He glanced up with a grin. "We were right."

Nuccio turned the laptop around so that LeVonte could get a good vantage point on it, "Watch the rear underside of Grant's car when it leaves the parking lot" He paused while they watched. "He just hit the pothole."

"Yeah!" Stop it right there." LeVonte stands up to get a closer look. "Something fell off the back end of the car."

"That was the cell phone detonator." Nuccio confidently stated.

LeVonte shook his head in disbelief, and let out a heavy sigh, "Since Prevscho is dead, what can we do to snag Ludvina and Sachovsky?"

"We have Rinaldo Perez and Ron Baumgartner working with their attorney to set up a meeting with Ludvina and her people," Nuccio grunted. "That will be the trap that snares the entire rat's nest."

"We better work fast. If anything leaks out to the press about this being a possible murder, we're all screwed."

"I'm holding you and your department responsible for that not getting out."

"Thanks a lot!" LeVonte sarcastically answered. "I'm doing the best I can here."

"My agents will bring Perez and Baumgartner in later, and we'll go over the strategy."

"What'll we do until then?

"Roll up your sleeves, and help me put together a strong case against these pricks," Nuccio answered with an arrogant grin.

At Mitch's cottage in the Summerland, several people were gathered on the lawn for the grand picnic. A volleyball match was just finishing, with Harry spiking the winning point across the net. Harry, Mitch, and Chris casually conversed as they walked away from the net.

"I got to compliment you, grandpa. You are a darn good volleyball player."

"I definitely move a little faster than when you knew me as an old man." He chuckled.

Chris flashed a flirty smile at Mitch and gave him an affectionate hip bump.
"Maybe we can all do this more often since Mitch is here."

Mitch's parents ran by as they conversed. Bobby was holding a frog in both hands, and chasing a squealing Doris, "Bobby!" Harry yelled. "You put that frog down, and quit scaring Doris."

Mitch glanced over at Chris and spoke under his breath, "That is way too bizarre."

"Your father is definitely a little heller." Chris giggled.

Harry and Mitch took a seat at a picnic table, but Chris hesitated, "I think I'll go see if I can help with the food, and let you two guys talk."

Harry noticed Mitch watching her admirably as she walked away, "That's quite a gal you got there."

Mitch only responded with a pleased grin as he continued watching her. After a few moments, he sighed and glanced over at his grandfather, "I used to love those old family picnics we had. Thanks for putting this all together."

"We always did have fun as a family." Harry beamed.

Mitch glanced around the yard for a moment, and chuckled to himself, "It's funny! Everyone seems to know who I am, but I can't figure out who some of them are."

"Some of us were pretty old by the time you came on the scene." Harry humorously quipped.

"Who are those two hot-looking chicks in the 1920's style clothes?" Mitch pointed across the yard. "They both came up, and kissed me on the cheek earlier."

Harry let loose with a hearty laugh, "Those hot-looking chicks are my sisters."

"Aunt Edith, and aunt Ethel?" Mitch shook his head in amazement. "No way!"

"As you can see, my father and I had our hands full, beating the wolves away from our door."

"No doubt!" Mitch laughed, while Harry pointed to someone else.

"Did you see your old childhood buddy, Steve Palmer?"

"Yeah! How in the world did he make it here?" Mitch questioned. "He was always a real hell-raiser."

"Obviously, he got his life straight before he passed on," Harry answered. "He's quite the gentleman now."

They both noticed Gabriel, as he sat by himself at the end of the pier, blowing out a tune on his trumpet. "That Gabriel is quite a strange guy," Mitch commented. "He's not very sociable."

"He's just rather quiet. That horn is his best friend."

A distant roll of thunder rumbled in from over the water. Both men watched with serious expressions as the clouds began to build in the distance. Everyone else paused to take notice of the unusual event as well. "A daytime storm," Mitch stated with dread.

Harry clenched his eyes shut, and slowly nodded yes. Mitch looked over at him with great emotion. "I think you already know it's me that's leaving."

"Gabriel told me the other day. I just didn't have the heart to tell the rest of you."

"At least I got a glimpse of what the afterlife has in store for me." Mitch sighed.

"You'll be back someday."

"And when I do, I promise I won't leave again." Mitch placed a hand on Harry's shoulder. "Please! Take care of Chris."

With tear-filled eyes, Harry gave him an assured nod, "She'll always be part of our family, Mitch."

"I love all of you very much."

"And we all love you, Mitch. You'll always be our boy."

The two men emotionally embraced, and as the clouds obscured the sun, they bid a final farewell, "Goodbye, grandpa!"

Mitch then turned and began his fateful march back toward the cottage.

Tilly cheerfully greeted him as he entered the kitchen where she was just taking a few casserole dishes from the refrigerator. "Mitch!" she kissed him on the cheek. "I just made a fresh pot of coffee. Can I pour you a cup?"

"Thank you! I think I need it."

She filled a cup and proceeded to put cream and sugar in it, as Mitch took a seat at the kitchen table, What's wrong, honey?" She asked as she set the cup down in front of him. "Aren't you feeling good?"

"I just have a headache." He answered with a slight chuckle. "I think I overdid it playing volleyball."

"Would you like some graham crackers too? I remember how much you used to like them."

"No thanks, grandma. This is just fine."

She leaned over and gave him another kiss, "You shouldn't push yourself so hard, honey. Your body is still recovering from that terrible accident."

Mitch responded with a loving smile, as she continued to advise him, "You just sit there awhile." She patted him on the shoulder. "I need to take these casseroles out to the food tent."

Mitch watched as she hurried away, and once she was gone, he sadly whispered to himself, "Goodbye, grandma." He glanced around the kitchen, taking in every little detail.

The storm rolled in closer..... he jumped when a loud burst of thunder cracked overhead. When he glanced out the window, he noticed everyone running for cover as the rain began to fall. Suddenly, Mitch clutched his head, groaning in extreme pain. It coursed through his body with such force, he spilled his coffee on the table. *Oh.....* Mitch glanced outside once again, and saw Gabriel standing alone in the open yard, gazing toward the cottage. He seemed to be oblivious to the falling rain. The scene caught Mitch off guard. The last thing he remembered was a flash of lightning that totally illuminated the room.

LeVonte and Nuccio held an afternoon meeting with Ron Baumgartner and Rinaldo Perez in the interrogation room of the police precinct. Nuccio sat forward seriously addressing everyone, "Okay! We're all set for this thing to go down tomorrow at 1500 hours."

"I would assume that you have a team in Miami ready to move on her connections there as well," LeVonte stated for verification.

"Precisely!" Nuccio answered. "We'll have people planted all over the bank."

Rinaldo squirmed uneasily in his chair, "There's one thing that concerns me about all of this." He paused. "Being that April, or should I say Ludvina is legally married to Mitch, can't she still claim what is rightfully hers, even if she is in prison?"

"That thought crossed my mind as well. It might take years to sort things out." Ron added.

Nuccio's cell phone rang, he quickly answered….. then took an intense expression as he listened.

"You have got to be kidding me," He remarked, and then listened a bit more. "We'll get down there as soon as possible."

Nuccio set his phone down, and glanced at everyone at the table with an expression of disbelief, "What was that all about?" LeVonte inquired.

Nuccio rested back in his chair, "I think we just got the miracle we needed." He shook his head with stunned amazement, before concluding. "Mitchell Grant just woke up."

A short time later, LeVonte and Nuccio arrived with Ron at the hospice site where Mitch was being housed. Ron wasted no time in hurrying to his bedside, while LeVonte and Nuccio stood back at a comfortable distance. "Welcome back, buddy. I missed you while you were gone."

Mitch looked up with tired eyes and forced a weak smile, "I could hear you, and everyone else from where I was in the Summerland."

Ron reacted with a puzzled expression, "The Summerland? Where in the world is that?"

"It's a place where dreams come true." He paused. "I stayed in a cottage by a lake, and all of my departed family were there. We were all young, healthy, and happy. We didn't have a care in the world."

Ron gently held his hand and listened as Mitch continued in a weak, but enthusiastic voice, "Even Chris was there, and she was just as pretty as I remembered."

"Really? Chris was there?"

Mitch slightly nodded with a sober face, "She was waiting there for me, and she still loved me after all this time."

"Wow!" Ron exclaimed. "I don't quite know what to make of all that."

"It was real," Mitch assured. "Don't take this personal, but I didn't want to come back."

"I can't say I blame you for that." Ron chuckled. "But I'm still glad you're here."

LeVonte turned to Nuccio with a raised brow and spoke in a loud whisper, "That's quite a story. Do you think it's the drugs talking?"

Nuccio seriously shook his head and became uncharacteristically emotional. He motioned LeVonte off to the side so that Mitch couldn't hear, "When I was serving in Afghanistan, there was a guy in my platoon that survived an IED attack." He paused. "He was in a coma for ten days, and when he woke up, he had a similar story."

"So, you think this place he's talking about is real?"

"Who's to say it isn't?" Nuccio shrugged. LeVonte pondered the possibility with a wide-eyed expression.

Ron settled into a chair near Mitch's bed and continued their conversation, "I think you already know that April tried to have you killed."

Mitch calmly blinked his eyes in acknowledgment, "Her real name is Ludvina Cherakova. She's a former Russian spy, and an operative in the Russian mob."

"I really know how to pick them. Don't I? Mitch grinned.

Ron motioned toward LeVonte and Nuccio, and they stepped closer, "This is Detective Clark and Agent Nuccio." He paused with emphasis. "With their help, we're taking her, and a lot of very bad people down." Mitch closed his eyes and responded with an accepting nod.

Just then, Dr. Howell breezed into the room from the outer foyer, "Gentlemen! I know you're all just as excited as I am that Mr. Grant is once again among the living. But he does need to get his rest."

Ron gave Mitch's hand a gentle squeeze, "I'll come back, and talk to you soon."

As the men began to file out of the room, Nuccio turned and went back to his bedside. He leaned in close to Mitch and spoke in a low tone, "Don't worry, Mitch. We got this." He assured. "And for what it's worth. I believe this place you spoke of really does exist." Mitch replied with a weak, grateful smile, and Nuccio responded with a quick wink, and a nod before departing.

The men all chatted with Dr. Howell as they strolled along the corridor, and into the reception area. "What are the chances of Mr. Grant making a full recovery, Dr. Howell," LeVonte asked.

"It's a miracle in itself that the man even woke up." He answered. "But he still has a long recovery road ahead of him. We have to be concerned with clots, aneurysms, and the simple fact that he's not a young man anymore."

"I suppose all of us could classify for that last fact." LeVonte chuckled.

"Unfortunately, yes." The doctor replied with an amused smile.

"I'll continue to have agents Sadler and Marion here with him until this thing gets resolved," Nuccio stated.

"My staff and I will take good care of him as well." The doctor assured.

"Thank you, Dr. Howell. LeVonte concluded as they reached the front door. "I hope you have a pleasant afternoon."

The three men departed and slowly walked to where their cars were parked in the unassuming residential neighborhood. Nuccio walked with a slower gait than the others and seemed to be pondering in thought. He paused his progress and looked up with an enlightened smile, "Wait up, you guys. I have an idea."

LeVonte and Ron paused to let Nuccio catch up, "Since Mr. Grant is now back among the living, I think it might be a good opportunity to change the will without Ludvina knowing."

"I get what you're saying," Ron answered. "I could get our attorney to erase her from the present will, and have Mitch be able to sign it."

"That will definitely throw a wrench into any plans she might have to inherit anything should Mr. Grant actually pass away."

"Exactly!" Nuccio smirked, as he turned his attention to Ron. "You have a few good hours left in the afternoon. Do you think the attorney could prepare a revised edition of that will, and have it notarized, and ready by tomorrow afternoon?"

"I can get right on it, and find out," Ron replied.

"I can drive him over there right now, and I'll give you a call later," LeVonte added.

"Great!" While you do that, I'll check on the progress of my other agents."

Nuccio watched as LeVonte and Ron swiftly departed. He couldn't hold back his enthusiasm as he prepared to get into his car, "Damn!" He chuckled. "I love it when a plan comes together."

In the cottage kitchen, Harry, Tilly, Bobby, and Doris all sadly sat around the small table. They all glanced at each other, waiting for someone to break the silent sorrow.

"I can't believe he's gone." Tilly emotionally remarked.

"I know," Harry replied. "I haven't felt sadness like this since I was alive."

"Isn't there something we can do, dad?" Bobby asked.

"Can't you talk to Gabriel?" Tilly added. "Maybe he can give us some kind of closure on the situation."

"I suppose I could try." Harry sighed.

Doris gazed out the window, and into the yard where the clouds had now cleared, and the late day sun now filtered through the trees, "I feel extra sorry for Chris." She remarked.

"I know," Tilly replied. "I tried to get her to come inside, but the poor dear is too heartbroken. She just won't budge from that chair."

Harry stood, and looked outside, "I'll go talk to her."

Moments later, Harry strolled out into the yard, while Chris held a vigil in one of the Adirondack chairs, longingly staring out over the lake. Harry approached awkwardly as her eyes never wavered from the glistening water. "Would you like Tilly and me to stay here with you tonight?"

Chris slowly shook her head no and continued with her endless gaze, "Can I at least sit down?"

She nodded yes, and Harry settled into the other chair, "If it's any consolation, I can say with certainty that he's missing you as much as you're missing him."

She finally turned toward him with great emotion, "It's just not fair!" She stated. "I waited here every evening for thirty-two years until he finally arrived, and now he's gone again."

One of the orange Tabby's jumped into Harry's lap and settled comfortably, "I know, honey." He replied. "I waited a long time for Tilly too, and Bobby waited even longer for Doris." He paused with emotion. "That's what you do when you truly love someone."

"If I would've just been more patient on that one night so many years ago, he and I could've had a lifetime together." She vented with frustration. "I think this must be punishment for that."

Harry glanced out over the lake in deep thought, as he stroked the content cat in his lap, "Honey! You can't keep beating yourself up over mistakes you made in life. You'll miss the blessings that you have here." He paused to let his words sink in. "Mitch knows now that you were faithful, and loved him all along. You need to get rid of that baggage."

She forced a smile, as tears streamed from her eyes, "I never thought I'd feel hurt like this again."

Harry gently set the cat on the ground, and it scurried off into the shadows of the yard, "We'll all get through this together, sweetheart. We're family."

They both stood up and embraced in an emotional hug, "Thank you, Harry."

"Now, are you sure you don't want us to stay?" He sighed.

She shook her head no, and smiled, "I just want to sit here until the sun sets, and talk to him like I always do."

Harry glanced back out over the water, "Somehow, I believe he'll hear you." He gave her an affectionate pat on the shoulder, then slowly strolled away, back toward the cottage. The sun was now close to setting, and it filled the bright green yard with a magnificent, magical glow.

As the close of another day arrived in the Summerland, Nuccio sat alone in a hotel room in another world, with his glass of Crown Royal. He sat reflecting on the many scars that lingered from a long, and difficult military career. He grinned and lifted his glass up, "To the Summerland." He toasted out loud, before downing the drink. He cringed at the bite of the alcohol, then added. "Hopefully, someday I'll see it as well."

The following afternoon, everyone took their places within the attorney's office conference room, waiting for April and her legal representative to arrive. Outside in the greeting area, Nuccio busied himself at a side desk, also waiting for the arrival. He took unassuming notice when she entered with her brash-looking attorney, Peter Zazny. The legal assistant greeted them immediately, "Welcome Mrs. Grant, and…"

"Peter Zazny" He asserted.

"Very well!" The assistant stated. "I will notify Attorney Belknapp that you're here."

The assistant exited the room, and Nuccio took subtle notice of the smug, confident glances that the two exchanged as they waited. Within a few short moments, the assistant returned and motioned for them to follow. "They're ready to see you now."

Nuccio waited until they were in the backroom before whispering into the hidden mic in his lapel. "Heads up, everybody. It's showtime."

Inside the conference room, April and Zazny exchanged greetings, and then took their place at the table, "Good afternoon, gentlemen." April boldly began. "This is my attorney representative, Peter Zazney."

All politely acknowledged him, and April followed with a fleeting, but flirty glance toward Rinaldo, before continuing with a domineering tone. "I'm sure Mr. Baumgartner is just as anxious as I am to get this over with. Can we get started?"

"Of course, Mrs. Grant!" Attorney Belknapp replied. "We'll begin with the reading of the agreement."

Meanwhile, in a bank lobby in Miami, Sergei Sachovsky had arrived, accompanied by his bodyguard. A dignified, young undercover agent glanced up from his desk and gave a slight nod to the bank manager across the way. The manager reacted with slight anxiety, as she quickly set her eyes back toward the papers on her desk.

The agent turned his chair away and spoke into his hidden blue tooth device, "The king is in the house." He quickly turned his chair around and kept a keen eye on the action.

Sergei's muscular bodyguard took a seat near an attractive and elaborately dressed undercover agent. The captivating woman sported a floppy white hat with an oversized designer handbag. She seductively crossed her shapely legs, emerging a flirty smile toward the gawking hulk. Sergei felt uncomfortable with the intense stares and stood impatiently, moving away before the bank manager ever acknowledged his presence, and called him over.

Back in Atlanta, Attorney Belknapp finished reading the agreement, and Rinaldo gave him a subtle nod when they made eye contact. "Are you satisfied by everything as it is, Mr. Zazny?" Belknapp asked.

"Yes." He assuredly agreed. "Everything seems to be worded properly."

"Very well!" He responded. "If you would pass the bank account number to Mr. Perez, we'll begin the transfer of funds."

Zazny passed the neatly folded paper to Rinaldo who would be conducting the transfer from his laptop, "Shouldn't we all sign the papers first?" Zazny asserted.

"With all due respect Mr. Zazny. Considering the large amount of money being transferred into my client's account, I would feel more comfortable signing after the fact." Zazny did not answer, but simply squirmed in his chair, while April blinked nervously.

Inside the bank, Sergei sat confidently as the bank manager waited for the transfer authorization to go through on her computer. "There we go, Mr. Sachovsky." She passed a document across the desk. "I'll just need you to sign this, so we can begin the transfer."

Sergei signed the document and handed it back to her without saying a word. She exchanged another hurried glance and quickly continued, "Okay! We'll begin the process, and it should only take a few moments." She looked up with a nervous smile. "Then we'll complete the transfer of assets into the account that you gave me."

Sergei grew impatient, while the transfer took longer than he expected. The manager glanced up, and calmed him with a smile."

"These darn computers have a mind of their own."

The bodyguard took careful notice as the female agent reached into her handbag, and she responded to his glance with a smile. "The problem with an oversized bag is that a girl can never find her lipstick."

At the desk, the manager made quick, alerting eye contact with the agent, before turning to Sachovsky."

"The transfer is complete, Mr. Sachovsky. Now, I can begin the transfer of assets from Grant Investments to the account you gave me." She quickly glanced up at the agent who was now strolling across the lobby toward them. "My computer is slow today, let me see if I can complete this on the computer at that desk over there.

She quickly evacuated her desk, leaving Sachovsky a bit suspicious. He turned to see the agent, who was already reaching inside his jacket for his gun. Sachovsky reached in his jacket just as the agent arrived with his gun already drawn. "Don't do it, Sachovky!"

The bodyguard alertly reached for his gun as well, but the female agent drew a gun from her purse first. "Don't even think about it, big boy."

Within seconds, agents planted throughout the lobby area converged. Sachovsky and the bodyguard reluctantly raised their hands as their guns were unholstered, and the two men were taken into custody.

"I guarantee, I'll be a free man before sundown." Sachovsky arrogantly remarked.

"Don't bet on it." The agent sarcastically grunted. "We have a whole trail of worldwide evidence that leads directly to you."

Sachovsky sneered at him, as another agent led him away. As he watched him depart, he talked into his Bluetooth, "The king and his court have been apprehended."

Inside the Attorney's office, Rinaldo waited nervously for Nuccio's signal in his earpiece, "It's going through. Just a bit slow."

April gave him a long, flirty glance from across the table, "It's finished." Rinaldo concluded.

"Very well!" Belknapp stated. "Now, we'll commence with the signing."

Just as April and Zazny signed the last copy, the door to the room flew open. Nuccio and LeVonte charged into the room with guns drawn, accompanied by a flood of other agents.

"Federal agents! Everyone, get their hands up now." Nuccio ordered.

Ron, Rinaldo, and Belknapp were quickly shuffled from the room by agents, while April and Zazny were taken into custody. April gave Nuccio a hard look as she was being cuffed. "I was still legally married to Mitch. I can fight this from prison." She grunted. "Besides, you all picked a fight with the wrong people. We're more powerful than you can imagine."

Nuccio sarcastically laughed, "We'll just add threats to a Federal Officer to your long list of charges, Ludvina."

"She's right, you know," Zazny added with an arrogant smirk. "We can drag this out in court for as long as it takes."

"Is that so?" Nuccio smirked. "I hate to rain on your parade, but…"

Nuccio picked up a copy of the agreement from the table and got right up into Ludvina, and Zazny's faces in an intimidating way. "The attorney switched the paperwork on you while the transfer was taking place. You both signed the wrong copy." He laughed. "You just signed Grant Investments and all of its' assets over to Ron Baumgartner."

"It won't hold up in court." Zazny snapped. "Mitchell Grant would've had to approve it, and in case you may have forgotten, he's dead."

"Sorry to disappoint you two again." Nuccio chuckled. But Mr. Grant is in fact very much alive, and this signature and time stamp proves it."

He points to the signature, and notary stamp with a smirky grin, while Ludvina and Zazny are flabbergasted beyond belief. "You lose! I win!" Nuccio proclaimed as he motioned to his agents.

"Get these two scumbags out of here." Nuccio exited the law offices triumphantly, amidst his agents as they led Ludvina and Zazny from the building in cuffs.

LeVonte, Ron, and Rinaldo all looked on, as they were led away. Ludvina gave them all a hard stare as she passed. "I'm glad to be finished with that evil bitch." Rinaldo stated.

Ron gave him a friendly tap on the back and exchanged a sly grin with LeVonte. "Hopefully you've learned not to trust seductive married woman, Rinaldo."

"Believe me! Never again!" He exclaimed.

Nuccio casually strolled over to them, "All you guys did great."

LeVonte motioned toward Ludvina, who was already secured in the back seat of a Federal car, "What'll happen with her?"

"Once she's convicted of all her international crimes, she'll spend the rest of her life at a Federal prison. Probably GITMO."

"It's safe to say that she won't be seducing anyone else with that pretty face any time soon," Ron commented.

"How much of their syndicate were you able to take down?" LeVonte further probed.

"We took down most of Sergei's people, and confiscated their assets." Nuccio sighed. "I'm sure it will lead us to other rat nests around the world. It's a struggle that never ends"

"At least the Miami connection is out of business as we speak," LeVonte replied.

"At least for now." Nuccio paused, then grinned. "I can guarantee that someone in the Kremlin is definitely crying in their vodka right about now."

All the men shared a hearty laugh, and LeVonte rested his hands on the shoulders of Nuccio and Ron. "I'm ready to get a beer, and celebrate." He announced. "Anyone else up for it?"

"Count me in!" Rinaldo quickly answered.

"Not me," Ron stated. "I need to go see Mitch, and tell him the good news."

LeVonte gave him an understanding nod, and turned to Nuccio, "What about you, Marine?"

"Sorry Army!" Nuccio chuckled. I really should tie up this paperwork, and get back to Washington." He shook his hand firmly. "It was a pleasure working with you, Detective Clark. You're damn good at what you do."

"Likewise, Agent Nuccio. It was an experience I definitely won't forget." He smiled and saluted. "Semper Fi, Marine."

Nuccio answered with a salute as well, "This we shall defend, Army."

LeVonte turned to walk away with Rinaldo, while Nuccio headed the other way. But after a few pondering steps, he turned back. "Hey, Vonte!"

LeVonte turned with a surprised expression, "Maybe I will join you guys for that beer." He motioned for him to follow along, and the three men strolled away together.

At the hospice, Mitch laid in his bed staring at the ceiling while a nurse checked his vitals. Agent Sadler paced in the far corner of the room, talking on his cell phone.

The nurse finished and straightened his pillows, "Is there anything else I can get for you, Mr. Grant?"

"Could I please get some water?" He asked with a shrill voice. "I'm thirsty."

Sadler strolled over to his bedside at that moment, "Good news, Mr. Grant." He enthusiastically announced. "I just spoke with Agent Nuccio. Your wife and her accomplices have been apprehended, so my services here will no longer be required.

Mitch replied with a sigh of relief, "So, what happens next?"

"We'll let you know." He placed an assured hand on top of Mitch's. "For now, just continue to heal, and get better."

Mitch replied with a weak smile, while Sadler responded with a wink and confident nod, "Take care of yourself, Mr. Grant."

Sadler strolled from the room and waved at the attendant at the reception desk. At the same time, Gabriel passed by, twirling his horn in one hand. Neither Sadler nor the attendant even noticed.

Mitch was glaring at the ceiling, with a tear rolling down the side of his face when Gabriel entered, "You're very sad." He stated.

Mitch was startled to see him, "Gabriel?" He glanced around the room. "What are you doing here?"

Gabriel calmly strolled over, and sat down in the chair by his bedside, "I wanted to check in on your progress. You were pretty busted up."

"The Summerland really wasn't a dream. Was it?"

Gabriel shook his head, "It's very real, Mitch."

Mitch's eyes wandered down, and he took notice of the horn, "Do you take that thing everywhere you go?"

He held the horn up and cracked an unusual smile that was quite different from his usual sober expression. "I never leave home without it."

The nurse entered with a cold bottle of water and brushed right by Gabriel as though he wasn't there, "Here's your water, Mr. Grant. Is there anything else I can get you?"

"No. This will be good for the time being. Thank you." The nurse left the room again, and strangely never acknowledged Gabriel's presence.

Mitch drank the cold water voraciously, then sighed as he rubbed his throat, "My throat's still raw from that breathing tube."

"You probably shouldn't be talking so much."

Mitch gestured toward the door, "She couldn't see you? Could she?"

Gabriel subtly shook his head, "Living people don't see me until it's their time to go."

Gabriel pondered his words, as he continued, "You were never meant to be taken from this world until you reached the age of ninety-two."

"Ninety-two? That's a long life." Mitch stated while Gabriel nodded and continued, "Just like Chris, your fate was altered by another human. But in your case, you were left tarrying between two worlds."

"I was happy. Why did you ever send me back here?"

"I know it seemed unfair." He paused. "But it was necessary in order for justice to be carried out appropriately."

"So that I could sign that will."

Gabriel nodded again, while Mitch looked toward him with all seriousness, "Please tell me this." He paused in thought. "What would've happened if Chris hadn't died in that accident all those years ago?"

Gabriel took a deep breath and gazed upward, "The two of you would've gotten married, and had two children. A boy and a girl." He nodded emotionally. "You would've had a happy life together."

Mitch sadly shook his head, "I would've given up everything I attained in life to have made that a reality."

"She is quite a remarkable woman, and man does she ever love you."

Mitch took a deep breath followed by another short swallow of water. He then glanced back at Gabriel, "So, if I'm supposed to be around until the age of ninety-two. How come I can see you now?"

Gabriel pondered his response for a moment, "Considering the happiness, and love you had in the Summerland, it was decided that I should come back, and give you a choice."

Mitch took on a baffled expression as he listened, "You can either continue with what remains of your life here, or you can go back to the Summerland, and continue where you left off there."

"For real?" Mitch questioned. "That's not a very hard choice."

"Despite your accident, you do have a fair amount of years left in this lifetime, Mitch." He shrugged. "A man of your wealth and stature could make quite a difference in this world, as you already have."

"I want to continue making a difference. But I can't live the rest of my life without the love I could've had with Chris." He emotionally shook his head. "Someone else can pick up the torch of charity, and carry it."

"If you're talking about Mr. Baumgartner, you should know that he has a much shorter expiration date than you do."

Mitch stared ahead in thought, "He always did have problems with his weight. Is that what gets him in the end?"

Gabriel nodded with a matter-of-fact expression, "He's a good man. We'll have a place for him in the Summerland." He gave an assured wink. "You're a good man too, Mitch. That trait obviously runs in your family."

Tears welled in Mitch's eyes, "I consider that the greatest compliment I could ever receive."

"So, I guess there's no changing your mind?"

Mitch shook his head, "My work is done here."

"Well! If you're ready to go now, I can get you back to the cottage before sunset." He smiled. "I'm sure Chris will be there waiting."

Mitch painfully reached over and retrieved a pen and notepad from his food tray, "I'm ready. But first, I need to leave a note for Ron."

It was nearing the evening hours by the time Ron reached the hospice. He enthusiastically marched through the front door and headed directly toward his room. Just before he reached the door, a crew of medical workers were solemnly leaving. One of them was pushing a resuscitation cart, "What's going on here?" He demanded.

The nurse motioned him off to the side, displaying a sorrowful expression, "I'm sorry, Mr. Baumgartner. Mr. Grant passed away a short time ago."

"How?" He was doing so good the last time I saw him."

"Believe me! I'm just as baffled, and devastated as you are."

Ron threw his arms up in total disarray, "Can I at least see him?"

"Sure. I'll walk you in." She respectfully answered. "We should have a few moments before the coroner arrives for his body."

Ron slowly entered, and approached his bed, while the nurse lagged behind, giving him some space. He stood observing him for a few long moments, and couldn't help but notice the peaceful expression on his face. "Well buddy, we did it. The people that did this to you are going away for a very long time." He painfully smiled. "I'm so sorry I didn't get here sooner." He choked up. "I'm going to miss you. I hope you truly are in that place you told me about."

The nurse stepped closer with a folded note in her hand and began to speak her mind.

"It was the strangest thing. I had just brought him some water, and a short time afterward, we heard what sounded like a trumpet blowing inside the room."

"A trumpet?" Ron questioned.

"Yes!" She exclaimed with a perplexed expression. "We immediately ran in, but no one else was here, and Mr. Grant had already passed." She handed the note to Ron. "He was clutching this note in his hand. It had your name on it."

She gave him a sympathetic pat on the back and quietly left him to read the note. He could almost hear Mitch's voice as he read it, "Thank you for being a true, and loyal friend through all these years. Someday, when you hear the sound of a trumpet, I'll see you again in the Summerland."

He closed his eyes and emotionally nodded yes. As he wiped the tears from his eyes and turned to leave, he paused to take notice of a large white feather that was laying on the floor. He picked it up, and examined it closely, before looking upward with an all-knowing smile.

The close of another day was nearing in the Summerland when Mitch slowly opened his eyes. All the pain and discomfort he had felt from his injuries was now gone. He sat up in bed, as a gentle breeze blew into the room, slightly lifting the curtains. He glanced around the familiar room in the cottage, and a smile exploded across his face. He paused before getting up to listen to the faint sounds of a distant lawnmower, and a dog barking somewhere outside.

He immediately made his way to the adjacent bathroom, and anxiously looked into the mirror, "Oh no!" He exclaimed. "This will not do!"

He clenched his eyes shut, and when he opened them, the middle-aged Mitch had transformed into the young, 23-year-old likeness that he had wanted to see. A confident expression came over his face as he admired what he saw. "Now, that's more like it."

Outside the cottage, Chris sat in the Adirondack chair, gazing out over the lake, as the evening sun slowly dived toward the horizon. Gabriel casually passed by on his evening stroll along the shoreline, "Good evening, Miss Christine!"

"Good evening to you as well, Gabriel!" She smiled.

He continued on without further word, and she watched as he paused near the shore to blow a quick, cheerful tune on his horn. He then gave her a departing wave before continuing on his way.

Unbeknownst to Chris, Mitch now stood behind her, observing the whole scenario, "Hey there, beautiful!" Mitch spoke with a sly grin. "Looks like I made it back just in time for the sunset."

Chris turned with an expression of shock, "Mitch!" She launched out of her chair with rocket speed and rushed into his embrace. They kissed with passion, while all the orange Tabby's surrounded them, meowing loudly with joy. At the far end of the yard, Harry pulled his riding lawn mower to a stop and watched the grand reunion. He glanced upward with a pleased expression, and mouthed the words, "Thank you."

The long shadows of the evening fell upon the grass, covering the yard with a golden glow, as the two lovers continued their embrace. Mitch Grant had returned to the Summerland, and those he loved dearly. Only this time, he was there to stay.

Tale Three:

The Darkness Between Two Lights.

It's said that we come from the light when we're born.

We carry that light within us in life.

And we're meant to return to the light when we die.

For many, that light dims, and their lives are plunged into darkness.

But for a special few, that light shines ever so brighter.

And they light the way for those souls lucky enough to be a part of their life.

Rob Prescott, a handsome, well-groomed man in his late forties, prepared to leave for the weekend from his job at the Prescott and Goldberg Architectural Firm. He fussed about in his office, as he grabbed his briefcase, and a bouquet, before hurrying into the main reception area.

He paused long enough to peek into the office space of his business partner, Art Goldberg. "Happy Friday, Art! I'm cutting out of here early, so I can beat the traffic on the 405."

Art, a grey-haired, youthful-looking man in his late sixties, glanced up from his work with a pleasant smile. "I take that you and Shelly have some big plans."

"Just dinner, and a sunset." Rob shrugged.

Art stood up and strolled outside his office to join him. "You two are still so much in love after all these years." He proclaimed with amazement. "I have to envy that."

Art's wife, Jenny Goldberg sauntered over from the reception desk to join in the conversation. She was a perky brunette in her late fifties with a heavy Jersey accent. "I can hear every word you're saying, Art Goldberg." She quipped as she struck a challenging pose, with her hands on her hips.

"Ah!" Art dismissed the approach. "I didn't mean it the way you took it. You know I love you, honey."

"Is that so!" She winked and flashed a sarcastic grin toward Rob. "When was the last time you brought me flowers on a Friday" She gestured humorously toward Art. "Can you believe this guy, Rob?"

Rob laughed, as Jenny shook her head, and returned to her desk. "Whatever! You and Shelly have a great weekend." He swiftly headed for the door but turned back. "Hey, Art! If you're going out on your boat, work a little more on that tan. I wouldn't want you to lose your reputation as the bronze god around here."

"Get out of here!" Art waved him off with a chuckle.

In the master bath of their Manhattan Beach home, Shelly Prescott carefully applied eye liner, while gazing wide-eyed into the bathroom mirror. She was a tall, naturally beautiful blonde in her early forties, who sported a cute smile that would enrapture even the hardest soul.

Shelly paused to listen, as she heard the front door open. She giggled with excitement, anticipating Rob's voice. "Sweetie! I'm home!" He called out.

She fussed with her hair for a moment and hurried out to greet him. "Happy Friday!"

They enthusiastically embraced, kissing passionately, before Shelly took notice of the bouquet Rob was holding. "Oh! Thank you for the beautiful flowers, honey." She joyfully admired the arrangement. "Such pretty colors!"

She kept talking as she hurried toward the kitchen, "Get the Mustang fired up while I put these in some water." Rob listened as she yelled from the other room. "We have to hurry! I made reservations for 5:15."

"Did you get the wine?" Rob called back.

"Yes! It's inside the cooler, there in the foyer." She shouted back, as she placed the flowers in a vase, and set them on the counter.

"Got it!" He replied. Shelly giggled with excitement, as she grabbed her jacket, and hurried from the room.

Outside, Rob backed out of the garage in his dark blue 1967 Mustang Convertible, just as his neighbor, Mark Faber was pulling into his driveway with his brand new Mercedes SL Convertible.

Mark was a short, thin man in his late thirties with an extravagantly self-righteous attitude. He leaped from his car and hurried across the well-manicured lawn to flag down Rob. "Hey, neighbor!" He yelled. "Taking the old 'Stang out for a cruise, I see."

"Shelly and I are going to dinner at the Turning Leaf, and then we're going to the beach to take in the sunset."

"You mean to tell me the old Leaf is still in business? I haven't been there in years."

"Still the best meal on the beach, for an affordable price." Rob's eyes wander to Mark's car. "Did you get a new car?"

"Top of the line SL," Mark responded with bursting pride. "Just picked that baby up this afternoon."

Shelly exited the house, sauntering along the walkway. Mark followed her with a keen eye. "Hello there, Shelly!"

"Oh, hi Mark! I haven't seen you around much lately." She nonchalantly replied.

"Well! The real estate market has been smoking hot, and I've been closing deals left and right." He bragged.

"Good for you!" Shelly replied as she got into the car. "Would you and Molly like to join us for dinner?"

"Thanks, but maybe another time." He flashed a fake smile. "We have reservations at the country club tonight."

Before either Rob or Shelly could say another word, Mark quickly inserted, "I wanted to ask you two for a favor." He sheepishly stated.

Both patiently listened while he hesitated to continue, "Our nanny is watching Millicent tonight. But she can't take care of her over the weekend."

Shelly quickly interrupted with enthusiasm, "We'd love to watch Millie this weekend."

Rob rolled his eyes and looked off the other way, "Are you sure? It'll be until Sunday night."

"Not to worry," Rob replied with a fake smile. "Millie's always a pleasure to have around."

"One of my clients invited Molly and me up to Santa Monica to stay on his yacht." He pridefully stated. "This guy is beyond wealthy."

"Oh! That's nice, Mark!" Shelly replied.

"You two are the greatest." He pointed with a grin. "I definitely owe you one."

"We'll just add it to the list." Rob mockingly joked.

"We'll bring her over in the morning."

"We'll be there, and looking forward to it." Shelly sweetly smiled.

Rob shifted the car into gear…. waved and tapped the horn, as they drove away. Mark pumped his fist with triumph as he strutted away.

At the Turning Leaf, Rob and Shelly were enjoying an after-dinner chat. The candle at the center of the table flickered brightly, and set a romantic mood, while they held hands across the table. "Do you ever notice how Mark always ogles over you like a piece of eye candy?"

"That's just Mark being Mark." Shelly giggled. "He does that to all the woman."

"I still don't like it."

"Oh, Rob!" She squeezed his hand. "You'll always be the only man in my life."

Rob took a swig of water and looked over, and past her shoulder at an attractive, well-dressed older woman. He then leaned in closer to Shelly. "Don't turn around and stare." He said in a near whisper. "Elizabeth Ashford is sitting three tables behind you."

Shelly also leaned in and whispered, "Who's Elizabeth Ashford?"

"She's a famous British actress who was very popular in the '80s and '90s." He answered while still casually watching her. "Oh! She's getting up to leave."

The woman sauntered by and paused to acknowledge them in a distinct British accent. "Hello!"

"Good evening, Ms. Ashford."

"I just had to stop, and compliment on what a handsome couple you two are."

"Well, thank you very much." Rob smiled. "I'm Rob Prescott, and this is my wife, Shelly. I've been a fan of yours for quite some time."

Elizabeth seemed quite flattered, but humbly waved off the comment, "I'm afraid I don't hear that as often as I used to."

She quickly turned her attention to Shelly, "And you, my dear, are stunningly beautiful.

"Thank you." Shelly blushed. "That's very nice of you to say."

"Well, it's quite true." She paused. "Would you by chance be a fellow thespian?"

Shelly was flabbergasted by the question, "Oh no!" She answered in a serious tone. "My husband and I have been married for twenty-four years, and I've never had a desire to be with a woman."

Elizabeth was dumbfounded, and staggered by her response. "Oh!" She reacted awkwardly. "Well, that's fine. I really shouldn't take up any more of your time. It was a pleasure meeting both of you.

"The pleasure was ours, Ms. Ashford." Rob politely replied.

Elizabeth departed with an uneasy smile, and Rob glared across the table at Shelly with stunned amusement. "What in the world made you respond like that?"

Shelly leaned in with a disdainful expression and whispered loudly. "Well! It was quite obvious that the old girl was interested in having sex with me."

Rob stared at her with a mixture of disbelief, and puzzlement. "Why would you ever think that?"

"She asked if I was a thespian." She responded with indignance. "That must be some new fangled name for a lesbian that goes both ways."

"Oh, Shelly!" He cuffed his hand over his mouth to contain his laughter. "A thespian is an actor or person of the theater."

"I didn't know!" She blurted out with frustration and embarrassment. "She probably thinks I'm just a ditsy blonde."

Rob shook his head and smiled with amusement. "We should get going if we want to catch that sunset."

A short time later, as they watched a beautiful sunset from Manhattan Beach, they snuggled close and sipped from their wine glasses. "Look at all those beautiful colors, Rob."

"I know." He pointed. "Those dark clouds accent everything."

Shelly glanced up at him admirably, "Are Art and Jenny going out on the boat this weekend?"

"Like every other weekend." He chuckled. "Art has an addiction to that boat and fishing. I guess that's his way of dealing with stress."

"Jenny certainly doesn't share that passion." She sighed. "She told me that she stays below deck, and reads a book."

"Well, I suppose that's an issue that's just between them."

"I know." She nodded. "But I guess I just want everyone else in our lives to be as happy as we are."

Rob gently kissed her on the forehead and smiled endearingly, "You are one special lady, Shelly Prescott."

Shelly shifted to try to get comfortable but winced with intense pain. She spilled her wine and moaned as she grabbed at her abdomen. "Are you okay, sweetie?"

She responded with frustration, as she took several deep breaths. "Every time I move a certain way, it's like someone's stabbing me in the lower abdomen."

"Dr. Griffin did say the cyst was about the size of a golf ball."

"It must be a golf ball with spikes." She stressfully exhaled.

"I think I better take you to the hospital, right now," Rob advised. "I'm sure they'd be able to move the surgery up a few days."

"Absolutely not!" She protested. "I want to spend this weekend with you and Millie. A drab hospital room is certainly not an option."

Rob carefully helped her to her feet, "In that case, I better get you home so you can rest."

Shelly buried her head into his shoulder and began to cry. "I'm sorry that I ruined such a perfect evening."

He wiped the tears from her cheek, kissed her, and tried to calm her down. "Listen!" He commanded while he looked her straight in the eyes. "The only thing we should be focused on right now is getting you to feel better. Okay?" Shelly emotionally nodded, as Rob proceeded to gather up the blanket, and cooler. He steadied her with his free hand as their bare feet plodded through the sand on their way back to the car.

That night, as they slept, the sound of the doorbell woke them up. Rob rolled over and glanced at the digital clock with squinting eyes, and groaned. "For crying out loud!" He blurted out. "It's 4:45 in the morning. Who's ringing the damn doorbell?"

He turned on the bedside lamp, while Shelly slowly sat up, and squinted her eyes against the light. "Surely, Mark wouldn't be bringing Millie over this early." She stated.

The doorbell rang again, and Rob quickly crawled from under the covers, causing their cat Matilda to jump off the bed. "I better get up, and go see."

Moments later, Rob made his way downstairs dressed in a robe, and night pants. He turned the outside light on and looked through the peep hole. There, he saw Mark standing spryly dressed in a Nautica polo and shorts. His nine-year-old daughter, Millie stood soberly next to him, still dressed in her kitty cat pajamas, furry slippers, and toting an overnight bag. "You got to be kidding me," Rob muttered to himself before opening the door.

"Good morning, Rob!" Mark announced in a perky voice.

"Isn't it a bit early?" Rob answered in an annoyed tone.

"Sorry, buddy! Molly and I wanted to get an early start."

Rob yawned and motioned to them. "Come on in."

Rob took notice of the shy little girl who looked up at him with her big blue eyes, magnified through thick-lensed glasses. His heart melted at her silent innocence. "Hi, Millie!"

"Hello, uncle Rob!" she answered, never wavering from her sober expression.

Mark quickly scanned the foyer area with widened eyes.

"Molly and I wanted to be at the Santa Monica pier by sunrise." He stated. There's a little place that serves the best mimosas."

Rob answered with a conjured smile, as Shelly made her way down the stairs, wiping the sleep from her eyes. "Hi, Mark! Hi Millie!"

"Hi, Aunt Shelly! The child's face lit up with a smile.

Shelly leaned down to greet the happy little girl, "We are so glad you're staying with us this weekend."

"Can I go to bed for a little longer? She answered as her expression turned sober once again. "Me and Mrs. Turner are very tired."

The little girl put her hand out, as though she was holding someone's hand, and Shelly reacted with a rather puzzled look on her face. "Sure sweetie! But who's Mrs. Turner?"

Before Millie could answer, Mark, interrupted, "That's just one of her imaginary friends." He rolled his eyes with embarrassment.

Millie showed no reaction to his comment, which created a rather awkward moment. He went down to one knee to address his daughter. "Now Millicent, you be a good girl for Rob and Shelly. Okay?"

Without answering her father, Millie turned, and slowly proceeded up the stairs, still holding on to the hand of the imaginary Mrs. Turner. Mark got a distressed look on his face as he watched her. "She's just tired. She usually sleeps late on the weekends."

In a barely audible tone, Rob muttered. "At least somebody does."

Shelly lightly elbowed him in the ribs, while Mark handed over the small overnight tote that Millie had left behind. He acted rather sheepish. "I think Molly packed everything that she'll need."

"If not, we'll make do," Shelly assured.

After Millie was upstairs, Mark whispered in a lower tone, "Mrs. Turner was the woman who lived in our house before we bought it. Millicent overheard us talking about how she died there.

"Oh! Yeah!" Rob blinked his eyes and yawned. "I heard a rumor that she had a stroke, and died."

Mark nodded matter-of-factly, "Because she lived alone, nobody discovered her body until two weeks later."

"Oh! How sad." Shelly commented.

"That's the reason I was able to buy that place at such a sweet price." Mark bragged.

A car horn honked loudly, and Mark looked out toward the driveway with urgency. "If the rest of the neighborhood wasn't awake, I'm sure they are now." Rob sarcastically stated.

"It's the queen summoning me." Mark chuckled. "I better get running."

"Have a great time, Mark," Shelly remarked.

"I'll see you on Sunday evening."

"We'll be here," Rob grumbled.

Mark reacted with nervous guilt as he hurried to leave. Rob and Shelly stood watching in the doorway as his Mercedes accelerated from the driveway. "Poor Mark!" Shelly exclaimed. "I have a feeling Molly calls all the shots in that relationship."

Rob answered with an agreeing nod and a grunt. "Let's go back to bed, baby."

Later that morning, Shelly was working in her art studio which she had set up in a spare room of the house. With an LA Dodgers cap turned backward on her head, she worked diligently on a canvas that rested on an easel in front of the large picture window. All around her were finished pictures of ocean and beach scenes, which was her favorite concentrated area.

Millie wandered in with the cat, Matilda following close behind. With wide eyes, she looked all around the room at the finished art pieces. Shelly glanced up and smiled. "Look who finally got out of bed."

Millie continued to take in all the works as though she never heard her. A grouping of pictures resting against a wall caught her attention. "I like your mermaid paintings."

"Well, thank you," Shelly answered as she continued with her work. "Which one of those do you like the best?"

"I like the one with the blonde mermaid sitting on the rocks." She smiled. "She looks just like you."

Shelly glanced up with a pursed smile, as she continued to work away at the canvas. "Since you like that one so much, I think it should be yours." She stated in a matter-of-fact tone.

The young child's face lit up with excitement. "Really?" Shelly gave her an assured nod and continued her work. "Thank you so much, aunt Shelly. I'll have my dad hang it in my room so that I can always look at it."

Millie then strolled over and watched with great interest as Shelly put the finishing touches on her painting. "That's very pretty!"

"It's almost finished. It's a full moon rising over the water." Shelly paused, "See the silhouette of the sailboat?

Millie stepped in for a closer look and nodded with excitement. She then curiously noticed the design painted on the side of Shelly's face.

"What's that painted on your cheek, aunt Shelly?"

"That is a peace sign." She paused to glance at the child. "We're taking you to the hippy fest down at the city park today."

Millie reacted with a puzzled expression. "What's a hippie?"

Shelly giggled, as she set her paint brush on the easel, and turned her full attention to the child. "Way back in the 1960s and 70s, there were people who had long hair, made their own clothes, and wrote songs about peace and love. Society called them hippies."

"I like peace and love." Millie soberly replied as she gazed at Shelly with wonderment. "Did you and uncle Rob used to be hippies?"

Shelly giggled and looked down to notice Matilda meowing, and rubbing affectionately against her leg. "I'm afraid Rob and I weren't around back then. But we also like peace and love." She answered as she picked up the purring cat.

Millie thought for a moment before speaking again, "Could you paint a peace sign on my face too, aunt Shelly?"

"I sure can, sweetie." She smiled. "I'll even print the word love on your other cheek."

"Cool!"

Shelly set the cat down, and went down to one knee to get closer to Millie. She then reacted with a wincing moan. "Are you okay, aunt Shelly?" Millie asked with great concern.

Shelly attempted to regain her composure, despite the intense pain, and nodded rapidly, "What's wrong?" The little girl emotionally persisted.

"Well!" Shelly began. "Aunt Shelly has a female problem that she needs to get taken care of."

Millie looked at her with an innocent, sober expression, "Is it a problem with your vagina?"

Shelly was taken off guard by the question, and looked away with embarrassment, searching for the right words to answer. "I suppose you could say that." She paused. "At least in that area."

"Do you need an operation?" The child continued to probe.

Shelly sighed and nodded yes, "My mommy had her tubes tied. Is that what you have to have done?"

Shelly uncomfortably cleared her throat. "It's a little more complicated than that. I have to go to the hospital on Monday, so I'll need you to say a little prayer for me. Okay?"

Millie responded with a sober nod, "Now, let's get your face painted up, kiddo."

Later, as the happy trio cruised down the Pacific Coast Highway in the Mustang convertible, Millie sat contently in the back seat. She had a large solar shield over her glasses, and a big dab of sunscreen spread over her little button nose. Shelly had put her long blonde hair into ponytail braids, and they flapped in the breeze. She and Shelly held pinwheels in the air that spun furiously, as the rhythmic sound of Richie Haven's "Here Comes the Sun" played on the car stereo.

A tough, rugged-looking biker pulled even with the car, and his hard expression quickly melted into a smile, as Millie waved at him. He gave a chuckling nod, and a thumbs up to all of them before continuing on his way.

At the hippie fest, the trio danced hand in hand, in a large circle with other attendants. Shelly bought a pair of love beads from one of the vendors and placed them around Millie's neck.

Later, they all sat and watched a beautiful sunset on Manhattan Beach. As they cruised home in the dark, both Shelly and Rob glanced back with a smile toward Millie who was now passed out, and sleeping soundly in the back seat.

As Rob carried the sleeping child into the house, Shelly bumped close and slipped her arm around his back,

"That day was absolutely magic." She swooned with a pleasing smile.

The next day, the trio visited a nearby farmer's market. Millie still proudly wore the face paint and colorful love beads that Shelly bought for her the day before. Rob and Shelly were occupied with bagging some vegetables, while Millie stared at something across the aisle.

She gave a wave in that direction, and Shelly noticed. "Who are you waving at, sweetie?"

"That man over there." She pointed. "He looks so sad.

Shelly looked in that direction, and shrugged, "What man? I don't see anyone."

"He's right over there." Millie insisted with much impatience. "He's wearing a long coat."

Both Shelly and Rob looked again and then exchanged a clueless glance. "I'd be sad too If I was wearing a long coat." Rob quipped. "It's almost 90 degrees today."

"I feel sorry for him," Millie stated, still looking in that direction. "He looks so lost."

"Oh! He'll be okay, Millie." Shelly smiled. "I'm sure he'll find his way."

Rob paid for the vegetables, and Shelly took hold of Millie's hand, "Come on, sweetie. Now we're going to a farm to get some fresh eggs."

"Will I be able to see the chickens?"

"I don't see why you couldn't." Millie beamed with excitement at the response.

Late that night, Mark and Mollie drove home from their weekend retreat. Barely a word passed between the two, as Mark stared straight ahead at the road, and Molly held a steady glare out the side window. Molly was a visibly spa pampered woman in her late 30s, with spray stiffened, sandy blonde hair, and a bit too much eye liner.

"We probably should've been on the road hours ago," Mark complained.

"If I had it my way, this weekend would've never ended," Molly grumbled. "The Finch's are definitely living the life I want."

"I think you and I are doing quite well." Mark countered, before quickly glancing her way. "You have to consider that the Finch's are billionaires."

Molly only gave a weary sigh in response, "I just hope we aren't taking advantage of Rob and Shelly's good nature by leaving Millicent for the entire weekend." He gave his wife another glance. "After all." He added. "They have a life too."

"Oh! They love taking care of Millicent." She grunted. "Besides, she isn't old enough to appreciate the finer things in life that we enjoy." Mark reluctantly refrained from carrying the conversation any further.

At the Prescott home, Millie sat between Rob and Shelly on the couch, with Matilda resting contently on her lap. They all laughed as they watched an episode of "Funniest Home Videos" on the TV. "I wonder if mommy and daddy forgot about me," Millie commented.

Rob and Shelly exchanged a quick, concerning glance, "Oh, sweetie! They probably just got a little sidetracked." Rob assured.

"They'll be here soon," Shelly added.

Millie giggled as Matilda raised her head to take notice of another cat that was meowing loudly on the TV. "I wish I had a kitty like Matilda."

"Do your parents know that you want a cat?" Shelly asked.

"Mom's allergic to them, so she said we can't have one."

The doorbell rang, and Rob sprang from the couch, "And, there's your mom and dad now."

The cat scuttled from Millie's lap as she and Shelly followed Rob to the door. Rob enthusiastically swung the door open to greet Mark and Molly. "Hey, you two! We were about ready to send out a search party." He stepped aside. And ushered them into the foyer.

"Time just kind of got away from us." Mark sheepishly answered.

"Santa Monica was marvelous," Molly added, in a tone of haughtiness.

The couple quickly turned their attention to Millie. "There's my little Millicent." Molly quipped, and Millie showed little enthusiasm with her mother. "What in the world is that on your face?"

"Aunt Shelly painted my face for the hippie fest."

Molly's expression turned to one of horror, "The hippie…what?"

Shelly quickly interjected herself into the conversation, "It was an event we went to at the city park yesterday."

Molly reacted with a haughty expression. "Oh! How modest!" She then critically examined the love beads around the little girl's neck, as Shelly continued.

"She didn't want to wash the paint off until you saw it."

"Well! It's coming off as soon as we get home, young lady. There's no telling how that paint will affect your complexion."

Millie somberly looked down, as Shelly displayed a sympathetic smile for the child. Millie walked over and grabbed the painting Shelly had given her. "Look! Aunt Shelly gave me one of her paintings."

Molly took the painting and held it up with a less than enthusiastic expression. "How cute!" She sarcastically quipped. "That mermaid looks like Shelly."

"It sure does," Mark stated, as he looked over Molly's shoulder. His comment drew a disdainful look from his wife.

Shelly responded to the uncomfortable moment with a nervous giggle and flashed a fake smile toward Molly. Mark tried to move the conversation along by turning his full attention toward his daughter. "What else did you do, sweetie?"

"We went to a farmers market, and then got eggs from a farm with real chickens."

"Wow! Real chickens?"

The child soberly nodded. "We also went cruising on California 1 in uncle Rob's Mustang, and listened to old-time music from the 1960s."

"Wow! The 1960s! That's even older than your dear old dad here." He joked as Millie responded with a giggle.

"Of course, we don't refer to it as California 1 anymore." Molly corrected the child. "The proper name is the PCH."

Mark ignored his wife's comments and stayed focused on Millie, "Nevertheless, you must've had a fun time, sweetie. I haven't seen you this excited for a while."

Millie looked at her father with a very serious expression, "We'll have to pray for aunt Shelly. She's having an operation tomorrow."

Mark looked up with great concern. "Nothing serious, I hope."

"She has a problem with her vagina."

Shelly looked away with embarrassment, and all the adults reacted rather awkwardly.

"Millicent!" Her mother scolded. "That's not the proper thing for a young lady to say."

Mark stepped in to smooth things over, "Just let us know if there's any way we can help."

Molly shot a stern look toward her husband, "That was a rather poor choice of words, Mark."

He could no longer hide his agitation with his wife, and he snapped back with a hard gaze. "I think Rob and Shelly knew exactly what I meant." Molly cowered down with a miffed expression, while Rob quickly intervened, trying his best to keep a straight face.

"By all means, Mark. We both appreciate your concern."

"We really should be going." Molly elbowed her husband in his side. "I'm sure Rob and Shelly would like some quality time to themselves."

Mark nervously nodded in agreement, while Millie emotionally hugged Shelly and Rob, "Thank you, aunt Shelly and uncle Rob." She held them both tightly for a long moment. "Say goodbye to Matilda for me."

"We sure will, sweetie." Shelly smiled.

Millie gave them both a final wave, as her parents awkwardly ushered her out the door. Mark turned before leaving and mouthed the words "Thank You" to both of them.

Shelly closed the door behind them, then turned to Rob with a frustrated groan.
"Sometimes that woman seriously challenges my good nature."

"You're far too kind, honey." Rob chuckled. 'I'll just tell it like it is. "Molly is a domineering, social-climbing bitch." He grunted. "It felt good to get that out." He shook his head. "I can understand why Mark has an eye for other women."

Shelly rapidly nodded with agreement, "I feel so bad that she treats Millie the way she does." She exhales her frustration and continues. "I just wish there was more we could do for Millie. She's such a little sweetheart."

Rob moved closer and placed his hands on her shoulders, "We have to try not to get too involved. After all, she's not our child."

Shelly looked away with hurt, and began to weep. Rob pulled her in close and tried to comfort her, "I'm sorry, honey. I didn't mean to…"

"I know." She interrupted. "I just wish that you and I could've had our own children."

Rob embraced her tightly, before holding her at arm's length, and looking straight into her eyes.

"We've been through this over and over." He paused. "The situation could remain the same, and I'd still marry you one hundred times over. I love you more than anything in this world." Rob affectionately kissed her on the forehead.

"I love you too." She sobbed.

"Come on! I need to get you tucked in." He smiled endearingly. "You have a big day tomorrow,"

She slipped her arm around his waist, and they slowly made their way up the stairs.

The next morning, the couple got up early to go to the hospital. Rob had pulled the Mustang up to the front door, and he helped Shelly into the passenger seat. "I'm so glad we're taking the Mustang." Shelly beamed. "It's such a beautiful morning."

"I knew you'd enjoy it, sweetheart."

Thoughts flooded through Shelly's mind as they drove along. She glanced over at Rob and smiled. "When I get out of the hospital, I need to buy art supplies for my students."

"Don't tell me the school district cut your budget again." Rob shook his head with frustration. "What are they doing with our tax money?"

"The arts are always the first thing to get cut." She sighed. "Some of those kids have so much talent too."

Rob took hold of her hand, and gave it a gentle squeeze, as she leaned back comfortably in her seat. "You know that old arcade building down by the beach?"

"Yeah!" Rob quickly glanced at her with wonder. "That's been on the market for at least three years."

"Wouldn't that be a great place to have an art center for the kids?"

"That's prime property, honey. They're probably asking a fortune for it."

"What if we had an investor?" She asked with a sly smirk. "Do you think we could talk them down on the price?"

Rob glanced over at her again with great curiosity, "Are you keeping something from me?"

She grinned like a cat that swallowed a canary. "Maybe."

"Are you going to tell me?" Rob chuckled.

"Sorry, Mr. Prescott!" She sarcastically exclaimed. "It's a surprise, and you're just going to have to wait until we get this operation over and done with."

"Every day is a surprise with you, honey." He smiled. "And I love it."

At the hospital, Rob waited patiently as the attendants prepared Shelly for surgery behind a closed curtain. Dr. James Griffin, a tall, dignified man in his mid-40s approached and quickly exchanged a firm handshake with Rob. "How's our girl doing, Rob?"

"She was pretty sick last night." He sighed. "She didn't get much sleep."

Dr. Griffin took a deep breath and gave a confident pat to Rob's shoulder. "Don't worry! I got this!" He assured. "She'll be back to her old self in no time at all."

The curtain opened, and the nurse wheeled Shelly into the corridor, "Well! Hello there, beautiful." The doctor quipped. "Are you ready to get this thing done, Shelly?"

Shelly gave a weak nod, as Dr. Griffin continued, "I understand the Dodgers have a pretty good team this year. When this is all over, I'll get four tickets, and we'll all go to a game. Just like we did last summer.

Shelly's eyes lit up with excitement, "I'd like that."

Dr. Griffin gave Rob an assured wink, before turning his attention back to Shelly. "I'll see you in the O.R."

Dr. Griffin departed, and Rob held Shelly's hand tightly, "I'll be here waiting for you." He smiled. "I love you, baby."

"I love you too." She answered weakly. Rob was reluctant to let loose of her hand as he gently kissed her on the forehead. He stepped away and watched with anxiety as the attendants wheeled her down the hallway.

Later, all appeared calm as Dr. Griffin tediously and skillfully operated on Shelly, while the nurses kept a close eye on her vitals. Suddenly one of the nurses spoke up in an urgent tone.

"Something's happened. Her breathing has shallowed, and her readings are dropping rapidly."

Dr. Griffin glanced up momentarily with much concern, as the situation escalated rather quickly. "Try to stabilize her. I'm almost done here."

"We're losing her, doctor." The nurse urgently announced. "She's crashing!"

"Prepare the epinephrine, stat!" His voice trembled with anxiety. "I have to get her closed up down here, or she'll bleed out."

Another nurse drew the vial, filled the syringe, and handed it off to the head nurse who quickly administered it. "Come on, Shelly girl!" The doctor urged as he closed the incision. "Done!"

The alarm on the vital machine went off, and all eyes darted at one another with urgency. Before anyone could react, the machine went to a long constant beep. "Code blue!" The nurse yelled. "She's flat lining!"

Dr. Griffin desperately gripped the paddles from the crash cart, and placed them on Shelly's chest, causing her body to jump on the table. They waited a few seconds, and the nurse shook her head. "She's not responding."

He hit her with another charge, but there was still no response, "Come on, Shelly! Come back to us!"

The nurse shook her head once more, and he set the paddles aside and began to administer manual CPR. Once again, there was no response. "Doctor! She's gone!"

He looked up at the nurse, emotionally holding back tears. "Should we call it?" She asked.

Dr. Griffin took a deep breath and looked up at the clock, "Time of death. Two fourteen PM."

Shelly's spirit left her body and stood watching with extreme confusion from behind the operating staff. Dr. Griffin sadly stood over her body for a moment. "I'm so sorry, Shelly!"

As Dr. Griffin and his staff slowly left the room, Shelly's spirit stood alone, looking with horror at her own lifeless body. She looked around the now empty room in confusion, "Oh my! She exclaimed. "What happened here? I was watching a wonderful movie of my life, and everything suddenly went black."

In the scrub room, Dr. Griffin sat on a bench with his head in his hands. The head nurse strolled over and sat down next to him. Shelly's spirit appeared in the room as they began to converse. "We did everything we could." The nurse assured.

The doctor leaned back against the wall and sighed. "This one was tough."

"We save some, and we lose some. It's part of our job, doctor." She nodded. "You know that."

"Except, in this case, she and her husband are good friends of mine." He paused with much anxiety. "Now, I have to go tell my friend that I couldn't save his wife."

There was a short, awkward silence between them, before the nurse stood, and gave a sympathetic pat to the back of his shoulder. She exited without another word, as Shelly sadly watched. "Oh my!" She exclaimed with much dread. "I really am dead."

Shelly's spirit returned to the O.R., and sat alone for a long period, staring at her lifeless body that was still on the table. She suddenly looked up in the corner and shielded her eyes. "I can hear you, and I know I'm supposed to go to that bright light, but I can't go now."

She stood looking up, "I never had an updated will, and I never had a chance to tell Rob about my surprise." She stated. "I can't leave him like this."

She waited, and listened to an inaudible voice, "If you would only grant me a little more time to tie up some loose ends, I'll happily go to the light." She pleaded. "Please just give me that chance."

Attendants suddenly entered the room and began lifting her lifeless body onto a gurney. They carefully laid a clean white sheet over the body, before they wheeled it from the room. The last attendant turned off the large operating light, and shut the door, leaving Shelly's spirit alone once again. "Oh my!" Her eyes searched the room with great anxiety. "What do I do now?"

In the Prescott and Goldberg lobby, Art entered with a bag of bagels, and a huge smile on his face. He held the bag up to Jenny, who sat behind her desk in visible distress. "I got your favorite bagels from the Manhattan Deli."

Jenny only responded with a sad smile, and Art quickly realized something was wrong, "Baby, what's wrong?"

"Oh, Art!" She exclaimed, fighting back the tears. "Shelly didn't make it through surgery."

Art was shell-shocked by the news. He set the bag of bagels on Jenny's desk and slumped into a nearby chair, "Oh my God!" He put his hand to his head. "Poor Rob!"

"I know. I'm absolutely numb with grief."

He thought for a moment and shook his head, "We need to be there for him. He doesn't have any other family."

"We will," Jenny assured. "But what about her family?'

"Both her folks are gone too, and her sister died in an accident a few years back." He sighed, before emotionally looking upward, and breaking into tears. "Dammit!"

Jenny quickly rushed to comfort him, "I know, baby! This is just terrible!"

Jenny sat on the arm of the chair, and massaged his back, while he wiped the tears from his eyes.
"Shelly was truly his soulmate." He paused to reminisce. "When he saw her for the first time, he told me, Art, the woman I'm going to marry just walked in the room."

Jenny teared up as well, "It's just not fair. They were so much in love with each other." She said as she pulled Art closer, and they consoled each other.

A few days later at the funeral home, Rob stood in obvious shock, as he greeted those who came to pay their respects. Art and Jenny loyally stood with him near the casket. Shelly's unseen spirit was present as well.

She wandered over and took a long look at her body in the casket, "I'm so glad Rob chose that dress. It was one of my favorites."

She strolled over and stood as close to Rob as she could, "Oh Rob! I wish you could hear me." She touched his arm. "I'm so sorry I left you this way."

Rob looked down at his coat sleeve with a confused look that Art noticed. "Are you okay?" He asked.

Rob looked off with bewilderment before answering, "I could've sworn someone just touched my arm."

Shelly's spirit became excited. "He could feel my touch."

At that moment, Mark and Molly approached. Mark gave Rob an emotional handshake, "Words cannot explain how bad I feel about all of this, Rob. I'm in complete shock."

"I know." Rob agreed. "It's totally surreal."

Molly strolled straight over to survey the body in the casket, while Mark remained with Rob, "I assume you know my business partner, Art Goldberg, and this is his wife Jenny."

"Yes!" Mark answered. "We've met a few times at your house parties." He respectfully shook hands with the couple.

Art and Jenny excused themselves, as they moved on to converse with another couple, "How is Millie taking all of this?" Rob asked with deep concern.

"Not well!" Mark sighed. "She's barely come out of her room since we told her."

Shelly's spirit reacted with remorse. "Oh! The poor baby!"

"Maybe I could talk to her." Rob offered. "It might be good therapy for both of us."

"I think that's a good idea, Rob." Shelly's spirit agreed.

"When you're ready, I think that's a great idea," Mark concluded.

Molly strolled back over, and Shelly's spirit took note of her low-cut, multi-shade, green dress, "Gee whiz, Molly. The least you could've done was wear a black dress, and maybe show a little less cleavage."

Mark and Rob shared another respectful handshake, "If there's anything you might need in the meantime, be sure to let Molly and I know."

Molly nodded with a half-smile and gave Rob a quick, tight hug that drew Shelly's ire. "You just watch where you're rubbing those silicon missiles, sister. I might be dead, but he's still my husband."

"Thank you both for being here." Rob sadly smiled. "It means a lot"

Mark gave him an assured wink, and wave, "We'll be talking to you soon, buddy."

Later, at the Faber home, Mark stood outside Millie's room and gave a light knock on the door. "Millicent!" He called out. Are you going to come down, and join us for dinner, honey?"

"I'm not hungry." She voiced from behind the closed door.

"Can daddy come in, and talk to you?"

"No!" She distressfully answered. "I just want to be left alone."

"Okay, honey." Mark sighed as he lightly leaned against the door. "I understand."

Inside the room, Millie sat on her bed, staring up at the mermaid picture on the wall, with tear-filled eyes. Shelly's spirit appeared in the room, standing behind her. "I like where you hung my picture."

The little girl froze for a moment, then turned around slowly. Her sober expression broke into a joyous smile. "Aunt Shelly!" She happily exclaimed.

Shelly's spirit appeared quite baffled by Millie's reaction, "I wished so hard for you to come back, and you did."

"Wait a minute!" Shelly paused. "Are you telling me that you can see and hear me?"

Millie nodded with enthusiasm, "Then it was true that you saw that man the other day at the farmer's market."

Millie gave another more serious nod, while Shelly moved closer, and sat down on the edge of the bed, "Okay!" She pondered. "Let me explain this to you." She nervously paused. "I'm here, but I'm not really here.

Millie took on a perplexed expression, and Shelly sighed, "Oh, dear!" She pondered again. "I mean, you're the only one who can see or hear me. At least as far as I know."

Millie was further puzzled, and Shelly continued with a frustrated sigh, "Let's try this." She paused. "Reach out, and try to touch my hand."

The little girl reached out and tried to touch her outstretched hand. "You can't feel it. Can you, Millie?"

"I can't feel it. But it's warm where your hand is."

"That's interesting." Shelly thought. "You obviously feel my energy."

"Why am I the only one that can see and hear you?" Millie curiously asked.

"I wish I knew." Shelly pondered. "You obviously have a very special gift."

"I'm so glad you're here with me."

"It's only temporary, honey. I need to go the light very soon."

"Where's the light?"

"It's a place that I can see off in the distance." She looked off into a corner of the room. "I think it must be heaven."

Millie smiled, and Shelly looked over her shoulder. She noticed someone curiously peeking around the corner of the closet door. "Who's that in the closet, Millie?"

The little girl turned around and answered with confidence, "That's Mrs. Turner."

Shelly is flabbergasted as the spirit of the feeble old woman stepped out from the shadows of the closet, "Mrs.

Turner?" Shelly addressed her. "You're the woman who used to own this house."

Mrs. Turner slowly nodded in response, "She can't talk." Millie said.

"I know, honey," Shelly stated with sympathy. "She had a stroke before she died."

Mrs. Turner pointed toward Millie and cradled her arms in front of her, "I know, Mrs. Turner." She stated with an understanding smile. "I love Millie too."

Shelly turned her full attention back to the little girl, "Even though you can see us, you can't tell anyone else. Okay?" She paused. "Others just wouldn't understand your gift."

Millie answered with a serious, understanding nod, "Can I try to hug you, aunt Shelly?"

"I guess you can try." She shrugged.

Millie reached out and caressed what others would see as open air. "It feels like a warm blanket."

"I can feel your energy too, sweetie." Shelly giggled, as the little girl hugged her tightly.

"I love you, aunt Shelly."

"And, both I and Mrs. Turner love you too," Shelly stated with much emotion. "Now, you need to go downstairs, and eat your supper." She nodded assuredly. I promise that we'll talk again. Okay?" Millie answered with a serious, sober nod.

A short time later, Millie indeed made her way to the dinner table, "Well! Look who finally came down to join us." Molly announced.

Millie didn't respond to her mother, but instead, commenced to fill her plate with food. There was an uncomfortable silence as everyone continued eating. Molly could not hold her silence any longer and turned to address Mark. "I thought poor Shelly looked terrible." She quipped. "They put way too much makeup on her face, and I'll never know why Rob chose that cheap-looking dress for her to wear."

Mark set his fork down, and looked as though he were ready to blow a gasket, "Out of mere respect, could you please keep your caddy remarks to yourself?"

Molly reacted with a grunt, and a shallow chuckle, "It's not as though she can hear us."

"How do you know that?" Mark challenged.

"Oh really, Mark!" She laughed. "Shelly's gone."

"Her spirit is still here." Millie interrupted. "She'll always be with us."

Shelly's spirit wandered into the room, "That's right, Molly! I'm here!"

"Oh, Millicent! That's a pleasant thought, but it's just not true."

"It is true!" Millie stood up in a huff. "Why do you have to be so mean."

"My thoughts exactly," Shelly added.

"Millicent!" Her mother scolded. "Don't you dare talk to me in that tone, young lady?"

Shelly focused on the salad dish near the end of the table, "Isn't that the dish you borrowed and never returned?"

She reached over and whisked it off the edge, and it shattered on the tile floor. "Oopsie!"

Everyone paused and took notice of the mishap. Molly turned her attention back toward her daughter with a stern look, "Did you do that, Millicent?"

"I didn't touch it! She yelled. "I wish you would quit calling me Millicent. I hate that name."

Mark placed his hands to his head and sighed as Millie stormed away, and out the front door. Mark then looked across the table at his wife with a disgusted expression. "Are you satisfied, Molly?"

"She's just having one of her usual temper tantrums." She grunted. "She'll get over it."

"Until you pour more fuel on the fire." He disdainfully remarked as he departed the table, and went in pursuit of his daughter.

Shelly strolled up behind Molly, with her arms firmly folded in front of her. "Way to go, Molly!" She sarcastically quipped. "I don't think you'll be nominated for mother of the year any time soon."

At the Prescott house, Rob wandered into Shelly's art room and glanced around at the pictures, and the art supplies. He spotted her LA Dodgers cap hanging from the knob of a chair, and had to clasp his hand over his mouth to hold back the rush of emotion. As though a reprieve from his sorrow, someone rang the front doorbell. He quickly tried to regain his composure, as he went to answer it.

As soon as he opened the door, Millie rushed in crying, and immediately embraced her little arms around his legs. "Hey, there kiddo!" He exclaimed. "What's wrong, sweetie?" He went down to one knee to get eye level with her.

"You look like you've been crying too, uncle Rob." She blubbered.

"Well! I guess we've both been having a tough time with all this." He forced a smile. "You want to talk about it?" Millie nodded yes, as she wiped the tears from her eyes.

Rob took her by the hand, and they sat down on the couch. Matilda jumped up and settled comfortably next to Millie. "Do your parents know you're here?"

"No, and I don't think they care."

"Oh, Millie! That's not true." He assured. "Your parents love you very much."

"Then, why does my mom have to be so mean to me?"

"I don't know." He searched for the right words. "I guess some people find it difficult to communicate with children."

"Shelly didn't." She countered.

Shelly's spirit appeared in the room, and Millie glanced her way as she stood listening. Matilda also noticed, and got up on all fours to look in that direction as well. All the while, Rob tried to carefully choose his words wisely in talking with the child. "Nobody could ever be exactly like Shelly." Rob's eyes teared up. "She was very unique." Millie listened attentively as he continued. "We could search the world over, and never find anyone exactly like her."

"Oh, Rob!" Shelly emotionally swooned. "That's so sweet of you to say."

The cat jumped off of the couch and strolled over to where Shelly's spirit was standing. It sat upright and stared straight at her. Rob took notice of the cat's strange behavior. "What do you see over there, Matilda?"

The cat meowed in response, and continued its' vigil, "Can you see me, Matilda?" Shelly asked, and the cat meowed once again.

"Oh, dear! I suppose I better leave the room before Rob gets suspicious."

Shelly left the room, and the cat promptly followed, while Rob and Millie watched. "That crazy cat!" He exclaimed.

Millie giggled, prompting a smile from Rob before he moved on on in a more serious note. "You know, Millie." He sighed. "Life isn't always fair, but we don't have any other choice than to accept what it serves up." He gently rested his hand on her shoulder. "Shelly may have been taken away from us, but nothing can ever take away the wonderful memories that we have of her." He paused. "Those memories will stay with us forever."

"I miss her so much already, uncle Rob."

"Me too." He replied with a wink and a nod. "But I can't think of anything that Shelly would want more than for you and me to always be there for each other. He paused with a smile. "Can I count on you for that?

Millie answered with a sober nod, and Rob held up his pinky finger, "Pinky shake?"

Millie giggled and wrapped her tiny finger around Rob's. She then hugged him tightly, "I love you, uncle Rob."

"I love you too, sweetie."

Rob's cell phone rang, and he glanced down at the screen before answering it, "Save your breath, Mark. Millie's right here with me."

He paused to listen to the muffled voice on the other end, "That's okay! She just wanted to talk." He nodded. "I'll walk her back over to the house."

He listened some more, "Will do, buddy!"

Rob ended the call and set the phone down on the coffee table, "That was your dad. He was very worried about you."

Millie only frowned in response, "Come on, sweetie! I better take you home now"

The next morning, Rob decided it was high time to get back into his work. He entered the reception area where Jenny was already settled in at her desk, "Good morning, Jenny!" He cheerfully greeted her as he breezed by.

"Good morning, Rob!" Jenny answered in a rather surprised tone.

Rob continued into his work space without another word. He settled behind his desk and immediately turned his attention to his computer screen. After a few moments, the curiosity got the best of Jenny, and she sauntered over to his desk with a very concerned expression. "Is everything, okay?" She asked.

Rob looked up with a carefree expression. "Yeah! I'm fine!"

"I thought you'd be taking the rest of the week off."

Rob paused with a sigh. "I've often heard it said that keeping busy is the best therapy for a broken heart." He spoke with an emotional smile. "Where's Art this morning?"

Jenny set her coffee down on the edge of the desk and took a seat. "He went out to get some bagels. He should be back soon." She sighed. " You know, I'm going to miss those long phone conversations I had with Shelly. She was truly my best friend."

Rob leaned back in his chair and smiled. "I do recall some of those marathon sessions. What in the world did you two talk about?"

"Just silly woman stuff, I guess." She looked away for a moment. "I've been upset for quite a while because all Art seems to want to do is go out in that damn boat every weekend. Shelly always had a way of making me feel better."

"She had that effect on everyone." He bravely bit back at the emotional rush. "You know, at least Art takes you with him out in the boat."

"I know. But sometimes I wish we could do other things. Just like you and Shelly did."

"Did you ever talk to him about it?"

"I'm afraid to say anything to him." She looked downward. "Sometimes, I just feel like a replacement in his life. I don't think he ever got over losing his wife and daughter in that accident."

"I know for a fact, that's not completely true. When you're not around, he talks about you all the time, and I know that he feels very fortunate that you came into his life when you did."

Jenny forced a short chuckle and wiped a tear from her eye, "We were two broken souls that needed each other."

Rob scooted his chair closer to Jenny, "I will say in his defense that you never get over losing someone that you love."

Jenny sighed, and continued, "I never told you this, but my first husband was an abusive bastard." She shivered at the thought. "I didn't think I could ever love again until Art came along.

Jenny choked back the emotion. "Just listen to me carrying on. You should be the one pouring out your heart to me."

"That's okay, Jenny." Rob gave an assured nod. "I think you needed to talk about this, and I'm glad I could lend an ear."

Rob glanced upward as if searching for divine help in knowing what else to say, "You should try to have a heart-to-heart chat with Art about this. I'm sure he probably doesn't even realize how you feel." He paused to further ponder. "Maybe I can drop a hint to him when the time is right."

Jenny cradled the side of Rob's face with her hand, as she stood up, and kissed him on the forehead. "You're a precious man, Rob Prescott. Now I know why Shelly loved you so much."

Shelly's spirit stood behind Rob, as Jenny sauntered back to her desk, "You're certainly right about that, Jenny." She stated with a forlorn smile.

Later in the day, Rob went to a local gym to exercise. He was doing everything he could to ease the sorrow over his loss of Shelly. As he sat on a machine, in between sets, he glanced around at the others who were also working out. Shelly's spirit stood nearby, supplying unheard commentary.

"I know what you're thinking, Rob. All these people in here are half our age, but you're far from being washed up, honey."

A well-built woman in her early 20s strolled by and shot a flirting smile in Rob's direction.

"Go ahead, and look, Rob." Shelly sighed. "I remember when my back porch swing looked like that too."

A young, and overly muscular guy, aggressively approached. "You almost done with the machine, pops?"

"Just one more set," Rob answered with a disgruntled expression.

The muscle head paused at the mirror in front of Rob, and struck a pose as if to intimidate, "Oh please!" Shelly rolled her eyes. "Are we supposed to be impressed?"

Later, in the locker room, Rob stood in front of the mirror, shaving. Shelly's spirit sat on a nearby bench, casually observing. A burly-looking man with an abundance of body hair swept by on his way to the showers. Shelly winced unpleasantly, as his body odor wafted her way. "I'm glad you never stunk like that, Rob." She commented. "The last time I saw that much body hair, it was on a grizzly bear at the zoo." She giggled.

Rob finished shaving and stood looking at himself for a moment. He glanced around to see if anyone was looking, before inhaling, and striking a quick pose. Just then, another man strolled from the shower and stared sarcastically as he passed. "Oh, Rob!" Shelly giggled. "I'm sorry, but that was painful to watch."

On his way home, Rob stopped at a local bar for happy hour. He squeezed into a spot at the crowded, square-shaped bar, and signaled to one of the bartenders. "I'll take a Coors Light draft." The bartender gave an upward tilt of his head to acknowledge his request.

Shelly's spirit squeezed into a tight spot between Rob, and a heavy-set woman. "Watch your elbow there, Missy. You're in my energy field." She commented.

She and Rob studied each life-weary face around the bar. Not a soul was familiar, but their expressions all told the same story. The bartender recklessly slid the beer across the bar to Rob, spilling a good bit of its contents in the process. As Rob took his first full swallow from the mug, several faces glanced his way with expressions that seemed to ask what his reasons were for being there. "Oh, honey!" Shelly exclaimed. "We don't belong here."

It was as though Rob had heard the comments, so he took another swig then nodded to the bartender, as he slid a ten-dollar bill toward him through the spilled beer. He wasted no time in getting out of there. As Rob got into his Mustang and started it up, he paused to glance at the bouquet of summer flowers that he had placed in the passenger seat. He painfully reflected for a moment before driving away. Shelly appeared in the back seat, and leaned forward, glancing at the bouquet. "I know those are supposed to be for me." Shelly sadly commented, "Such beautiful colors." She leaned forward and kissed Rob on the neck. Rob felt the energy…. it startled him at first….. but then he submitted to the emotion. The flood of passion forced him to quickly place his hand on the spot where she had kissed him.

Rob found himself suddenly distraught and needed to find someplace to relax. A quiet spot vacant of people. So, he decided to hit the beach…. In the backseat was a blanket he could lay out and sit to watch the sunset. Little did he know, but Shelly was right there with him. Across the way was a young couple in a romantic embrace. Rob smiled at the sight.

"They remind me of how we were. So much in love." Shelly sighed. "I wish there were some way of you knowing that I was right here with you." She continued watching with him. "Oh! The sunset is so beautiful tonight."

Rob sat for a few moments, then rolled up his pant legs, grabbed the bouquet, and started walking toward the water's edge. Shelly hurried to keep up. He paused in the moist sand, laid the flowers at the waters' edge, and whispered, *"it's not quite Friday, but happy Wednesday, sweetheart."*

As Shelly sadly watched, the gentle waves quickly engulfed the flowers. "Happy Wednesday, honey." She sadly whispered.

Later, after setting the flowers adrift, Rob went to the Turning Leaf, and sat at their favorite table to eat supper. He stared at the empty chair, troubled with being alone. Yet, still unaware that Shelly's spirit was indeed with him. Suddenly Rob's deep thoughts were interrupted, "Well! Hello there, handsome."

He looked up, startled to see Elizabeth Ashford standing there, "Good evening, Ms. Ashford."

"Where is that beautiful wife of yours?" She asked.

Rob hesitated, trying to fight back the tears, "Shelly passed away earlier this week."

"Oh, dear!" She sorrowfully exclaimed. "I am so very sorry."

Shelly's spirit vacated the chair, as Elizabeth sat down, "I don't mean to pry. But what on earth happened?" She shook her head emotionally, "She was so full of life when I saw both of you here last week.

Rob took a deep breath, "She went in for a routine operation on Monday morning, and died in the operating room."

"I don't know what to say. This must be so very devastating for you," Elizabeth replied. She looked down at Rob's plate, "Please pardon my intrusion. I never meant to interrupt your meal."

"That's quite alright, Ms. Ashford." He smiled. "I'm finished eating."

"In that case, let me pick up your tab, Mr..."

"Prescott! But please call me Rob." He stuttered, "You don't have to do that."

"Oh, but I insist! And, I would very much like you to join me for a stroll on the pier." She smiled endearingly. "It's such a beautiful evening."

"Very well," Rob responded with a slow, thoughtful nod.

"And please do call me Elizabeth." She stated with a grin. "I feel like such an old woman when someone addresses me as Ms. Ashford."

A short while later, Rob and Elizabeth slowly walked along the boardwalk, while Shelly's spirit followed close behind. "I love the crisp night air this time of year," Elizabeth declared.

"It's amazing," Rob added.

"If you don't mind me asking, how long were you and Shelly married?"

"Twenty-four years."

"Ahh! Twenty-four glorious years." She shook her head with amazement. "You both were so very fortunate."

"We certainly were," Shelly commented.

There was a short pause in conversation as they continued to stroll along. "Several years ago, when I was a young woman, I dated this young man back in England. His name was Nigel." She pleasantly reminisced. "I was an actress in the theater, and he was a carpenter who constructed the stage sets."

Rob listened attentively as she poured out her memories. "Like you and Shelly, we were so very much in love."

"What became of the two of you?"

She sighed, "One night, a Hollywood executive caught my performance, and I accepted his offer to come to the States."

"Didn't Nigel go with you?"

"Oh, no!" She shook her head. "He wanted no part in leaving England and his family."

"Didn't you stay in touch?"

"We did for quite some time." She emotionally paused. "But eventually, he quit answering my letters." They paused at the end of the pier and leaned against the railing as she concluded, "I was devastated." They both stared out at the star-filled darkness over the ocean, as she continued the story. "By the time I was able to return to England, I discovered he had taken up with another woman, and married." She fought back tears, "I suppose I should've moved on myself, but I never quite got over him."

Rob reacted with surprise, "But you were such a beautiful, and successful actress. Certainly, you must have had several worthy suitors over the years."

"Oh yes!" She laughed. "But I was far too caught up in my career to ever attempt love again." She sighed. "I regret that now because time simply slipped away from me." She pondered for a moment. "I should've given love another chance. I would've given up a lifetime of my fame and fortune if only I could have spent even half that time with a man I truly loved."

"It's never too late to find love, Elizabeth."

"No, it isn't. But the chances certainly dwindle with each passing year." She paused with a caring smile. "You're still a young man, Rob, don't let your broken heart prevent you from ever loving again. I'm certain that's what Shelly would want."

Rob struggled emotionally, while Shelly's spirit stood close by. "She is so right, Rob." She nodded. "You should listen to her."

Rob almost reacted as though he heard Shelly, "Thank you for sharing that story, Elizabeth."

She smiled at him through tear-filled eyes, "Now, young man, would you be kind enough to escort me back to my car? It's getting way too late for a woman of my age to be out and about."

"It would be my pleasure to do so." He entwined his arm with hers, and they slowly strolled away.

Later that night, as Rob prepared to call it a day, he paused to listen to the sound of chirping crickets that drifted in through the screen of the open bedroom window.

He stood in his night clothes, staring at the empty bed. The agony of the moment ripped through his body, and pulled him to his knees. He knelt next to Shelly's side of the bed, and buried his face into the mattress. Shelly sat in the dark corner of the room distraught over the fact she could not do anything to ease his pain.

Matilda, the cat jumped onto the bed, and affectionately rubbed her head against Rob. He smiled and gave her a quick rub on the chin, as she purred loudly. The incident brought him slight relief, and he decided to get back up, and strolled back to his side of the bed. As he proceeded to crawl under the covers, and settle in for the night, Shelly strolled over and laid down next to him. Matilda noticeably snuggled in close to her energy.

"I wish I could hold you in my arms once again, and feel the warmth of your body." She folded her arms tightly and shivered. "It's cold and dark where I am. It's like being in darkness between two lights." She glanced off into the corner. "On one side, I can see into your world. On the other, I see a brightness that beckons me." She sighed. "I know I'm supposed to go to it. But I can't go until I know you're okay." Shelly smiled and gently stroked Rob's cheek with her finger. Rob smiled and unconsciously touched his face in that spot. Then, as Shelly amicably watched, he drifted off to sleep.

The next day, Rob's office was alive with activity, as he and Art worked diligently on an account. Art entered Rob's work area, carrying a large roll of architectural drawings. "I just put the finishing touches on these plans for the Horton Bridge account."

"Great!" Rob exclaimed. "Let's look them over together, and we'll try to get them out to the contractor later this afternoon."

Art spread the plans out on a nearby work table, and Rob looked over his shoulder, "This is some of the best work that you and I have done." Art stated with enthusiasm.

A few seconds later Rob's phone rang, he grabbed it to answer but looked puzzled to see the caller's name. "Hello, Gina….." He waited for her to take a breath, "Hold on! Settle yourself down, Gina. I'll try to help if I can." He paused. "Can you tell me where Jim is right now?" He continued listening, grabbing a pen and notepad from his desk. Art observed with great concern.

"I know where it's at, Gina. Don't worry! I can get there within the next hour." He listened a bit more and impatiently nodded. "I promise I'll drive him home." Rob ended the call and took a deep breath.

"Is everything okay?" Art asked.

"That was Dr. Griffin's wife." He sighed. "He hasn't been to work since Shelly died, and he's been drinking heavily every day."

"Sounds like he has a problem that I'm all too familiar with." Art stated with concern.

"Do you feel like doing an intervention?"

"I was hoping you would ask me that."

"Good!" Rob nodded. "Let's get these plans ready for Jenny to ship out, then we'll go."

A short time later, Rob and Art entered the dark lounge and quickly spotted Dr. Griffin sitting at the bar by himself. He appeared to be quite buzzed already, as he held a drink close to his lips, twirling the liquid content, and staring hypnotically into the mirror behind the bar. He hadn't shaved or combed his hair in what appeared to be several days. When he saw the two men approaching in the mirror, he turned around with surprise. "Rob! What are you doing here?"

Both Rob and Art settled at stools on either side of him. "Gina called me. She's worried sick about you."

Dr. Griffin sighed, and set his drink down on the bar. "I'm ready to talk about this, if you are." Rob suggested, and Jim instantly became emotional, "Everything was my fault. Shelly should never have died." He threw his hands up in frustration. "I'm so sorry, Rob!"

Rob tried to calm him down as best he could, " Listen to me! It wasn't your fault, Jim." He paused. "None of us knew that she had a defective heart valve. It went undetected for years."

"I should've caught it." He balked. "I was her doctor."

"You were her doctor. But you're not God." Rob stated seriously. "From the time she was born, her heart was like a ticking time bomb. We're just fortunate that we had her in our lives for as long as we did." He placed his hand on his shoulder with assurance, and gestured toward Art. "This is my business partner, Art Goldberg."

Art and Dr. Griffin exchanged cordial nods, "Let's go sit at a table, and talk." Rob motioned to a booth in a far corner. "I think Art has something to say that you need to hear."

The men all got up and settled down at the table. Art then leaned in close to take control of the conversation. "I know we all thought the world of Shelly, and losing her hasn't been easy on any of us." He paused to stress his point. "But hearing this just might help set you straight."

Shelly's spirit also settled at the table to listen as Art began to recant. "About 20 years ago, Rob and I were working late one night, trying to meet a deadline on a job." He paused. "I had promised my wife and daughter that we'd go out to dinner that night."

Dr. Griffin straightened in his chair and listened attentively. "When I realized I'd be late, I told them to go on ahead without me, and meet me at the restaurant." He paused again, finding it difficult to continue. "On their way there, a guy ran a red light, and T-boned their car." He emotionally sighed. "They both died." Dr. Griffin winced at the revelation.

Art looked away with pain, while Rob laid a sympathetic, and supportive hand on the back of his shoulder. "For a long time, I blamed myself for not being there for them." He shook his head. "I didn't want to live anymore, and like you, I started drinking heavily to ease the sorrow." He looked gratefully at Rob. "If it hadn't been for Rob, Shelly, and my Rabbi intervening, I probably would've ruined my career, and eventually drank myself to death."

Dr. Griffin gave a sympathetic, understanding, nod as Rob proceeded to insert his thoughts. "Things happen that are beyond our control, Jim. You couldn't save Shelly, but just think of all the other lives you've saved over the years."

"I couldn't have said it better myself." Shelly enthusiastically proclaimed, while Art continued.

"I'd be lying if I said that time heals. I think about my wife and daughter every day, and I will until the day I die. But there is one thing I will tell you with certainty." He added with assurance in his voice. "You won't find any answers at the bottom of a glass of booze, Doc." He shut his eyes tight, and nodded. "Don't go down the same path that I did."

Jim sat silent for a few moments in pondering thought, before he glanced up at the two men.

"Thank you both." he said. "I really needed to hear that."

Shelly spoke her mind as well, though she knew she couldn't be heard. "Yes!" She nodded tearfully. "You guys handled that quite well."

Dr, Griffin gratefully shook Art's hand, while Rob placed a friendly hand on his shoulder. "Come on! Let's all get out of here." Rob stated. "You shouldn't keep Gina waiting any longer."

The three men got up to leave, but Shelly remained seated in fond reflection, smiling contently.

Afterward, Art returned to the office and approached Jenny at her desk. "Did everything go okay?" She asked.

"Yes." Art nodded. "We got the doctor home safely, and since it was late in the day, Rob just dropped me off, and went on home."

"I know that wasn't easy for you." She stated in an almost cautious fashion.

Art acknowledged her with a weak smile, and she quickly changed the subject.

"FedEx picked up those plans a little while ago. They should have them first thing in the morning."

"Fantastic!"

Art fidgeted with his car keys, appearing to want to say more, "You know, Jenny. I don't say this, or show it as often as I should." He began. "But I am so fortunate to have someone as wonderful as you in my life."

Jenny looked up at him with much emotion, "Oh, Art!" She stood up, embracing him as her eyes filled with tears. "Thank you so much!" She kissed him. "You'll never know how much I needed to hear you say that."

Shelly's spirit appeared, and stood close by, observing the tender moment. She smiled, and nodded her approval. "Way to go, Art!"

Meanwhile on the busy 405, Mark was a stressful case as he sat in bumper-to-bumper rush hour traffic. He hit the auto-dial on his cell phone and adjusted his Bluetooth as he waited for an answer. Finally, Rob's voice came across on the in-car speaker. "Hi, Mark! What's up?"

"Rob! Buddy! Pal! I realize it's Friday, but can you do me a big favor?"

"Maybe." He paused. What's going on?"

"Well! I got this last-minute deal that I have to close on, and I'm stuck in a stinking traffic jam."

"Okay! I'm stuck in that same mess."

"And Molly's busy with a Women's Club meeting."

"Get to the point, Mark. I'm growing old as we speak."

"Millicent's guidance counselor called us at the last minute, and wanted us to come in for a meeting." He sighed. "There's no way we can make it. Can you go instead?"

"I don't know if that's a good idea, Mark. The counselor specifically wants to meet with you."

"If she won't talk to you, then just tell her we'll have to reschedule, and Millicent can ride home with you."

Rob let out an audible sigh. "When do I have to be there?"

"In-kind of like an hour."

"In an hour?" Rob roared. "I'll have to drive like a maniac."

"I knew I could count on you, buddy. I won't forget this."

"Wait!" Mark hung up before Rob could say another word.

At the elementary school, Rob hurried into the counselor's office, where Millie also waited patiently. The counselor, Linda Rodriguez, a stern-faced woman in her late 30's, peered at him over the top of her spectacles as he took a seat next to Millie. "Hi, uncle Rob! Where are my parents."

"They couldn't make it, honey."

She looked downward with a frown, and Rob immediately turned his attention toward Ms. Rodriguez. "I apologize for being late. Traffic was crazy today."

"So, you're Millie's uncle?" She asked.

"Not exactly. I'm Rob Prescott." He nervously paused. "I'm the Faber's neighbor. They had a last-minute emergency, and couldn't make it."

Ms. Rodriguez never changed her hardened expression, as she stared across the desk at Rob.

"I'm sorry Mr. Prescott. Since you're not related to Millie, I'm afraid I can't continue with this meeting."

"Wait!" Rob exclaimed. "I am like an uncle to her. We're very close." He paused. "My wife, Shelly Prescott used to be a teacher here at the school."

Ms. Rodriguez completely changed her demeanor and placed her hand to her head.

"I am so sorry, Mr. Prescott. I never made the connection."

"Thank you."

Shelly's spirit appeared behind Rob and Millie and listened in as she continued. "Everyone here at the school, including me, thought the world of Shelly. Please accept my condolences."

"Oh really, Linda!" Shelly huffed. "Is that why you and the others used to call me little Miss Perfect behind my back?"

Millie sat in her seat, rocking back and forth nervously as Ms. Rodriguez continued, "I usually don't speak with anyone else other than the parents. But considering the circumstances, I suppose it would be okay."

Rob nodded in agreement as she slid Millie's report card across the desk for him to view, while Shelly looked over his shoulder. "Straight A's!" He looked up. "This is great!"

"That's our little Millie!" Shelly proudly added, and the little girl glanced at her with a smile.

"Millie is a very intelligent child, Mr. Prescott."

Rob proudly winked at Millie, as Ms. Rodriguez hesitated, and continued. "As good as she is with her studies, she's lagging a bit behind in her social skills."

"She's just a little shy," Rob assured.

"You do know that she stays off to herself, and talks to imaginary friends?"

Rob glanced over at Millie, who listened attentively, "I'm aware that Millie's attention is often focused on other things, but she has a creatively active mind."

Linda pursed her lips tight and nodded, "Do you know if the Faber's have consulted with a child psychiatrist?"

"Oh! This woman is definitely out of line." Shelly ranted, while Rob grew increasingly uncomfortable.

"Millie!" Rob turned his attention to the child. "Could you wait outside in the hall for uncle Rob?"

"Can I wait outside on the front stairs?"

"Sure! Just don't wander away from the school."

"Okay, uncle Rob."

She gave a short wave at Shelly as she departed the room, and Rob took a deep breath, "Ms. Rodriguez! Millie is just a little girl, and insinuating that she has a problem while she's here listening does not remedy the situation."

"You tell her, Rob!" Shelly fumed, as Rob continued.

"I used to be the same way when I was her age, but I grew out of it, and I certainly didn't need a psychiatrist."

"Nevertheless, I do plan to consult with her parents on this matter."

"That's fine! But I'd still like you to refrain from talking about this in front of Millie."

"With all due respect, Mr. Prescott. I am the professional, and I do know what is best for her."

"That kid means the world to me, Ms. Rodriguez. I would never want her to think she was anything other than normal." He stated with rising anger. "I think your handling of this is anything but professional."

"Preach it, honey!" Shelly added.

Linda took a deep breath, wanting to say more, but Rob stood up, and cut her short, "I think we're done here, Ms. Rodriguez." He proclaimed. "It would be best if you continued this conversation with the Faber's"

He flashed a fake smile, and politely exited the office. Shelly, on the other hand, remained standing firm with her hands on her hips. "I guess he put you in your place, Linda."

Rob stormed out of the front doors of the school, with Shelly's spirit close in pursuit. He immediately noticed an overweight boy, and a small group of kids bullying Millie. "Oh no! I'm putting an end to this, right now." Rob stated as he quickly moved toward the situation.

"Watch your temper, honey," Shelly warned.

The boy held Millie's glasses at arm's length and taunted her, "Give me back my glasses!" She yelled.

"Silly Millie four-eyes!" He teased, while the other kids laughed.

"Hey, fatso!" Rob quipped. "Give her back the glasses."

He soberly handed them back to her, "What's wrong with you kids?" He scolded. "Were you all raised by morons?"

"You wouldn't talk to me like that if my dad were around." The fat boy remarked.

"Oh yeah!" Rob exclaimed. "Then maybe your dad and I should have a little talk."

"He'd kick your ass, mister!"

"We'll just have to see about that. Won't we?"

"Oh Rob!" Shelly exclaimed. "Maybe you shouldn't have said that."

In the wake of the other kids scattering, the fat boy stormed away without saying another word. Rob then turned his full attention to Millie, "Are you okay?"

She slowly nodded as she placed her thick spectacles back on her face. Rob then took hold of her little hand, "Come on, honey! Let's go home!"

Rob was still fuming mad when they got into the car. As he secured Millie's seat belt, he could tell that she was still visibly upset as well. "If there's one thing that I absolutely can't tolerate, it's a bully." He stated.

Shelly listened from the back seat, and nodded in agreement, while Millie stared out the passenger window. After a few long moments, she turned her attention back toward Rob. "Uncle Rob! Is there something wrong with me?"

"Absolutely not, sweetheart!" He quickly glanced over. "You are beautiful, perfect, and very unique. Never forget that."

She only answered with a pleased smile, as he continued, "If there's anyone who can't see that, then they're the ones who have the problem." He nodded intently. "And, if any of those bullies ever bother you again, I want you to give them a good swift kick in the jimmies."

"Oh, Millie!" Shelly exclaimed. "Uncle Rob is just upset. He really shouldn't have said that either."

After Rob drove Millie home, she entered her bedroom and tossed her backpack on the bed. She looked up to see that her Mermaid picture was missing from the wall. Immediately, she stormed from the room in a huff. "Where is my Mermaid picture?" She yelled. Molly was preparing dinner in the kitchen when she calmly confronted the raging child.

"What did you do with my Mermaid picture?" Millie demanded.

"Oh, honey!" Mommy thought it might be best to take it down so that it wouldn't remind you of Shelly, and make you sad."

"You had no right to do that," Millie screamed. "It's my picture!" The child trembled with anger. "Why do you hate Shelly so much?"

Shelly's spirit stood nearby with her arms folded in front of her. "I think I know why."

"Millicent! That's ridiculous! I never hated Shelly."

"You're a liar!" Millie charged. "And I wish you'd quit calling me that stupid name. My name is Millie!"

Mark entered the house amid the heated argument and quickly tried to intervene, "Hey! Hey!" he stood between them. "What's going on here?"

"She took my Mermaid picture." Millie stomped in a raging fit.

Molly simply shrugged when Mark glanced her way for an answer. "You really shouldn't have done that, Molly." He glared at her with disdain. "That picture belongs to Millicent."

Millie turned her rage toward her father. "Millie! Millie! Millie! That's my name! Why can't you both call me that?"

Mark tried to further calm the situation and sternly addressed his wife. "Where is the picture, Molly?"

"I put it in the storage closet." She answered sheepishly.

"Go get it, and put it back where it belongs," Mark ordered.

"Go get it yourself!" She angrily quipped. "Can't you see I'm busy fixing your lousy meal?"

Shelly reacted, as she and Millie took it all in from off to the side. "Oh my! This is getting a bit intense."

Just then, the doorbell rang, and Mark raised his arms in the air. "Saved by the bell!"

Mark opened the front door to see a towering, broad-built man in his mid 30's staring down at him. "Can I help you?" Mark politely asked.

"Are you Millie Faber's father?"

"Yes, I am!" Mark proudly proclaimed.

"I'm Billy Sigorsky's father." He scowled. "I understand you called my kid fatso and asked if he was raised by morons."

Mark was clueless, and stammered, while Shelly placed her hand to her head, and reacted. "Oh! Oh!"

"There must be some sort of mistake, Mr. Sigorsky." He stuttered. "I have no idea what you're talking about."

Sigorsky became enraged, as Molly and Millie took a stand behind Mark.

"No, no, Faber!" he pointed his finger. "Don't try to say my kid's a liar."

"Mr. Sigorsky!" He pleaded. "Can't we just talk this out in a civil manner?"

"I'm calling nine, one, one, Mark," Molly announced as she marched from the room.

"Better yet, shrimp." Sigorsky sarcastically grinned. "Why don't you walk your rich, privileged ass outside, and we'll talk about it under my terms."

"Oh, Rob! What have you done?" Shelly vented with frustration.

Millie suddenly stepped forward from behind her father, and bravely confronted the big man. "You leave my daddy alone, you big bully."

"Shut up, you little geek!"

Before Mark could retaliate with words, Millie reared back, and kicked the big man hard in the groin, driving him down to one knee with pain. "Millie!" Mark hysterically cried. "Why did you kick that man in the...?"

"Uncle Rob told me if anyone tried to bully me, I should kick him in the jimmies."

Shelly couldn't help but be mildly amused. "Oh boy!"

Mark's puzzlement over the situation, turned to sudden enlightenment, and he quickly offered aid to Mr. Sigorsky. "Are you okay?"

Sigorsky replied with a stunned nod and strained voice. "I think I better leave now."

The big man struggled to his feet, as Mark helped him. With a defeated glance toward Millie, he retreated down the walkway, still grasping his groin with obvious discomfort.

Mark stepped back into the safety of the house and sniffed the air. "Is there something burning?"

Molly hurried away toward the kitchen, "Oh no! Our supper!"

Later, after things settled down, Millie sat on her bed, reading a book. There was a slight knock on the door, and Mark entered carrying the Mermaid picture. Millie's eyes lit up when she saw it. "Can we talk?" Mark asked.

Millie sat up on the edge of the bed, and nodded yes, while Mark hung the picture back in its place. "Thank you," Millie murmured, while Mark settled next to her.

"And thank you, for saving me from that big brut today."

Millie giggled, and Mark continued, "Ms. Rodriguez called me this afternoon, and we talked a bit."

"I don't like her at all," Millie remarked.

"Honey! You need to quit talking to these imaginary friends." He sighed. "We both know that they're not really there."

"But daddy! They are!" She maintained. "I can see things that other people can't see."

"Come on, sweetie! You know that's not true."

"But it is." She insisted as she glanced over his shoulder. "I can see Shelly standing behind you right now, and Mrs. Turner is here too."

"Oh, honey!" Shelly exclaimed. "I was hoping you wouldn't tell him that."

Mark turned to look, then glanced back at Millie, "Okay." He bit his lower lip in clever thought. "If her and Mrs. Turner are actually here, then why can't I see them?"

"I don't know!" She vented with frustration. "But they're both here."

"Alright." Mark pondered for a moment. "If Shelly is really here, and she can hear me, I want her to tell you something that only her and I would know about."

"Oh my!" Shelly paced, "What should I say?"

Mark patiently waited as Shelly tried to think of something to say. She suddenly blurted out the first thing she could think of, "Janet Hartman!"

Millie took on a puzzled expression as she turned her attention back to her father. "Well! What did she say?"

"Janet Hartman." The little girl cluelessly shrugged.

Mark immediately panicked and jumped to his feet, "Okay! Okay! Enough said on that matter."

Mark glanced at the Mermaid picture, then toward the spot where Shelly was supposedly standing. He hesitantly reached out in that direction to see if he could feel anything.

"Shelly?" He questioned. "Are you really in this room?"

"Yes, Mark." She sighed. "I'm here, and you need to remove your hand from my boob."

Millie giggled, and Mark quickly turned. "What did she say?"

"She said you're touching her boob."

Mark quickly pulled his hand back and looked all around the room. "I won't even attempt to touch Mrs. Turner."

Millie giggled again, while Mark sat back down, and firmly placed his hands on the little girl's shoulders. "We absolutely cannot tell mommy about this. She'll have us both thrown in the nuthouse."

Millie gave an intentional nod, "I won't tell anyone, daddy."

"We'll talk some more later." He nervously sighed. "Daddy needs to go rest now." He kissed her on the forehead. "It's been a pretty tough day."

"Okay, daddy." She nodded again.

Mark quickly moved to exit the room, breezing right by Shelly's spirit. "Goodbye, Mark." Shelly giggled. He paused at the door, and stressfully glanced around the room once more, before departing.

At the Prescott home a short time later, the doorbell rang just as Rob was passing through the foyer. He swung the door open, and an almost hysterical Mark rushed in before Rob could invite him in. "Come right on in, Mark." He sarcastically smiled.

"Do you have time to talk?"

"Somehow, I don't think I have much of a choice." He laughed. "I'm just fixing supper for myself. Can I get you a beer?"

"I just might need a six pack after the day I just had."

Rob motioned for him to follow to the kitchen. "I'm cooking up some goulash. There's enough if you want to join me."

"No thanks. I just had a burger and fries from McDonalds."

Rob glanced at Mark awkwardly, as he popped open a can of beer, and handed it off to him. "Didn't Molly feel like cooking tonight?"

"She burned it!" He rolled his eyes. "Long story, but she's on the warpath."

"Did Millie get something to eat?"

"I got her a happy meal."

Mark chugged practically the whole can of beer in one gulp. Rob observed, while filling his plate from the skillet. "You weren't lying." He strolled over, and sat down opposite of him at the table. "I guess you really did need that beer." He gestured toward the refrigerator. "There's more. Just help yourself."

"Thanks, buddy."

"So, what's on your mind, Mark?"

"For starters, you know that fat kid that was bullying Millicent at school today?

Rob slowly nodded with his mouth full of food, as Shelly's spirit appeared on the scene, and also took a seat at the table. "His gargantuan father paid me a visit this evening."

"Oh wow!" He rolled his eyes. "I think I may have been responsible for that happening."

"I figured that out." Mark sarcastically remarked. "Anyway, just when I thought this goon was going to kick my ass, Millicent hauled off, and kicked him in the nuts."

Rob nearly choked, as he tried to contain a burst of laughter. "Are you serious? She actually did that?"

"Yeah! The big guy went down like a giant redwood." He smirked. "I understand you were responsible for her doing that as well."

Rob gave a reluctant nod, while Shelly silently observed, "I'm sorry, Mark." He sighed. "It just really pissed me off to see someone bullying a sweet little kid like Millie."

Mark got up to grab another beer from the refrigerator. "After he finds out what she did to his father, I don't think he'll be bullying her anytime soon."

Rob laughed, and Mark reluctantly did as well. Even Shelly couldn't resist joining in on the amusement. "I have to be honest." Rob continued to laugh. "I wish I could've been there to see that."

Mark took a swig of his beer and leaned back in his seat. "You do know how Millicent claims she sees and hears things that we can't?"

Rob rolled his eyes and nodded, "Ms. Rodriguez did bring that up at the meeting. What about it?"

"I think she really can. The kid has some sort of a special gift." He leaned in closer and lowered his voice. "Shelly was in her bedroom tonight, and so was Mrs. Turner."

"You don't need to whisper, Mark. I can still hear you." Shelly teased.

Rob quit eating and looked at Mark very awkwardly. "How many drinks did you have before you came over here?"

"Believe me on this. I'm stone-cold sober." He stated with all seriousness. "I reached out to where Millicent said Shelly was standing, had my hand on her boob, and could feel the warmth."

Shelly giggled, while Rob continued to stare with disbelief, "Run that by me again."

"Look!" He exclaimed. "I swear it's all true, but the clincher came before that."

Rob cocked his head, and squinted toward Mark, as he continued his story. "Just to prove whether she was there or not, I asked Shelly to tell Millicent something that only she and I would know about."

"What did she say?"

"One name!" He paused with emphasis. "Janet Hartman."

"A name that would make poor Mark tremble with anxiety." Shelly chuckled.

Rob appeared quite baffled, "Isn't she that hot-looking brunette that's a realtor at your firm?"

Mark reluctantly nodded in response.

"How does she fit into all of this?" Rob cluelessly shrugged.

Mark took a deep breath before he answered, "A few years back, when you had one of your house parties, Janet and I had a few too many cocktails." He sighed, "Needless to say, we ended up having a little rendezvous in your upstairs bathroom."

Rob was taken back with surprise, "You do know that her husband is a retired professional wrestler?"

Shelly listened to the exchange with amusement, "I know!" Mark rolled his eyes. "Sometimes that damn appendage between my legs overrules any sliver of common sense that I might have."

"You got that right," Shelly remarked.

Rob took a deep breath and shook his head, "Okay. How does Shelly fit into all of this?"

"I thought we locked the door, and Shelly walked in on us."

"That lock's been broken since we moved in here." He paused. "Poor Shelly must've been horrified."

"You know it, honey." She remarked. "It took a while before I could use that bathroom again."

"Anyway. That was our little secret, and to my knowledge, Shelly never told anyone."

"I sure didn't." She added.

"Shelly was always good at keeping secrets." Rob replied.

Rob walked over to the kitchen counter in deep in thought, "If all this is true, there's so much that I'd like to say to her."

"Oh, Rob!" She exclaimed with emotion. "There's so much I want to say to you too."

"It's all true, Rob," Mark stated in all seriousness.

Rob pondered the situation further, "Do you suppose Millie could help me communicate with her?"

"It's certainly worth a try. It might help you find closure, and maybe you could convince her to move on to wherever dead people are supposed to go."

"We have to make sure this stays between the three of us," Rob warned. "If anyone found out, they'd throw us all in a psychiatric ward."

"Believe me, Rob! I couldn't agree more."

Rob stared away in deep thought while Mark kept the conversation alive with a bit of apprehension.

"While we're on the subject of Shelly, I have one more thing that I need to get off of my chest."

Rob turned to listen, "I was totally head over heels in love with your wife."

"Yeah, Mark!" Shelly laughed. "I think that was pretty obvious."

Rob stared hard at Mark for a moment, before bursting into laughter. Mark was visibly offended by his reaction. "What the hell is so funny about that?" Mark asked. "That wasn't an easy thing to admit to my best friend."

"I'm sorry, Mark." He chuckled. "But every guy that met Shelly, fell in love with her. I mean, she was perfect. How could you not love her?"

Shelly giggled.
"You do have a point there, Rob." Mark sighed.

"All that might be true, Rob," Shelly stressed. "But you were the only man I ever loved."

Mark stood, and strolled over, leaning against the counter next to Rob. "I never told anyone else this, but I fell out of love with Molly a long time ago." He paused in thought. "I started cheating, and thought I could find what I was looking for in another woman."

"What were you looking for exactly?"

"What you and Shelly had. I was insanely jealous."

"What exactly does Molly want?"

"I really don't know." He cluelessly stated with frustration. "We were happy until she got pregnant with Millicent. It was hard labor, and she came into the world with a lot of issues." He paused. "Molly was never the same after that."

Rob pondered the conversation before continuing, "Marriage isn't an easy thing, Mark. And sometimes things aren't as perfect as they appear." He emotionally paused. "Shelly had three miscarriages and a still-born baby."

"I'm sorry, buddy. I didn't know."

"It was tough on both of us. We wanted kids, and it just wasn't meant to be." He paused. "The love we shared for each other got us through it."

Shelly nodded emotionally. "I could've never made it without you, honey."

Rob gave Mark a friendly pat on the back of the shoulder. "Millie's a great little kid with a lot of love in her heart. You're blessed to have her." He emotionally paused. "She might be legally blind without those thick glasses, but as we both now know, she can see a lot more than we could ever imagine."

Mark gave an exaggerated gesture of agreement, as Rob continued. "I also know that she was diagnosed with attention deficit disorder as well. But from where I stand, the only deficit I see is that she's not getting the attention she needs, and deserves from you and Molly."

"Bingo!" Shelly exclaimed.

Mark emotionally nodded in agreement once again, while Rob got teary-eyed. "All the fancy cars and aspirations for wealth can't make up for what you already have with that sweet little girl."

"You're right, Rob." He nodded rapidly. "The one thing I want more than anything is to be a good father, and a loving husband."

"If that's the case, you need to talk it over with Molly, and see where she stands."

"Oh yes, Mark!" Shelly exclaimed. "He's definitely right about that."

Mark absorbed the advice, and took it to heart.

When he finally went home, he entered the bedroom where Molly was already under the covers, reading a romance novel. "Where have you been all evening?"

"I was over visiting with Rob." He replied.

She glanced up from her book with an expression of disdain, "It would've been nice if you had told me where you were going."

Mark sat down at the edge of the bed and stared at the wall. "Why do you have to be so difficult with Millie and me?"

"You mean Millicent."

"No, Molly!" He clenched his eyes shut, as though holding back his rising rage. "She wants us to call her Millie, and that's what I'm going to call her from now on."

Molly set her book down and turned her full attention toward her husband. "What prompted the change in your attitude?"

"I just think it's high time for me to be a better father to my child."

"I suppose that means I'm a failure at being a good mother and wife?"

Mark slowly stood up, without making eye contact. "If that's what you want to maintain, then so be it."

He entered the walk-in closet and gathered his pajamas, and a blanket, before confronting her once more. "It's obvious that Millie isn't the little princess that you always hoped for, and as far as I'm concerned, I could probably never earn enough money to make you happy."

"That's not true Mark, and you know it." She charged.

"Isn't it, Molly?" He paused to gauge her reaction. "Maybe you and I should just get a divorce, and you'll be free to find whatever you really want in life."

"Is that what you want?" She shot back in a rather timid tone.

"It's not what I want." He sighed. "But under the circumstances, maybe it's the best thing to do."

Molly reacted with shocked silence, not knowing how to reply. Her silence only further infuriated Mark, as he moved to exit the room. "I'll just sleep on the couch tonight." He marched out, without another word being said.

Moments later, Mark changed into his pajamas and prepared to bed down on the couch for the night. He turned the lights off, fluffed up his pillow, then settled in, staring at the ceiling in deep thought. The light came back on in the room, and Molly slowly paced toward him. "I don't want a divorce, Mark."

Mark sat back up, and Molly settled at the edge of the couch next to him. "I do love you and Millicent…I mean… Millie." She sighed. "I know all about those other women you cheated with, and I also knew you were in love with Shelly." She nervously nodded. "I knew she would never cheat on Rob, but I was still insanely jealous of her." She laughed. "I even knew about you and Janet Hartman."

"How did you know that?" Mark asked with surprise.

"I'm a woman, Mark!" She sarcastically replied. "We know these things."

They shared a brief laugh, then Mark became serious once again. "I was very stupid, honey."

"Well, yeah!" She exclaimed with emotion. "But I suppose if you were going to be in love with someone other than me, Shelly would've been a good choice." She sadly smiled. "I could never match up to her as a wife, or a mother."

"That's not true, Molly."

She shook her head to negate his comment, "You saw in Shelly, everything you wanted me to be."

Unbeknownst to either of them, Shelly's spirit stood in the shadows of the room, listening closely. "No!" Mark shook his head. "I saw the qualities in her that you had when I married you, and I wished you could be that way again."

He put his arm around Molly and pulled her in closer. "I'm just as much to blame as you are." He nodded. "We have a beautiful little girl that we hardly know because we're too busy trying to climb the social ladder. He looked up with frustration. "I want to change all of that."

"I do too, Mark!" She replied with surprise. "I only wanted those things because I thought that's what you wanted."

"Wow!" He sighed. "Am I an idiot, or what?"

"I think we both are." She vented, before pondering her next words. "Do you think it's too late to change things?"

"I don't know!" Mark answered with frustration. "But I'm willing to give it another try if you are."

Molly emotionally nodded in response. "You bet I am, sweetheart."

They embraced emotionally and kissed. Shelly still stood in the shadows, now teary-eyed. She forced a smile and whispered to herself. "Well played4e3mjkh c!"

Molly took Mark's hand and motioned to the stairs. "Will you come back to bed with me?"

"You bet!"

Early the next morning, Molly opened the door to Millie's room and peeked in. She opened the door the rest of the way and watched as the child peacefully slept. Millie stirred and squinted her eyes toward the door, "Is someone there?"

"It's just mommy checking in on you, honey."

Millie reached for her glasses on the nightstand and placed them on her face. Molly slowly sauntered in and sat at the edge of her bed. "Did you sleep well last night?"

Millie nodded, and Molly glanced up at the Mermaid picture that hung over her bed, "I shouldn't have taken your picture down yesterday. Can you forgive me for doing that?"

The little girl soberly nodded again, "Your father and I talked last night. We agreed that we haven't included you enough in our lives." She emotionally smiled. "I promise you, that's all going to change.

Millie sat up straight and listened attentively, "You're our precious little girl, and we love you very much."

They exchanged joyous smiles, "If you're ready to get up, you can come downstairs, and help me make pancakes. Would you like that?"

Millie nodded with excitement and crawled out from beneath the covers. Molly held her hand out, and the little girl gripped onto it. As they prepared to leave the room, she glanced up at her mother.

"Mommy!"

"Yes, Millie."

A big smile graced the little girl's face. "You called me Millie."

"Yes, I did." She nodded assuredly. "That's what I intend to call you from now on."

"I love you, mommy." Molly went down on one knee, and hugged the child tightly, as tears rolled down her face.

Shelly and Mrs. Turner stood in the corner, unnoticed by even Millie. They both reacted with enthusiasm, and joy at the sight of the tender moment. Shelly glanced up into the opposite corner of the room with an ambitious stare. "I'm almost done here." She whispered with tears welling in her eyes. "Just give me a little more time."

A short time later, the whole family sat at the dining table enjoying Saturday breakfast. Mark voraciously devoured his plate of pancakes. "These pancakes are so good." He commented.

"I helped mommy make them." Millie enthusiastically responded.

"I know you did. That's why they're so good."

He exchanged a quick wink and a smile with his daughter and continued talking. "How would you like to go see uncle Rob this morning?" He paused. "I think he has something he needs to talk to you about."

"I'd like that." She enthusiastically replied.

"But Mark!" Molly sighed. "I thought we were going to spend the day together as a family."

Mark gave her an assured wink, "Right now, it's raining, and this is something that Millie and I need to do." He paused with pleading eyes. "I promise you that it won't take long, and we'll all do something really fun later on." He glanced over to Millie. "Isn't that right, honey?" The little girl nodded with enthusiasm, and Molly responded to both of them with an understanding smile.

The doorbell rang at the Prescott home, just as Rob was passing by the foyer. He quickly answered the door and found Mark and Millie standing there under their umbrellas. He quickly herded them in from the deluge. "Come on! Get in here where it's nice and dry."

"It's like a monsoon out there." Mark quipped.

Rob took their umbrellas and set them opened on the tile floor to dry. For a long moment afterward, there was an awkward silence between the three, until Mark decided to speak first.

"Millie!" he hesitated. "Uncle Rob would like to communicate with aunt Shelly. Do you suppose you could help him do that?"

"I can try." She answered.

Rob reacted nervously, as he anxiously glanced around the room, "Is Shelly here with us now?"

Millie responded with a rapid, serious nod. "She's standing right behind you, uncle Rob."

Rob swung around quickly, hoping to catch a glance, but nothing was there. "I'm here, Rob! You just can't see me."

Mark reacted uneasy in the moment and motioned toward the kitchen. "Maybe I should just go in the other room."

"I just made a fresh pot of coffee," Rob answered. "Go ahead, and help yourself."

As Mark left the room, Rob put all of his focus on Millie. "Is there any way that I might be able to see and hear Shelly, just like you do?"

The little girl shrugged and looked to Shelly for an answer. "Oh my!" Shelly exclaimed. "Let me think this over for a minute." She pondered, "You two need to sit down on the couch next to each other.

Millie took hold of Rob's hand, as they sat down. "Okay!" Shelly began. "Let's try this."

Millie looked toward where Shelly was standing, while Rob observed. "Take off your glasses, Millie."

The little girl removed them, and Rob set them on the side table. "Can you still see me, honey?"

"I can see you clear, aunt Shelly. But everything else is fuzzy."

"Good, sweetie! That means you're seeing me with your third eye."

The little girl got a puzzled look on her face and put her hand to her forehead. "I have a third eye?"

Rob also reacted awkwardly as he listened. "No, sweetie!" She giggled. "That means you're seeing me with your mind." She took on a more serious demeanor. "Now, I want you two to hold hands."

Millie placed her little hand into Rob's giant palm. "I'm going to place my hand lightly on the top of your head" She did so, and waited. "Can you feel my energy?"

"I can feel it!" Millie exclaimed, with excitement. "I can really feel it!"

"Wow!" Rob reacted. "It's like an electric current passing between us."

He looked past Millie with astonishment, as the apparition of Shelly appeared. "Shelly! Oh, honey! I can see you!" He shook his head. "It's amazing!" Mark curiously peeked out from the kitchen and quietly observed.

Shelly's voice trembled with excitement. "Can you hear me too?"

"Yes, baby!" He emotionally replied. "I can hear you too."

"Just don't let go of Millie's hand, or you'll break the connection."

Rob reacted with anxious emotion, while Millie remained quiet, with her eyes closed. It was almost as if she were in a trance.

Mark quietly sneaked from the kitchen and took a seat at the dining room table. "Hi, Mark!" Shelly said. "I know you're sitting at the table behind me."

"She knows you're here, Mark."

Mark awkwardly reacted and raised his cup toward the living room to address her. " Hi Shelly!"

Rob's jaw dropped with awe as he gazed upon the spirit of his wife. "Oh, honey!" He sighed. "I miss you so much." A tear escaped and trickled down his face. I miss everything about you. Especially that nervous little giggle of yours."

Shelly giggled, and Rob smiled with amusement. "Yeah! That's my girl!"

The cat entered the room and settled on the floor between them. It sat straight up and stared straight at Shelly. "Matilda's here with us. She can see you too."

"I know." Shelly nodded, as she endearingly gazed at the feline. "My little fur baby." She smiled. "I miss her so much."

The cat meowed in response, and they both laughed. Shelly then looked upward into a corner of the room, and her demeanor became very serious. "I have to go to the light soon. But I want you to know that I love you so much, and I am so proud of you." She smiled endearingly. "You are so kind-hearted, and you've made such a difference in so many people's lives."

"I had an excellent teacher," Rob replied.

"We made a great team, honey."

Rob pondered in thought, searching for the right words to say. "Once you go, will I ever see you again."

"Oh yes!" She enthusiastically exclaimed. "I'll be watching you from a distance, and when it's your turn to go into the light, I'll be the first one to greet you."

"I can't wait!"

"You'll have to learn to wait." She sighed. "You have to promise me that you won't quit living because I'm no longer there." She emphasized. "Life is so beautiful, and it goes by so fast. Don't miss one second of it."

"My heart is going to be broken over you for a long time." He emotionally stated.

"I know." She answered with a sympathetic smile. "But I'll echo what Elizabeth told you that night on the pier. "If you ever have the chance to love again, don't let the opportunity pass you by."

"It would be hard to love anyone as much as I love you."

Shelly responded with a smile and motioned toward her urn, which rested on the fireplace mantle. "I want you to take my ashes, and scatter them on the beach where we used to watch the sunsets." She intently nodded. "I can't think of any other place I'd rather be."

"I promise I'll do that, honey."

Shelly looked away and smiled. "Remember that last day we were together, and I told you I had a surprise?"

"I remember."

"In the top drawer of my desk, in the art studio, there's a notarized letter that you need to present at our bank." She paused with emphasis. "There's a money market account in my name that's worth 3.8 million dollars."

Rob reacted with shock. "Shelly! How in the world did you accumulate all of that money?"

Shelly slyly grinned with pursed lips. "My sister and I inherited it when our parents passed away. I then inherited her half when she died." She paused. "I was saving that money for our retirement years, and wanted it to be a surprise."

"You were always full of surprises."

Shelly giggled at his response, then pondered in careful thought. "I want you to take some of that money, and try to buy that old arcade building we talked about."

Rob finished her statement with an all-knowing smile. "…As an art center for the kids."

"Exactly!" She glanced back at Mark, who watched attentively. "I'm sure Mark could help you get it for a decent price."

"I think we can work on that."

"Don't forget, honey. Even though you can't see me. Just think of me, and I'll always be there."

Rob nodded, while Shelly jokingly took a no-nonsense stance. "One more thing before I go, mister." She grinned. "You have to promise me that you'll go into my studio, and begin painting again."

"I promised you that a million times." He chuckled with amusement. "But this time, I promise I will do it."

Shelly looked toward the light once again, then back at Rob. "It's time for me to go now."

"Is there any way that I can kiss you goodbye?"

"We can try." She shrugged. "I'm new to all this too."

They moved slowly toward each other, with only Millie between them. Without breaking the energy chain with the little girl, their lips softly came together. After a few long, passionate seconds, they moved apart again. Rob emotionally covered his mouth with his hand.

"I could feel your energy."

"I could feel yours too." She giggled. "It was beautiful!" She emotionally sighed. "I guess this is goodbye, for now, darling."

Rob quivered with emotion. "We'll see each other again. I just know it!"

Shelly then turned toward the light, and her jaw dropped with awe. "Oh, Rob!" She cried. "You should see all the beautiful colors." She paused to marvel at the sight, then beamed with further excitement. "I can see my mom and dad, and my sister and our unborn babies are there too."

Rob nodded rapidly, while Shelly looked off to the side, and extended her free hand outward. "Come on!" She coaxed. "You can come too. There are people over there who have been waiting a long time for you."

Rob looked in the direction she was talking with a puzzled expression. "Who are you talking to, honey?"

Shelly glanced back at Rob with a grin. "Mrs. Turner."

The old woman took hold of Shelly's hand and gazed with wonder at the light. Rob could now see Mrs. Turner, and he shook his head with amazement. "Here we go!" Shelly told her.

Shelly giggled as her hand lifted from the top of Millie's head, and she slowly walked into the light with Mrs. Turner.

There was a loud whoosh sound as the spirit portal closed, and Rob looked upward, whispering sadly to himself. "Goodbye, sweetheart."

Millie opened her eyes and looked up at Rob with much emotion. "They're gone, uncle Rob."

Mark slowly rose from his seat, wiping away tears that had escaped from his eyes. He also sadly looked upward and whispered. "Goodbye, Shelly."

Rob embraced Millie and kissed her forehead. "Thank you so much for that, sweetie."

The rain had quit falling outside, and Rob looked over her shoulder to notice a beam of sunlight now streaming through the living room window. "How about that?" He announced with a smile. "The sun finally came out."

"It sure did," Mark replied enthusiastically. "I think that's a signal of a new start for all of us." He and Rob exchanged a brotherly hug, and Millie embraced them both.

In the days and months that followed, life continued as usual for all those who loved Shelly dearly. But many things changed as well. Rob continued the Friday night ritual of dinner at the Turning Leaf, and watching the sunset from Manhattan Beach. It was a routine that helped him feel connected to Shelly, even though she was no longer there. As one would expect, there would always be a Friday in which the weather wouldn't cooperate. That day happened about three months after Rob saw Shelly for the last time.

As he finished the days work at the office, he strolled over to his office window, and watched the rain pour down in a deluge. His mind wandered, as he gazed out, and he never noticed that Art had entered the room.

"Looks like you might have to alter those plans for tonight, partner." Art announced as he casually sauntered closer.

Rob smiled in response, and turned his attention away from the rain. "I'll still go out to dinner. I hate cooking."

Art glanced toward the storage closet, and headed in that direction. "I just came in to get something I stashed in here earlier." He swung the door open, and retrieved a bouquet of flowers.

"Flowers?" Rob chuckled.

"The keys to a woman's heart." Art laughed. "You taught me that." He playfully bowed toward Rob. "Jenny and I have started our own little Friday ritual."

"The flowers are far more effective than a bag of bagels."

"Hey! Those are genuine New York style bagels."
They both laughed.

"If this weather clears, are you going out in your boat this weekend.?"

"I put the boat up for sale."

"No way!" Rob exclaimed with surprise. "What prompted that?"

"I think it's about time we start doing some things that Jenny enjoys doing. It's time to change things up." He conlcuded with an assured wink, before quickly moving to another subject. "I almost forgot to tell you. Doctor Griffin has been coming regularly to the AA meetings. He's doing good."

"I'm happy to hear that." Rob smiled. "Since you and Jenny won't be out on the boat tomorrow, I hope you'll show up for the ribbon cutting at the Art Center. It's at 2PM."

Art looked upward with sudden enlightenment. "Jenny did have that marked on our calendar. We wouldn't miss it for anything." Art gestured toward the door. "We're getting out of here early. Would you care to join us for dinner?"

Rob shook his head no in response. "Maybe some other time, buddy. Thanks all the same."

Art gave a quick, understanding nod before departing to the outer office.

Rob couldn't resist peeking out of his office, as Art presented the flowers to Jenny. He smiled to himself as he watched the couple embrace lovingly.

Later, when Rob arrived at The Turning Leaf, he walked briskly from his car under the shield of his umbrella. As he passed by the ramp to the boardwalk pier, he paused to take notice of a lonely soul with an umbrella at the end of the pier. Elizabeth Ashford stood there, gazing out longingly into the fog over the Pacific Ocean. It was as though she were waiting for her long lost lover to appear through the mist. He thought for a moment about joining her, but then thought better just to let her be.

Satisfied with his decision, he continued on his way, as the rain fell even harder.

Later that evening, he returned to a dark and silent house. Matilda purred loudly at his feet, prompting him to take the cat comfortably into his arms. As he passed the room that once served as Shelly's art studio, his heart skipped with emotion, and the cat curiously gazed into the room as if searching for her. He started to proceed down the hall, but decided to go back.

He flicked the light on in the room, and looked at the painting of the moonlit sailboat that was still on the easel. It was the last piece that she had painted. He gently set the cat down onto the floor, and picked the painting up to view it more closely. "You certainly had a wonderful talent, sweetheart." He whispered to himself.

He carefully placed the painting down among some of her other finished work, and glanced around the room. He could feel her presence very strongly, and could hear her voice clearly in his mind, telling him to start painting again. He spotted some blank canvasses, and placed one onto the easel. He then looked to a nearby table top, where

Shelly kept all of her paints, and supplies. He grabbed the LA Dodgers cap that still rested on the back of her folding chair, and placed it on his head backward, just as she had always done. He smiled to himself as he looked down at Matilda, who watched him with curious eyes. "I guess now is a good time to start, old girl."

Friday nights were different at the Faber residence as well. Millie sat atop her bed working diligently at her homework when a slight knock was heard at her bedroom door. Mark entered cradling a little Tabby kitten in his arms, and Molly followed close behind.

Millie leapt from the bed with excitement when she saw it. "Is she really mine?"

"She's all yours!" Mark answered with assurance as he carefully handed the little kitten off to his daughter.

Molly went into a sneezing attack, and everyone looked her way with concern.

"Don't worry!" She exclaimed while trying to recover. "The kitten stays! Mommy will just have to get used to taking anti-histamines."

Millie happily cradled the purring kitten, while Mark answered his wife with a smile, and a wink.

The rains finally ceased late the next morning, and gave way to a sunny afternoon. In the months after Shelly's death, Mark and Rob were able to broker a deal for the old beach arcade building. On this joyous ribbon cutting day, Rob glanced up proudly at the bold lettering above the entranceway that read "The Shelly Prescott Art Center."

"We made it happen, sweetheart." He whispered with a smile.

"Everyone who was part of Shelly's life was in attendance, including at least half the population of the Manhattan Beach Community. Countless children were eager to rush through the doors as soon as the ribbon was cut, to see what fun opportunities awaited them.

The memorable afternoon gave way to a beautiful summer evening, and Rob felt it was the perfect time to set about the task of scattering Shelly's ashes. He carefully let them sift through his fingers as he strolled along the beach near their favorite spot. When he was finished, he paused to watch the sinking sun over the oceans' horizon, and talked to her spirit in a low tone.

"It's finished! You're a permanent part of this place now, and someday I will be too."

A brief, light breeze blew in from the Pacific, tossing his hair to one side. He smiled, knowing it was Shelly's way of letting him know that she was there.

Several months later, Rob was in his yard as Mark and his family were backing out of their driveway in an aqua green 1966 Thunderbird convertible. Rob quickly crossed the lawn to check out the classic car. "When did you get this?" He asked.

"I sold my Mercedes to one of my clients last week, and then I saw this on the showroom floor of a classic car dealership." He beamed with pride. "What do you think?"

"Isn't it cool, uncle Rob?" Millie asked with much excitement.

Rob eyed the car with admiration. "It's absolutely beautiful!"

"Now you and I can go to car shows together, buddy."

"Yes, we can." Rob chuckled.

"Do you have any plans today?" Molly asked.

"Not really." He shrugged. "Just hanging around the house. Maybe working on a painting."

"It's a beautiful day. You should come with us, Rob?" Mark suggested. "We're heading down to the art show at the park."

"I wouldn't want to intrude on your family time."

"Nonsense! We'd love for you to come along," Molly urged.

"Besides, uncle Rob." Mark quipped with a clever smile. "You are family."

"Yeah, uncle Rob! Can you please come with us?" Millie added.

Rob looked back toward his house, and then back at them with a grin. "Let me run, and lock my doors."

Later, as they all strolled through the park, checking out the vendor booths at the show. Mark took note of how enthused Rob was with some of the works. "You should think about doing the circuit." He suggested. "You're a very good artist in your own right."

"Maybe someday." Rob sighed.

A particular picture caught Millie's eye, and she ran over to the booth to get a closer look. "Uncle Rob!" She yelled with excitement. "Look at this one."

Rob strolled over to also get a closer look. "You're right, Millie. That is very nice work." He carefully picked up the framed art, and held it at arm's length. "See how well the artist blended the colors?"

Millie nodded, as the artist, a tall, attractive blonde woman in her early 40's approached. "I see you two have an eye for colors."

"Yes! I happen to be an artist too." Rob stated while motioning toward the painting. "I really like the method you used in this work."

"Well! Thank you very much." She extended her hand, "My name is Kim."

Rob shook her hand and noticed her pretty smile. "Pleased to meet you, Kim. I'm Rob.

Millie took the opportunity to force her way into the conversation. "My name's Millie." She smiled. "You're very pretty."

Kim and Rob were both amused by the child's comment. Kim knelt down to speak to her, "Thank you so much for that compliment, Millie. You're very pretty too."

Millie smiled with delight, while Rob motioned toward the painting. "I'd be interested in buying this."

"That particular piece is one hundred and seventy-five dollars."

"Fair enough!" He exclaimed with a wink. "I'll take it."

Kim was overwhelmed as Rob handed her a credit card. "Great!" She gasped. "You're my very first sale of the day."

"Obviously, other people don't have an eye for true art." He replied

"Let me wrap that up for you, Rob."

Mark and Molly had been checking out work at another booth and paused at a comfortable distance to observe the exchange. "Are you thinking what I'm thinking?" Mark asked.

"Maybe." She replied. "She's tall, blonde, and she's also an artist."

"Not to mention, she's damn good looking too."

Molly jokingly elbowed Mark in the ribs. "You would notice that."

Rob tried to make conversation as he watched Kim carefully wrap the picture. "Have you done the circuit very long?"

"I've been painting for quite some time. But this is my first year on the circuit." She paused, as she handed him the wrapped picture. "It's something I always wanted to do, and when my husband passed away, I…" She became overwhelmed with emotion and was unable to finish her sentence. "I'm sorry." She added while wiping away a tear. "It's only been a year since I lost him."

"I totally understand," Rob replied with great sympathy. "I lost my wife about six months ago."

Kim took a deep breath, and nodded, while Millie carefully followed the conversation with her big, innocent blue eyes. "It looks like we have more in common than just a love for art." She stated.

"It isn't something you get over easily," Rob added.

Kim smiled at him and Millie. "Maybe I'll see you two around at one of the other shows."

"That's a good possibility." He replied.

"It was good to meet you, Ms. Kim," Millie stated.

"It was good to meet you too, Millie."

She turned her attention back to Rob, and nervously nibbled at her lower lip. "Well! You take care, Rob."

"You too." He awkwardly answered.

Rob turned to walk away, after exchanging a long last look, and Millie impatiently tugged at his pant leg to get his attention. "Uncle Rob!"

Rob glanced down at her. "What, Millie?" She motioned for him to bend down so she could whisper something in his ear. As he listened to what she had to say, he took on an enlightened expression. He then turned, and with slight hesitation, strolled back toward Kim's booth.

"Excuse me, Kim." He nervously cleared his throat, as she turned, and smiled. "I was just wondering…" He awkwardly stammered, while she patiently listened. "I was wondering if you might like to go out for dinner when you get finished here today?"

Kim was quite surprised by his question, and rolled her eyes in response, seeming to be speechless. Rob was quickly discouraged, and embarrassed by her reaction. "I can understand if you'd rather not." He stammered even more. "I just thought it would be nice to talk a little more."

"No! No!" She exclaimed with equal embarrassment. "I just didn't know how to react. It's been quite a long time since someone other than my late husband asked me out." She looked away for a moment, as if pondering. Then glanced back at Rob with a grin. "Actually, I think I would like to have dinner with you."

"I think she likes you, uncle Rob," Millie stated with a sure nod.

Both Kim and Rob reacted with amused embarrassment at the child's bold comment. "Kids say the darnedest things." Rob chuckled.

Kim awkwardly nodded in agreement and responded with an eager question. "Can you come back around 5:30?"

"5:30 it is." He replied.

Still observing, Mark and Molly exchanged wide-eyed expressions over the unfolding event. Rob gave a slight wave to Kim, before taking Millie's hand and joining her waiting parents.

As they all departed, Mark and Molly exchanged a quick high five while they walked a bit ahead of Rob and Millie. "I love it when a plan comes together." Mark proclaimed.

"I know," Molly replied with a clever grin. "Isn't love grand?" They both laughed, as they hooked arms, and Molly leaned in to kiss Mark affectionately on the cheek.

Millie smiled as she watched her parents walking ahead. "I think everything is going to work out alright, uncle Rob."

"I think you're right about that Millie." Rob glanced upward at the sun with a smile. For a brief moment, he could've sworn he saw Shelly smiling back at him, and by the expression on Millie's face, he knew she had seen her as well.

About the Author

Brian was born and raised in Erie Pennsylvania, and has been involved in some capacity of writing since a very young age. After graduating from Penn State University, he lived several years in North Carolina and then Florida, where he presently resides. His accomplishments cover a wide spectrum from writing Psychology Textbooks, several essays on Metaphysics, articles on health and fitness, songwriting, and screenplays. He is also the author of The Balanced Journey, a common sense guide to living from a Spiritual and Metaphysical point of view. (Amazon Publishing, 2012).

In 2017, he retired from FedEx after 21 years of service, and began a new career as a script doctor for the movie industry. He is also very active in Historic Preservation, causes that support our Military Veterans, a fan of Classic Rock Music, and is an avid fitness enthusiast.

Additional Books by Brian Jay Nelson
branchview.info

- The Branchview Series

- The Unexpected Journey
- The Epic Showdown
- The Portal of Time

www.ingramcontent.com/pod-product-compliance
Lightning Source LLC
Chambersburg PA
CBHW060300100726
47907CB00002B/225